DEDICATION

To all of my family, who never doubted me for a second. To my Wordwraiths, for helping to make my dreams a reality and supporting me without fail along this journey. To the rest of my incredibly supportive author community, including the IndiePubbers and my Glorious Ladies of Romantic Fantasy, for listening to me whine on the bad days and cheering alongside me on the good days. And to all those readers who have shown such enthusiasm for my stories that I can't stop writing, even on the hardest days. This book exists because of you. Thank you.

BOOK 1

BARGAIN AT BRAVEBANK
THE LEGACY OF LUCKY LOGAN
J.R. FRONTERA

**Published by
TIN CAN**

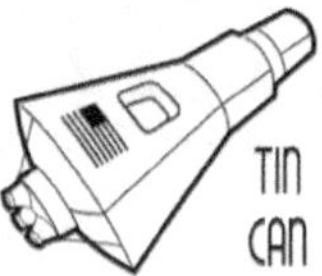

**An imprint of Wordwraith Books, LLC
705-B SE Melody Lane #147
Lee's Summit, MO 64063
http://www.wordwraiths.com**

Version 1.0

http://www.jrfrontera.com

Cover art by Duy Phan
Cover typography by J. Caleb Design
Formatting by Charity Chimni
Maps by renflowergrapx

BOOKS BY J.R. FRONTERA

All books available on Amazon.com and most other online retailers, wherever books are sold.

THE LEGACY OF LUCKY LOGAN

(scifi western)

Bargain at Bravebank

Bastard of Blessing

Bones in Blackbird

Demon at Devil's Deep

(and more coming soon)

N'SPACE

(humorous space opera)

Galapalooza

The Starburst Inn

STARSHIP ASS

(humorous space opera)

Of Sporks, Overlords, and Moon Worms

Of Donkeys, Gods, and Space Pirates

Of Donkeys, Dogs, and Rogue Bits

Of Donkeys, Cogs, and Hot Bodies

COMPLETE

For a fully updated book list check out https://jrfrontera.com.

FREE BOOK ALERT!

Before he was a rancher and a family man, Logan Delano was a 15-year-old orphan, running in an outlaw gang led by the ruthless Paul Johnson. In the wilds of the Independent Americas, under the merciless eye of Kill 'Em All Paul, having any kind of conscience just might land you dead. Unfortunately for Logan, it seems he's still got part of his…

Download your free copy of LUCKY LOGAN at the link below and saddle up for a gritty, gun-slinging tale of just how far one young outlaw will go to survive…

www.jrfrontera.com/posse-up

WORDWRAITH BOOKS

PRESENTS

A NOVEL PRODUCED BY

J.R. FRONTERA

PAT STEVENS

VICKY MEYER

COVER ART BY

DUY PHAN

COVER TYPOGRAPHY BY

J. CALEB DESIGNS

FORMATTING BY

CHARITY CHIMNI

MAPS BY

RENFLOWERGRAPX

AND STARRING
ROGER CLARK
IN THE AUDIO PRODUCTION

THE LEGACY OF LUCKY LOGAN
BOOK 1

WRITTEN BY

J.R. FRONTERA

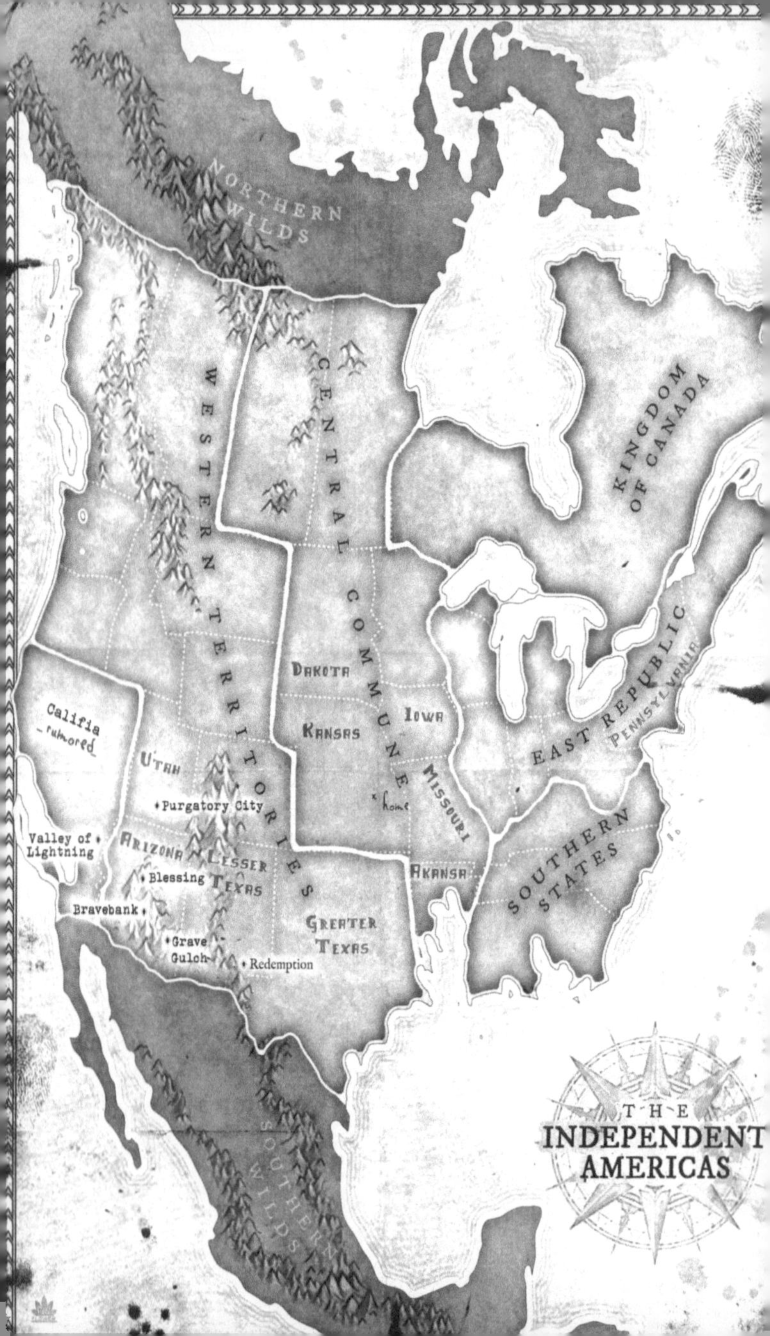

NORTHERN WILDS
KINGDOM OF CANADA
WESTERN TERRITORIES
CENTRAL COMMUNE
EAST REPUBLIC
PENNSYLVANIA
DAKOTA
IOWA
KANSAS
MISSOURI
Califia
rumored
UTAH
Purgatory City
home
Valley of
Lightning
ARIZONA
LESSER TEXAS
SOUTHERN STATES
Blessing
Bravebank
AKANSA
GREATER TEXAS
Grave
Gulch
Redemption
SOUTHERN WILDS
THE
INDEPENDENT
AMERICAS

Califia
—rumored—
WESTERN
UTAH
Purgatory City
Valley of
Lightning
ARIZONA
Sonoita
Blessing
Bravebank
Holding
Tank Pool
Nah's hideout
Peridot
Grave
Gulch
WESTERN TERRITORIES
LESSER TEXAS
CENTRAL COMMUNE
KANSAS
GREATER
TEXAS
SOUTHERN
WILDS
THE
INDEPENDENT
AMERICAS

A PREDICAMENT

"You've come quite far enough, young man."

The voice, clear and hard as steel and undoubtedly feminine, echoed against the bare rock of the cliff face that loomed ahead on the red dirt path.

I gave a sharp pull on the reins, bringin' my dusty sorrel mount to a halt, stiffenin' in the saddle.

It was her. It had to be her. I drew in a slow, deep breath as my heart quickened. *For Chrissakes, Van, settle down. This is what you've been waitin' for. Don't lose yer nerve now.* I swallowed hard in a suddenly dry mouth and tightened my hold on the reins. "I ain't gone far enough till I find Ethelyn," I called out in reply, keeping the brim of my hat low as I took in the path ahead, squintin' fer a sign of movin' shadows, ears pricked for sounds of shiftin' gravel or the cock of a hammer.

Nothin'. Not a shadow out of place, no sound 'cept the soft breeze whisperin' against the smooth rock face, the far-away shriek of a hawk circlin' for prey.

For a heartbeat I worried my information had been wrong.

I worried Holt had been right.

I worried I'd come all the way out here fer nothin'.

But then a slim figure dressed all in black stepped out from behind the pale, carved rock ahead, abruptly enough to make my horse throw up his head and snort in alarm. I sat steady in the saddle as he shifted uneasily beneath me, never takin' my eyes off her.

Nine-Fingered Nan.

She looked different in person than she did on the posters. Older. Taller. More fierce. Like she could drop you dead with just a nod of her head. And accordin' to some of the stories about her, she could. Long wisps of silver-white hair fell from beneath her black, broad-brimmed hat, floating about her shoulders. She stood straight and proud and seemingly immune to the heat of the noon-day sun beatin' down upon us, her cold blue eyes borin' hard into mine. She had a gun belt over her skirts holding a matchin' set of pistols, a shiny golden buckle that winked in the sun, and a bandoleer across one shoulder.

I tensed. Sweat trickled down between my shoulder blades. My horse gave a nervous whicker.

Nine-Fingered Nan made no move for her guns. Yet.

I was all too aware then of my own pair of irons weighing heavy on my hips. Slowly, gently, I set the reins down over my saddle horn, lettin' my hands sit loose atop it, ready to draw if I needed to.

She tilted her chin up, lettin' the sun splash across her wizened, weather-worn features. Her pale eyes narrowed. "Yer the brother."

It weren't a question. So I didn't answer. Instead I bit off a question of my own, hoarse and rough. "Where is she?"

Nine-Fingered Nan's wrinkled lips twitched. It

might have been a smile. It might have been a smirk. "Not here."

I clenched my teeth together hard, resistin' the urge to draw. I was in no mood for games. Not after everythin' I'd done to get this far. "Then *where*?"

"How should I know?"

My heart throbbed in my throat, rushin' in my ears. Somehow I got the words out around the rage. "I know you have her," I snarled. "Hate to tell ya, but yer man Lloyd Renneker squealed. Had to carve him up real good 'fore he'd talk, but talk he did. I know you know where she is. Stop wastin' my time."

Her expression didn't change at my outburst. Didn't even waver at the news I'd cut up and bled out one of her crew. "Your information is bad, boy. Your sister ain't here. Never was. Never will be. You're huntin' a ghost. Your sister is dead."

The words hit like lead, suckin' all the breath outta me. The terrified part of me, the guilt-ridden part that dredged up that night over and over again in nightmares, that hated myself for not getting back to Ethelyn sooner, that urged me to drown myself in whiskey or 'shine or the nearest lake and be done with it, that part of me knew it could be true. But the other part of me, the part that burned for whatever justice I could get, that kept draggin' me on day after day for year after year, chasin' rumors and whispers that a girl named Ethelyn Delano was still alive … that part of me refused to believe.

Ethelyn was still alive. Lloyd Renneker had said so. And he'd said she was with Nine-Fingered Nan, about to be sold for an exorbitant sum to a wealthy merchant overseas.

"You lie," I rasped. I intended to draw, right then

and there, and put a bullet between the eyes of Nine-Fingered Nan.

But the gun blast that roared against the rocks weren't mine.

My horse dropped to the ground like a stone and I hit the dirt path with a grunt, ears ringin'. Disoriented, I struggled to pull my leg from beneath the dead weight of the sorrel as Nine-Fingered Nan crunched across the gravel-strewn ground in her worn black boots, straight at me, one of her pistols smokin' in her hand.

Her right hand. The hand with the missin' trigger finger.

Some people said it'd been my own pa who'd shot off that finger. They said she'd drawn a gun against him, and he'd shot her gun right outta her hand, and taken that finger with it. They said he coulda killed her, but on account of her bein' a young woman and all, he hadn't.

They said he'd meant it to be a lesson to her.

They said it had only made her meaner. Angrier. Deadlier.

I weren't sure if I believed those stories … until now. I gaped wide-eyed at her as she approached, heart poundin' fit to choke me. *Get up already or you'll be as dead as yer goddamned horse!* I tugged my leg free at last and sprang to my feet, reachin' fast for the pistol at my hip.

It blasted from my hand with a stingin' spark soon as it cleared leather, sendin' a sharp lance of pain through my palm, then a third shot exploded pain through my left thigh. I cried out as I hit my knees. Blood splattered into the dirt. My eyes watered and I ground my teeth, gaspin' at the hazy air in ragged breaths.

My whole left thigh was on fire, pulsin' angrily around the ounce of lead now buried in it, and my right hand throbbed somethin' terrible, too.

Nan stopped a few paces in front of me and leveled the barrel of her gun at my forehead.

I considered the pistol still on my left hip. Considered the point-blank range of the one pointed at my head.

Slowly, I lifted my hands.

My stomach turned. Holt had been right. I was a full-blown idiot for comin' out here. Gone on a death wish. Dead man walkin'. Plenty of men older and wiser and faster and smarter than me had come after Nine-Fingered Nan. And they were all dead.

And Nan was still standin'.

"Call me a liar again," she whispered.

I knew better. I couldn't help Ethelyn if I was dead. I forced myself to look up into those cold, hard eyes, and wondered why I wasn't dead already.

"I just want my sister back," I said, voice gruff with pain. Maybe Nine-Fingered Nan was still human, somewhere down deep in that murderous soul of hers. Maybe she had even had someone else she cared about once. A husband. A child. A sibling of her own. "I just want her back. What do you want fer her? Money? You gonna sell her? Name yer price."

One of Nan's silver-white eyebrows lifted, just slightly.

For a moment a blaze of hope lit through me, dullin' the pain of the bullet in my leg. Nan *did* have her. Or at least, Nan knew where Ethelyn was. That hard, expressionless face had cracked, just a bit, just enough to let me glimpse what Nine-Fingered Nan loved the most: cold, hard cash.

The grizzled old gunslingin' woman took one step closer, sneerin' down at me. "A stupid young fool like yerself could never afford it, that's fer sure."

I ignored the insult. She was right, anyway. I *was* a stupid young fool for comin' here. Or at least, for comin' here alone and thinkin' I could get out alive. But then, she hadn't killed me yet. I took a breath, took a gamble. "I'll owe you," I said evenly.

It was as much a death sentence as lettin' her put a bullet through my head right then and there, but at least it was a chance for Ethelyn to be free. No one wanted to owe Nine-Fingered Nan 'less they were impossibly desperate, so I'd heard. Or 'less they had a death wish.

Well, I *was* impossibly desperate. And I guess I had a death wish, too.

She eyed me for a long, silent moment, the only sound the distant shriekin' of that circlin' hawk. Then she tilted her head to one side, the shadow of her hat brim slidin' long down her shoulder. "The son of the infamous Lucky Logan, willin' to be ol' Nan's little errand boy?" Her face split in a terrible grin. Then she laughed, the sound bouncin' around inside the carved-out cliff face. She laughed and laughed and laughed.

I took it. I stayed quiet. I stayed on my knees with my hands raised, the bullet hole in my leg leakin' blood into the dirt. I let her have her moment.

Pride would get me nothin' but dead when it came to Nan. And not dead quick, neither. She'd made that obvious when she'd shot my horse out from under me. So I waited for her to finish laughin'. I'd waited nine years for this chance. I could wait a few minutes more.

When she finally stopped, she wheezed for air and swiped tears from her leathery cheeks with her gun-free hand. Then she took a deep breath and shook her head. "You got stones, boy, I'll give you that. And maybe, maybe if ya had yer pop's reputation, that'd be a suitable offer. But I don't know that you've proved yerself yet. Least not well enough to rest me assured I'd get my money's worth outta you."

The desperation—that impossible desperation—surged in my chest. She couldn't say no. This was my only chance to get Ethelyn back. After all this time, all the nightmares, all the drink, all the murderin'… there was nothin' else after this. Nothin' but dead ends and death. "Then give me a chance to prove it to you," I said, the words tumblin' out in a rush. "You ain't killed me yet. Why?"

Her gaze sharpened at the question, but I pushed on.

"You coulda killed me three times over already. But you didn't. Why?"

Her lips pursed, the blue glare narrowin' as her pistol arm straightened, bringin' the barrel and its mortal payload closer to my skull. "Testin' the merit of Lucky Logan's get," she said quietly. "So far I have to say I been sorely disappointed."

I swallowed, but held her stare. Tried to slow my breathin', which had gone all quick and shallow. Lookin' down the barrel of a gun had never been a favorite past-time of mine, but doin' it bleedin' and at the mercy of Nine-Fingered Nan was far worse than any of my past experiences with such a thing. In all those cases, I'd still been armed, and the other man dead by my gun 'fore he could get off a shot. "I didn't come here to kill you," I said, just as quietly. It was a half-truth. I'd always planned to kill her if she didn't give me Ethelyn. But as Holt always liked to say, *The best laid schemes of mice and men often go awry, and leave us nothing but grief and pain, for promised joy.* I looked down the barrel of Nan's gun and gulped back the bitter laugh. How perfect was that ridiculous rhyme of his now?

Oh, if only he was here now to see how royally I'd fucked this up. If only he was here now to lend me another gun in this fight.

"I came here to get my sister back, is all," I said. "No other man—or woman—who's drawed against me is still livin'."

I saw her understand. Saw it in the softenin' of her jaw, the slight lowerin' of her gun. She knew it was true. I might not a' had the reputation of my infamous pa, no, but I *did* have one. Or was startin' to. And if she knew who I was, then she'd know what people said about me.

And out here, that was the third best currency to bargain with. Right after cold, hard cash and cold, hard bullets.

I weren't as good as my pa. Not yet. But there was no arguin' I had no qualms about killin' … not when it needed to be done.

She dropped her pistol abruptly back into its holster. "Fine. We'll see what yer made of before killin' ya outright. You get back to Bravebank alive and with yer wits intact, you'll find my man at the poker table in the Stag Saloon."

I almost didn't hear her. The relief made me dizzy, light-headed. "Ethelyn?" I asked breathlessly. "Where is she?"

"She'll be safe enough. Lest you die in the desert." Nine-Fingered Nan gave an amused snort. "You make it to Bravebank first, boy, then we'll discuss terms."

I nodded, vision blurred with tears despite myself. "But … you have her? You know where she is?"

Nan rested her gnarled hands on the twin pearl grips at her hips. From my vantage point, the stump of her right index finger was clearly visible. It tapped restlessly against the gleamin' pearl. "Ya said I did," she snapped. "Didn't ya?"

I nodded again. Renneker had said so, yeah. And he'd been one of hers. One of hers for a long time now. Well, till I'd ended him, anyway. Would he have lied?

Would Nine-Fingered Nan lie now?

Of course she'd lie to you, ya dumb sonuvabitch! I could hear Holt screamin' the words even now. Of course she'd lie.

But what I'd told her earlier was true. All my searching had led here, to her. This was it. The end of the trail. If Nan didn't have Ethelyn, then I didn't know where to look next.

Make it to Bravebank first, then she'll discuss terms.

She had Ethelyn. She must have.

I kept noddin' like an idiot. Mostly 'cause I couldn't get any more words out.

And mostly to convince myself Nan had to be tellin' the truth.

"Ya got ten minutes to get the hell outta here,

boy," Nan growled. "'Fore I change my mind." And with that she turned and walked away, boots crunchin' on the gravel. She disappeared into the ancient cliff dwellin', and with a start I saw six others emerge from their hiding places as well and follow her. Four men and two women. Likely her most trusted lieutenants. But they'd never even had to announce themselves. Nan had easily dispatched me all on her own, without even breakin' a sweat.

I felt a fool, all right, a colossal fool.

But I was a livin' fool, and that was somethin'.

I'd wanted to leave here with Ethelyn. Instead I was leavin' with a sore hand, a new hole in my leg and a massive debt to Nan that would probably get me killed. But it seemed the only way forward.

For now.

Holt would be furious. Havin' a debt to Nan meant I'd be just what she'd said: her little errand boy. Jumpin' at her beck and call didn't sound particularly pleasant, but if that's what it took to get my sister free, that's what I was gonna do. It'd mess up his plans real good, but, well … ain't that what his favorite sayin' was all about?

I closed my eyes and sank slowly down to all fours, suckin' in a few deep breaths to settle the fear still coursin' through my limbs. Then I winced and swore; moved my left leg just a bit and cried out at the shock of pain. *Fuck*, it hurt. Blood soaked my pant leg. I wondered if the bullet had sunk into the bone. Wondered if it was broken. Sure felt like it.

I wondered if I might lose the leg. That'd be a sweet sight all right: Lucky Logan's hobbled son.

I shook my head and shoved such thoughts away, then used the body of my poor dead horse as leverage to get to my feet. The pain flared, takin' my breath away. I stood a moment, balanced on my good leg, and waited for it to pass. Breathed through it.

There was surely no way I could put weight on my shot leg. I could tell that much easily enough. So I reached down and pulled my rifle from its scabbard, leanin' on it heavily like a crutch as I looked off the edge of this rocky rise out across the stretch of river below and then beyond, to the mountainous desert that led toward the town of Bravebank.

And my heart sank as I realized my predicament.

No horse. No supplies. A gimp leg. A wound bleedin' like a stuck pig. And miles and miles of desert between me and Ethelyn's freedom.

II

A GRAVE MISTAKE

I feared I had made a grave mistake.

But it was too late to turn back now. Too late to tell Nine-Fingered Nan that she and her deal could both go to Hell. Too late to decide I should have put a bullet in her brain the second I first laid eyes on her. Too late to take back my willingness to owe her a debt that would probably get me killed.

I stopped in my trek across the burnin' hills. My hat brim shoulda shielded my eyes from the sun's infernal glare, but out here it seemed to hardly help. The unendin' onslaught of light dazzled my vision. Sweat stung my eyes and made my shirt cling to my skin. The throbbin' agony in my left leg had finally subsided into a warm ache, but I wasn't so sure that was a good thing. I'd tied my bandana over the bullet hole; stuck my rifle down inside my boot and tied it to my leg too, to make a crude kinda splint. And I'd cut a length of my saddle girth and cinched it tight around my leg above the wound, but there was a thin trickle of blood still paintin' a long trail of red in the fabric of my pants.

The heat, the distance, these hills, and havin' only one good leg was killin' me, already.

I wouldn't have to wait to die on an errand for Nan at this rate.

I'd die here. Now. In this damned desert without a soul in sight.

Shadows in the shapes of birds slid over me, soundless, and raced ahead, then circled back again. Vultures. Bastards had been followin' me since I'd left Nan's rocky hide-out.

They knew. They always knew.

I lifted my hat from my head briefly to swipe at the sweat on my brow with my forearm. The heat came off the rocks in waves, making everythin' waver. I wavered where I stood, too. Sometimes it was hard to tell what was caused by the heat and what was caused by exhaustion and blood loss.

I blinked hard and shifted my saddle bags on my shoulder. I'd taken what I could manage to carry off my dead horse, sure, but there was only so much one man could hold. And only so far one man with a bullet in his leg could walk.

If only she hadn't shot my horse.

I'd liked that horse, damnit. He'd been my best one yet. Cost me twenty-five dollars. Shakin' my head, I uncapped my one canteen—also rescued off my saddle—and allowed myself a small sip. Not that it would matter.

Wouldn't matter that my horse was dead. Wouldn't matter that I was out twenty-five dollars, plus the cost of that perfectly good saddle. Wouldn't matter that I had half a canteen of water left.

I was makin' slow progress. Too slow.

The birds would have me soon enough. Or one of those mountain lions, maybe. Long before I reached the outskirts of Bravebank.

Damnit, Van. How could you be so stupid?

I closed my eyes, but it seemed the sun still burned there, straight through my eyelids. Burnin', always burnin'. Burnin' away my eyes, my mind, my soul.

I thought of Ethelyn then, and the last time I'd seen her. Nine years ago. In the black of night. Both of us splattered with blood that wasn't ours. And her eyes … her big green eyes wide in terror, the whites shining in the dark. Her small fingers clutchin' hard at my arm.

She had begged me not to go. *Begged* me.

But we couldn't stay there. So I'd promised I'd be back soon as I could. And I'd gone, anyway. I'd left her there, huddled in some woods a distance out back of our burnin' house. Alone.

Three days I was away, that's all. Three days.

When I'd returned … she was gone.

Three days away and I'd lost my sister for nine years.

I drew in a sharp breath of air that tasted of furnace. I swallowed though I had no more spit. And I started hobblin' forward again. I trudged onward through that red dirt and rock, mostly draggin' my left foot behind me as I had done for all the last miles.

The sun was steadily droppin' toward the horizon I aimed for, lightin' the way toward the town of Bravebank. Pointin' the way, and blindin' me, too.

Mockin' me.

With every step I heard Nan's voice in my mind: *Get to Bravebank alive and with yer wits intact first, boy, then we'll discuss terms.*

My right hand fell to the pistol on my hip. The pistol with the dent of another bullet in its cylinder now. I suppose it was some small mercy she hadn't taken off my finger, too, in some twisted sense of poetic justice for the finger my pa had taken from her.

But maybe it hadn't been him who'd shot that finger off of her, after all.

My own fingers, all full five of 'em, curled around that worn grip, and I winced as sharp pain stabbed into that palm again. Well, no matter. The fingers still worked, and if I had to draw I could still draw.

I used the grip's familiar feel to bolster my resolve. If I ever saw Nine-Fingered Nan again, I was gonna kill her.

No more talkin'. No more negotiations.

She thought this was a game, fine. I'd play it just long enough to end it. For good. She thought the desert'd kill me? Thought she could dismiss me to go die in the wastes while she sold my sister off, anyway?

Well, I'd show her.

I'd show her just what Van Jensen Delano was made of, all right. I might not a' inherited my pa's luck, but Holt knew as well as anyone else who'd ever spent any time with me that I'd sure as hell inherited his stubbornness. And Mama's, too.

Holt often said I been cursed with a double-barreled shotgun of mulishness.

It almost made me laugh now, half outta my mind with blood loss and heat and sloggin' through the endless desert.

If not for that, I'd'a for sure been dead a long time ago. And probably Ethelyn, too.

And as much as Holt cursed that trait of mine, it'd served the ol' bastard well enough on plenty of our jobs. He'd never complained about it, then.

And so I walked on.

I held the memory of Nan's disdainful sneer in my mind, and Ethelyn's terrified ten-year-old face, and kept on walkin'. Into the shimmerin' fire of the settin' sun. Toward Bravebank. Toward Ethelyn's freedom. Toward Nine-Fingered Nan's eventual end.

Toward my own salvation.

I awoke to harsh whispers and the vague feelin' of hands pattin' at my body.

It didn't take thinkin' to react. I reached for my guns as I surged up sittin' with an angry yell, and the bandits tryin' to rob me jumped back with startled cries of their own.

It took me a good long minute to realize both my hands were still empty.

I blinked hard in the darkness, tryin' to make my swimmin' vision clear. The chill of the desert's night air hit me then and I shivered violently, though my skin was still wet with sweat.

Then one of the robbin' bastards laughed and held up two pistols of his own.

No, wait. They was *my* pistols. The backwater sonuvabitch had *my* goddamn guns!

"Lookin' fer these?" he drawled. He held them forward, lettin' 'em slip down and dangle from his index fingers by their trigger guards.

I gritted my teeth. I wanted to leap up and wrap

my hands around his throat. Throttle that smirk right off his sunburned, pock-marked face. But I was only sittin' down, and already the ground was rockin' under me, everything lookin' like the sun was still up, waverin' and shiftin'.

His partner chuckled. "Always disarm those ya gonna rob first," he quipped. "Even if ya think they're dead."

"'Xactly," the man with my guns said, and he grinned like a fool as he tucked 'em into the rim of his pants.

Rage burned in my throat. I was gonna kill 'em. Both of 'em.

The problem was, they had my saddle bags, too, and my canteen. They had everythin' off me already, and I had nothin' left.

"Well, wha' should we do wif 'em now?" the one who didn't have my guns asked his sonuvabitch friend. He held a big revolver, an older model, the kind that sometimes jammed and blew up in yer hand. But the kind that'd punch one big hole in the guy you were amin' at if they didn't blow up in yer hand. The one most folk around here called the Gambler, on account of the fact you took a gamble every time you pulled the trigger. He had it pointed at my chest.

I took a quick look around best I could with my wobbly vision while they debated. I didn't recognize anythin'. I had no idea where I was. The river weren't too far away; I could see the moonlight shimmerin' off it to my right. But then, I'd been followin' the river southwest all day, so its presence didn't help me figure out where I was at all.

I didn't remember passin' out. I didn't remember hittin' the dirt.

But I must have lost consciousness at some point, then dropped in my tracks, right in the open. Right in a prime spot for lazy bastards like these to find me.

My frantic searchin' stopped at the sight of their horses. Two perfectly good horses, standin' patiently not too far away. Loaded with saddle bags of their own, and bedrolls. And more canteens. I tried to swallow. By God was I thirsty.

"Mebee sell 'em?" the one holdin' the revolver suggested to his friend.

But his friend shook his head. "Nah. Lookit 'em. He's mostly dead already. Wouldn't fetch much."

"Shoot 'em, then?" his friend suggested next.

I wished they'd stop talkin' bout me like I wasn't sittin' right there, plottin' how to murder 'em both. But I suppose I couldn't really blame 'em. I surely felt mostly dead. Wasn't sure I coulda got up off the ground anyway, even if my life depended on it.

Which it might.

It was all up to how this debate of theirs turned out.

The one with my guns studied me with beady black eyes that glinted in the light of the full moon. It cast our shadows out long across the sand, as if it were tryin' so hard to live up to the fierceness of its bigger, brighter cousin. But its pale, silvery light didn't burn away your sanity like the sun's did. It only cloaked the scrawny man sizin' me up in hard, silver angles as he spat into the parched dirt. "Nah. Be a waste of a bullet. Lookit that leg a' his. It'll get 'em. We don't need ta do it."

His friend appeared irritated at this assessment. "Well wha', then?"

The man with my guns stared at me for a long, silent moment, and I glared back at him, bracin' myself with both hands against the ground to keep from swoonin' over. Then he smiled, but I noticed he didn't get no closer to me. They were both out of arm's reach, damn it all.

I didn't even have my knife to hurl at 'em. They had that, too.

The skinny, pock-faced fella shrugged his narrow shoulders. "Nothin'," he answered simply. "Leave 'em fer the buzzards. Let's go."

He turned and made for his horse. With *my* guns, and my saddle bags, and the little bit of water I had left.

His friend seemed unsure. He looked from his no-good partner to me and then back again. "You sure?"

"I'm sure." The other man didn't even look back. He was so sure I weren't no threat he couldn't be bothered to waste any more time on me.

I made some sort of growl and lunged toward the ankles of the one still standin' there holdin' a revolver at me. He yelped and staggered backwards, and my reachin' hands grabbed only dust and gravel.

The other fella laughed at his friend and swung up on his horse. "C'mon, Clint. Stop foolin' around. Let's go 'fore this night gets any older. I wanna get some female company 'fore dawn."

I could see Clint's face darken even in the moonlight, embarrassed at bein' startled by the likes a' me. He grumbled, namin' me foul names, and shoved his revolver back into its holster. Then he scuffed a boot into the ground, givin' me a nice shower of the same dust and gravel that was still gripped in both my fists.

I ducked my head just in time, but my hat was missin', too. I shut my eyes as the grit rained over me, then coughed.

Clint grumbled under his breath all the way to his horse.

I struggled to my feet, anger blockin' the pain of my leg, the throbbin' in my right hand, the exhaustion, the thirst. My vision narrowed, but I could still see the silhouettes of Clint and his sonuvabitch friend. And that was all that mattered.

I swayed and staggered, but somehow managed to keep upright. "Leavin' already?" I husked. My voice sounded like stones in a set of rusty gears. "But we was just gettin' to know each other."

Clint turned to face me just as he was about to mount up, the full moon highlightin' his widened eyes and open mouth.

His friend just shook his head, one hand goin' to rest on the grip of my gun as he leaned forward on his saddle horn. "You wanna die quick, boy? Keep talkin' and I'll letcha."

I widened my stance a bit, plantin' my boots into the ground to steady myself. Felt like the whole world was rockin' somethin' fierce now, but I hoped this sunuvabitch couldn't see that. I hooked my thumbs into my belts. My *empty* belts. "You wanna die slow?" I asked in return.

He straightened in his saddle at my threat and looked to his pal.

Clint, for his part, clambered up on his own mount in a hurry and reined it around to face me.

I saw his right hand drop back down to his revolver.

Then the pock-faced thief chuckled. He looked me over again, like he was makin' fer sure I couldn't really deliver on my threat, and sighed. "I kinda like you, kid." His fingers slid off my gun and went back to his reins. "Too bad we won't be seein' ya around again." He tossed me a mock salute. "Adios." He turned his horse and waved for Clint to follow after, and Clint did so, lookin' over his shoulder at me fer a second longer before turnin' his attention to the trail ahead.

I swore and hobbled after 'em quick as I could, but I hadn't really thought this far ahead.

'Course he hadn't believed my threat ... but I'd had to say it, anyway. I couldn't just let a pair of highwaymen rob me blind without tryin'.

And I sure as hell was gonna try.

I saw a pile of the red, rough rocks that littered much of the land in the Territories off to my left, and a few chipped pieces on the ground 'bout as big as my palm. I stumbled over to 'em and scooped one of the bigger ones up just as Clint and his bastard friend kicked their horses into a trot.

I hurled the rock after 'em with all my strength, aimin' fer the one who still had my guns.

The rock thumped into his horse's rear and the animal startled, jumpin' sideways with his ears pinned and kickin' out with both back feet. It was enough to unseat his thief of a rider, who hit the ground with a grunt.

I ran at him fast as I could manage, half-limpin' and half-lurchin', and tackled him just as he was comin' to his feet.

He gave another grunt as my weight came down on top of him, but I'd already yanked my pistol from his waistline. I pressed the barrel into his middle and fired.

The shot was half-muffled by our bodies, but he jerked as the bullet tore through his gut, and his eyes grew wide and white as the moon, watchin' us impassively from on high with her cold, pale gaze.

Clint gave a yell of mixed surprise and horror, snappin' my attention to him, instead.

I rolled off his pal just as he fired, takin' my left pistol with me, too, and his bullet sent up a spray of dirt right next to his friend. I landed on my back and brought both pistols to bear on Clint, firin' simultaneously.

My twin shots hit him in the chest, leavin' an arc of blood as he went clean off his horse, sprawlin' limp to the ground. His horse swiveled its ears and pranced in place, snortin' nervously. But it didn't bolt.

That was a good horse.

There was movement from the skinny man I'd tackled and I reflexively shifted my guns to him. He froze. We were both still layin' flat out on the ground, only I had loaded irons in my hands, and he was only just reachin' fer his.

Had been reachin'. Till he'd seen my two barrels swing toward him again. "Easy now," I prompted. "I said you'd die slow, remember?"

His face contorted into a scowl, mostly anger, but some pain, too.

A bullet to the gut was a bad way to go, I'd heard.

He glared at me hard, right in the eyes. And his reachin' hand twitched.

I fired again, point blank, tearin' up his left shoulder real good.

His screams echoed out across the distance, over-lappin' the noise of my gunshot.

"I did warn ya," I said as he writhed in the dirt. "Twice."

He looked back at me with eyes full of murder and hate and agony.

I drug myself up outta that same dirt and staggered again to my feet, keepin' my pistols aimed straight at him. I was feelin' plenty of agony myself. "Now," I rasped, "you just throw your gun my way, nice and slow." I fought hard to keep my own pain outta my face. Fought hard to keep my hands steady.

"You can go fuck yourself," he spat.

I gave him a smile. What else was I gonna do? The fella was just about as stubborn as me. I shoulda put a bullet in his forehead then, but I'd told him I was gonna let him die slow, and I liked to keep my promises. He wasn't going to talk himself outta that.

I limped around him, bein' careful not to break eye contact. He'd shoot me the second I looked away, no doubt. I went to his right side, and he watched me warily, a sheen of sweat now glistenin' on his brow. His breathin' was harsh and ragged, his jaw clenched tight.

Well, maybe with that shoulder bleedin' out like it was, he wouldn't last as long as I would have liked. But that couldn't be helped now. "Hands up," I ordered.

He slowly complied. At least with his right hand. His left was still clutchin' at the hole in his gut. And

I imagined it was suitably useless now, given the state of that shoulder. I also imagined he thought I'd come nice and close to grab his gun fer myself.

But I knew better. I'd learned that lesson years ago. So I focused on his right hand, the one that could still move, and blew another hole straight through his palm.

His screamin' was more like shriekin' now, and I stepped backward as he flopped around bad as a fish tossed outta water.

Clint's horse, steady though it was, shied sideways at all the motion and commotion.

I just stood and watched fer a minute.

Then, satisfied he could no longer shoot me in the back as I left, I turned stiffly and hobbled away from him, over to Clint's horse. I holstered my weapons back where they belonged, then heaved myself up into the saddle. I nearly blacked out as I swung my stiff, splinted left leg over the cantle, but I clutched the horse's mane in my white-knuckled fists and somehow managed to pull myself back from the darkness, settlin' heavy into the saddle seat.

The horse shifted uneasily beneath me.

"Easy," I whispered. "Easy there." I was talkin' as much to myself as to the horse. The night seemed to have gotten darker despite the full moon. No matter how hard or how much I blinked, my vision just wouldn't clear. It took a lot of effort to detangle my fingers from the mane and get them on the reins, and more effort still to nudge the horse forward.

It took a few uncertain steps and then stopped.

The thief I'd shot fulla holes spat curses at me from the ground. Some real bad ones. And some real creative ones.

I twisted in the saddle to look down at him. "Too bad I won't be seein' you around again," I said, echoin' his own words back to him. Poetic justice, that's what Holt'd call it. And that it was. I gave him the same mock salute he'd given me, too. "Adios."

And I forced my heels into the horse's side and closed my eyes, concentratin' on stayin' in the saddle as she picked up into an easy lope. I leaned precariously to one side before draggin' myself upright again.

The thief's screamin' and cursin' was growin' fainter behind me.

Good.

He should have just left well enough alone.

I slowed the horse again. I wasn't gonna last long at a lope. It was hard enough to keep my seat at a damned walk. Clint and his sonuvabitch friend were no-good bastards, but they'd been right about one thing: I was mostly dead already.

I lifted my face to the sky, squintin' at the stars and tryin' to orient myself. But the cursed moon's light washed some of 'em out, and the rest kept slidin' and jumpin' all over the place. I shut my eyes again and rubbed at 'em with two fingers.

You ain't never gonna be able to tell where you're goin' in this state. You can hardly keep yerself sittin' up straight!

The horse kept ploddin' along, calm again now that'd we'd left the scene of carnage behind.

I remembered what the pock-faced thief had said about wantin' female company 'fore dawn, and a shred of hope flickered to life inside me. Bravebank was the only town in this desert for a lot of miles. That meant he and his pal Clint had most likely been headed there when they'd found me. And if they coulda got there 'fore dawn, the town couldn'ta been too far away now.

I slumped in the saddle, lettin' the reins go slack. The horse could find the way from here, surely. They always seemed to know the way to the nearest barn.

And this time, that's exactly where I wanted to go.

I let myself relax, one hand reachin' for the canteen looped over the saddle horn.

Approachin' hoofbeats brought me to high alert again and I had one gun out and aimed toward the noise long before my sluggish mind caught up to what I was seein'.

A riderless horse appeared outta the cloud of dust it was kickin' up. Eventually I recognized it. It was the horse of the man who'd taken my guns. The horse I'd hit in the ass with a rock. The horse that'd thrown its rider so I could kill him slow.

I holstered my pistol as the second horse drew up alongside its companion and snorted. It dropped into an easy walk to match our pace. I lifted my brows. Apparently these two had been together awhile now, and one couldn't stand to be without the other. Well, one horse was surely better than none. And two horses was better than one. Maybe I could even make back my twenty-five dollars.

Maybe.

I pulled up the canteen and uncapped it, then took a long swig. It felt like a brick in my hand, and puttin' the cap back on was far more difficult than it shoulda been.

Damnit, Van. Get it together. You gotta make it.

Nine years of searchin'… you can't let it end here, not when you're so close. You're almost there now.

I wrapped my fingers in the horse's mane again, hopin' it'd be enough to keep me in the saddle. I was fadin', I could feel it.

Just so tired.

All I wanted to do was sleep. Close my eyes and let it all go. Just fer a minute…

MORE THAN ONE KIND OF VULTURE

It was pain that woke me a second time.

Sharp, piercin' pain, shockin' out from the bullet hole in my leg.

I yelled and lurched up before I'd even fully realized I hadn't been awake in the first place. I threw out a hand blindly, the sun searin' my vision. The world was a blur of white and heat, 'cept the few dark shapes lurkin' close. And one was over there near my leg.

It fluttered back a few steps as my hand came at it, and that's when I knew they must be vultures of the animal variety, instead of vultures of the human variety.

Both kinds of vultures were bad news, in my opinion. And one not necessarily better or worse than the other. Not really. Not when you were in my kind of state.

I flung out my hand again. "Get!" It came out a harsh whisper instead of a shout.

The bird only watched me. Unafraid. Patient. Like it knew if it just waited a few minutes more, I'd lie back down and go quiet. Fer good.

I gritted my teeth and tried to conjure up a good swear, but I was too exhausted even for that. I groped for my gun, found it still on my hip. Well, least the birds couldn't take those from me, unlike their human counterparts. I drug it outta the holster and half-rolled toward the feathered bastard. I propped myself on both elbows. Had to hold the damn gun with both hands.

Had it always been this heavy?

A sharp peck on the back of my right calf brought me swingin' round again to the one behind me. "Damn you!" I spat. "I ain't dead yet!"

Not yet. Though I was surely closer to it than I would have liked.

It raised its wings and hissed at me.

"Go to Hell," I growled back. I pulled my trigger.

The others took off with loud cries of protest as their comrade fell, but I lifted the barrel and squeezed off two more shots at 'em, fer good riddance. Got one of 'em, and it dropped like a rock back to the dirt. I was gonna take another shot at the one still flyin', but then I saw that dented cylinder roll upward toward the hammer and I stopped myself. Didn't want to be takin' any more gambles. Lord knew my luck had turned out shit enough as it was, and my right hand was already all hot and swollen.

I swore and fell back into the burnin' dirt myself. Shoulda used the left pistol, instead. Closin' my eyes, I felt for it now, and exhaled loudly when my fingers found it, safe and sound still where it belonged.

And then some clarity returned to my poundin' head.

And I sat up with a start, and looked around at the shimmerin' stretch of desert surroundin' me best I could with that cursed sun bakin' me good as a fish in a pan.

I'd had a horse, hadn't I? And water. And supplies.

But there surely was no sign of any of that now. Not even any hoofprints in the dirt. I squinted and rubbed at my eyes. But my view didn't change.

I suppose if there had been a horse, its tracks coulda been covered over by the wind by now. However long it had been. How long had I been lyin' here comatose in the open again, tryin' to die?

Long enough for the birds to think I was their next meal, I guess.

Had I imagined Clint and his sonuvabitch friend?

I didn't think so, but then, I wasn't sure of much anymore.

'Cept the fact I was surely gonna die if I didn't find Bravebank soon.

It couldn't be that much further. I had to make it.

I pushed my gun back into its holster and then pushed myself up off the ground, my left leg stickin' straight out in its makeshift splint, stiff as a board. Sweat ran in rivulets down my face and my back. My arms shook, my vision dimmed, and a wave of nausea rocked me. I sat back down hard, the world tiltin' sideways.

I tried to hold myself up, to brace myself, but this time it didn't do no good. I collapsed anyway, the world still rockin'. I wanted to keep goin'. I had to keep goin'. I reached out with one hand, clutchin' at a fistful of dirt and gravel as if it were a hold on life itself.

I crawled forward. Or sorta crawled. More like slithered on my belly, movin' westward still inch by inch. I was glad then that Holt hadn't come. I surely didn't want him to see me like this. And I was even gladder that Nine-Fingered Nan had been left miles behind in her cliff-face refuge. If she ever knew what she'd done to me here, she'd probably laugh until she finally croaked.

I groaned, a bit of dust kickin' up into my face with my breath. *Don't be a fool. She knows exactly what she did to you.*

That's why she'd demanded I meet her man in Bravebank instead of makin' me a deal right then and there. Why she'd shot my horse. Why she'd shot me in the leg instead of the head. Why she'd made my sanity a condition in her agreement to give me a chance to earn Ethelyn's freedom.

All so carefully arranged.

All so expertly manipulated to kill me. After makin' me suffer awhile first, of course.

Damn her to Hell. Damn her straight to Hell. I pulled myself forward another inch. I couldn't let her win. I couldn't let Ethelyn go. Everythin' in me screamed to keep goin', but my body was givin' out. It didn't care what I wanted anymore.

I slumped into blackness.

Somethin' jostled me.

I heard voices again. The damn vultures just wouldn't leave me alone. I made to reach fer my guns with heavy, sluggish arms, and there was an alarmed string of words in response. I couldn't tell what the vulture was sayin'. Whether or not that was 'cause of my own disorientation or 'cause they was speakin' some foreign language, well, I couldn't sort that, either. But that didn't matter. I'd kill 'em either way.

'Cept I couldn't seem to get my hands around my guns.

Another voice answered the first, and this one cut through the haze of my dehydrated, bled-out, sun-dazzled wits. A woman's voice.

I couldn't understand her, neither, but my heart jumped in my chest anyway, thinkin' of Ethelyn. I attempted to roll over, to sit up. Where was I? Who were these people?

Women didn't often travel with bandits of the Territories ... but then, there was Nine-Fingered Nan. She'd been a lady once. Maybe. Now she was the Devil Incarnate.

This woman here could still be a vulture, certainly.

Now there were *two* female voices talkin', runnin' over each other into nonsense. And a boy's voice, too. ***What the hell? Who brings a kid out here?***

I tried to drag my eyes open, tried to leverage myself up on one elbow. I felt cool wood underneath me, a stark difference from the hot, dusty ground. *What in—*

Somethin' came down over my nose and mouth. A sweet-smellin' cloth. I reached up in attempts to yank it away just as other hands took my shoulders and pushed me down flat to my back again. My eyes came open at last, but there was only blurry figures around me. My surroundin's were dim, claustrophobic.

Looked like a man sittin' over me, though, the

one holdin' the cloth to my face. I grabbed at his arm, but he was damn strong. Maybe if I hadn'ta just spent two days or more walkin' in the desert with a bullet in my leg, I coulda taken him easily.

But not now.

His arm was rigid, the muscles in his forearm hard beneath my clawin' fingers.

"Easy, son, easy now. Calm down. This is for your own good…"

The words filtered through my kickin' and gruntin', but gave me no reassurance. I'd heard such words before, and what followed had never been particularly pleasant. Not to mention this bastard seemed bent on suffocatin' me. And I surely didn't see how that could be fer my own good.

Though maybe there was a few lawmen out there who might've thought puttin' me out of my misery was fer my own good.

Maybe this fella agreed with 'em.

I felt the sleep comin' on, and my beatin' at the man's arm and chest weakened. My arms dropped to the wooden planks beneath me, suddenly heavy as lead. Despite my best efforts, my eyes closed. My thoughts of Ethelyn, of dyin', of Nine-Fingered Nan, drifted off.

"That's it," the man whispered, only now it seemed his words had gained the comfort he'd obviously intended, whether or not it was genuine. I eased into them. "That's it. Just relax. Go to sleep. You're in good hands, now."

Suffocatin' hands, I thought, still breathin' into that sweet-smellin' cloth, slow and deep now. *Damn yer … suffocatin' hands, you … no good … sonuva…*

Next time I came conscious, it was slow and peaceful. No voices this time, no hands on me, no pain. Least, no pain fer awhile. Felt like I was floatin'. No burnin' sun bakin' me. No hot dirt and rock searin' my skin. No sharp peck of vultures tryin' to make me a meal.

Gradually, awareness came back to me. There was somethin' soft under my back and my head. The light through my eyelids was subtle, not blindin'. The air smelled different … like fire smoke and somethin' savory. And there were sounds, too, muffled but unmistakable: the creak of footsteps on floorboards, quiet conversation, the sound of a knife choppin'. Choppin' what, who knew. Maybe vegetables. Maybe meat.

My gut twisted at the familiarity of it and I drew a sharp breath as memories came floodin' back.

My fists gripped sheets.

I was in a house. I was in a damned house. A house so similar to the one I'd used to know…

My eyes flung open. I stared up at a beamed wooden ceiling. Daylight filtered in through a window to my right, framed in pretty lace curtains. The sight of 'em hit me like a punch in the gut.

Mama'd had curtains like that.

They'd burned up just as nice as everything else in the house.

Includin' her.

A choked noise escaped me and I sat up, then reeled. That's when the pain came back, all at once and somethin' fierce. My whole left thigh felt like it'd been laid open and carved up. I clutched at it and cried out, and that's when I noticed the shape of it didn't look quite right under those crisp white sheets tucked in around me.

Footsteps came runnin' and the door to my left banged open. I jerked my head toward it to see a middle-aged woman gapin' at me. Instinctively I fumbled fer my guns, but I weren't even wearin' my gun belt no more. All I had on was a union suit, and I wondered how that'd happened.

The woman left the doorway, runnin' off yellin' fer someone.

I remembered the women I'd heard talkin' when that man had tried to suffocate me, and figured these were probably the same people. She was probably runnin' off to get the man who'd tried to suffocate me, to tell him he didn't do such a good job of it.

I needed to get out of here. Didn't matter that I was damn near naked, or that I didn't have my weapons. Didn't matter that the room was spinnin' fit to put me right back down into the bed. I'd grabbed the edge of the blankets to throw them back when another person appeared in the doorway; a young woman.

The sight of her stopped me cold. Now it was me who was gapin'. I hadn't expected the other woman I'd heard to be so near my own age.

Then the older woman returned, with a tall, thin man in tow. He wore small, round spectacles and had a well-oiled mustache that pointed upwards on the ends. From that and the spotless condition of his fancy dress shirt and silk vest, I knew right off he was one of those so-called "learned" men. Had he really been the one tryin' to suffocate me?

The bastard was stronger than he looked.

"No, no, no, *no*!" he said quickly, shakin' his head as he came across the room at me. "You cannot be up! Lie back down before you hurt yourself!" He shoved me back down into the pillow with unceremonious force. "You are very, *very* lucky to be alive, son. But if you do not rest now, all of my hard work will be for nothing!"

Well, I understood his words alright now, but he had a heavy, lilting accent. "I ain't lucky," I growled. "And I ain't yer son."

His finely groomed eyebrows lifted above his spectacles. "Perhaps not, but I *did* save your life. You are welcome."

"I didn't say thank you." Even as I muttered it, my eyes shifted from him to the older woman I assumed was his wife, and the young woman I figured was his daughter. Both of 'em looked unsettled, concerned. The wife gripped the choppin' knife in one hand, white-knuckled. So they were the smarter ones in the family, it seemed.

"I am quite aware," the man stated wryly. "But nonetheless, it is done."

Was it? I weren't so sure. Not with the fire that burned in my leg now. It hurt worse than it had in the desert. I turned my gaze back to him. "You shouldn'ta done that," I croaked. "You shouldn'ta brought me here." I'd learned long ago, helpin' people most often just got you dead quicker. And this man had a family. He was even more an idiot for riskin' 'em like that.

The man scoffed, reachin' to the bedside table to retrieve a stethoscope. So what was he, then, some kind of doctor? "Son, if I hadn't of found you and brought you here, you'd certainly be dead, and the buzzards feeding on your carcass."

I swallowed hard, knowin' that was no lie. But that didn't mean I'd wanted the help. Didn't mean I was gonna owe him for savin' my life. I couldn't afford to owe anyone, and I already owed Nine-Fingered Nan everythin' I had left. "I told you, I ain't yer son," was all I said.

He pursed his already thin lips at my response, then stuck the stethoscope into his ears and tried to press the other end of it to my chest like he was gonna listen to my heart. I knocked his hand away.

His wife in the doorway took a step forward, the knife liftin' a bit as if in warnin'.

I met her hard stare over the man's shoulder. As if? No. It was surely a warnin'. Her face spelled out her thoughts clear enough: *Harm my husband and I'll carve you up like a holiday ham.*

"I need to listen to your heart," he said, oblivious to the murderous glare his wife was borin' into me. "Your leg was terribly infected when we found you. I think the infection was stopped at the leg, but I need to be sure."

I looked at him again, tryin' to understand him. Tryin' to figure out why he wanted to help a man like me. Some stranger he'd found half-dead in the desert. His accent marked him as a foreigner. Probably come here from across the sea. Maybe that was it, then. Maybe he just didn't understand how things worked over here yet.

If he didn't sort it out quick, though, the damn fool and his whole family'd end up as dead as I would've been if he'd just left me where he found me.

Just as dead as Mama and Pa.

"Why," I blurted harshly. "Why'd you help me? You shouldn'ta done that."

He blinked behind the thick round glass of his spectacles. "Why? What kind of question is that? I'm a doctor, son. I took an oath. Not only that, but the Good Book says—"

"*No.*" The word tore outta my throat, unexpected tears burnin' in my eyes. I closed them so the man and his family couldn't see. I struggled to keep my composure, a grief fresher than I'd felt in years rakin' at my insides. It had to be this damned house. The lace curtains. The mention of the Good Book, that Mama'd liked to read from every night as she'd knelt and said her prayers.

"No," I choked out again. "Stop. Stop it." I opened my eyes and stared straight into the man's confused face so he'd know how serious I was. "Stop helpin' people. Stop quotin' the Good Book. Forget your oath." I lifted a hand to point at his wife and daughter and then gestured out yonder, out beyond the adobe walls of his house. "Take yer family and go back to wherever you came from 'fore you all end up dead."

He drew back a bit at my words, then looked over his shoulder to his wife and daughter. Maybe he was tryin' to decide if I'd meant that as a warning or a threat. It didn't matter, so long as he listened.

Then the floorboards from the other room creaked a little, and another face appeared between the shoulders of the wife and daughter. A boy's face, maybe ten years old, and I remembered the child's voice I'd heard when I'd been delirious. I'd hoped that'd been part of a dream.

It seemed it wasn't.

His mother noticed him there and scolded him in their native language. I couldn't make out what she was sayin', but her tone and her body language said she was orderin' him away. His wide, dark blue eyes stared straight at me, and his mouth hung open a little.

I glared at him, too.

His mother's words became more urgent, and he finally, reluctantly moved out of sight again. Who knows where he went, but that didn't matter, either.

I wasn't stayin' here, anyway. I couldn't. I shook my head and pushed myself sittin' again. "I gotta go. I can't stay."

The man reached out toward me and opened his mouth to protest my movements, but I threw back the covers before he could stop me.

And froze.

My left thigh ended in a stump. The rest of my leg was missin'.

MACHINE PARTS

Well, there was somethin' there, all right, but it surely weren't my natural leg. It was some kind of mess of metal, all long pipes and gears, and it laid on the mattress where my leg shoulda been, exposed through the cut ribbons of union suit left there.

I stared at it, a horror rushin' through me like I'd never felt. And then a rage. My body trembled, my heart throbbin' wild in my chest. Heat flooded my face as I brought my eyes back to the skinny man. The doctor. The man who had taken my leg.

Murder musta been clear on my face, 'cause he went deathly pale and held up his hands palms out, as if surrendin'. "I was trying to tell you," he said quickly, "your leg was terribly infected when we found you. Infected, and dead. There was no way to save it."

My mouth worked. But the rage was takin' all the words. "You," I finally whispered, then had to swallow. I tried again. "You … you *took my goddamn leg off*!?"

"As I said, I saved your life!" He was indignant now. "The flesh of your leg was dead. The tourniquet you put on…" He shook his head. "It was on too long. It stopped the infection from spreading it seems, yes, but there was not enough circulation in the leg. I'm sorry. It was all that could be done."

"I … you … you sonuva…" The room was spinnin' again. I felt sick. I leaned over the side of the bed and retched.

The man jumped back, but there was hardly a thing in my stomach, and I didn't make much of a mess. His wife was surely glad for that. I spit, my breath comin' harsh and ragged. My left thigh—the half of it left—still pulsed as if it'd been laid open. But now as I looked at it closer, I saw instead that the metal contraption had been attached to it. Flesh and metal fused together.

I retched again and squeezed my eyes shut. I clutched at the sheets and the edge of the mattress, thinkin' I might actually faint. That'd be a good one … faintin' clean away right in front of the women. I clung hard to consciousness, hangin' on to the anger to anchor me.

"I … I'm sorry," the man said again in his thick accent. "It is always a difficult thing to lose a limb. But if you had kept the leg, you'd have died. Do you understand?"

I understood, all right. I understood this man had picked me up outta the desert, drugged me, and performed some kinda unholy surgery on me. Some kind of twisted, dark experiment that had fused my body with a tangle of cold, hard, lifeless metal. "You took my leg," I repeated.

"Yes," he said again. "To save your life. It was the only way, I assure you. And I would argue the false leg I have provided you is an advantage, not a disadvantage."

I took a few deep breaths, the anger helpin' to bring me back from the edge of blackness. "An …

advantage?" I lifted my poundin' head to stare at him. "An advantage? You *chopped off my goddamn leg!*" I lunged outta the bed at him, but I was weak and clumsy and minus one leg.

The metal one didn't work like a flesh and blood one, and he stepped easily outta my reach. I crashed to the floor instead, landin' heavy with a cry as a new flare of pain gripped my thigh.

"Please do not exert yourself," the man urged. "You must rest or your body may still reject the false leg and you will die despite my efforts."

"Good riddance," his wife said from the doorway.

"Hanna!" the doctor said, aghast.

I saw her booted feet step toward me and looked up from where I was curled on the floor to see her brandishin' the choppin' knife. She held the point of it at me, aimin' at my forehead, though her husband put his arm out in front of her to stop her advance.

I wasn't sure if he was tryin' to protect her from me … or me from her.

"I told my husband to let you die," she whispered. "I told him you were trouble. That you were not worth it. I could tell it from the looks of you. But he would not listen. My husband is a decent man. A good man. Better than you could ever hope to be. He is too kind. He cares about those he should not care about. And so he saved you. And look what it has gotten him. Nothing." She spit at me, and the wad of saliva fell just short of my face. "No gratitude. No thank you. No kindness. Just curses and anger."

"Hanna," the man said softly, but she would not be silenced.

"Go and leave if you wish. Die alone in the wild like the dog that you are. Like you should have died days ago. I will not mourn for your passing. I think no one will."

She pressed the knife's handle into her husband's hand, gave him a fierce glare, and then spun on her heel and marched out of the room. Her daughter turned and hurried after her, leavin' me alone with the man.

The good, decent doctor who had cut off my leg.

He looked down at me then with an expression I did not expect: sympathy.

I rolled onto my back and closed my eyes against it. Damn fool. He was surely goin' to end up dead. "You should have listened to your wife," I croaked. "I ain't worth savin'."

I was a fool, too. A fool and a failure. I hadn't stopped those men from killin' Mama and Pa, or from burnin' down our house and everythin' else we owned. I hadn't kept Ethelyn safe; I'd left her and she'd disappeared. I hadn't killed Nine-Fingered Nan when I'd had the chance, and now my leg was gone. I'd finally found the end of my searchin', finally thought I had a chance to get Ethelyn back, after all these years, and instead I hadn't lasted even two days in the desert 'fore nearly bein' buzzard food.

How long had I been here, in this man's house?

How far away was Bravebank from here?

How long would Nine-Fingered Nan's man be waitin' in the Stag Saloon?

After all of this, after everythin', Ethelyn could already be gone. Shipped off. Sold. And Nan laughin' at the both of us as she counted her cash.

"Nonsense," the man said quietly, bringin' me

back from the mires of my misery. "Everyone deserves to be saved. Everyone deserves a second chance."

It was my turn to laugh, a choked, bitter sound. "That's the biggest pile a' horseshit I ever heard."

I could think of a few people who surely didn't deserve to be saved. Nine-Fingered Nan chief among 'em. I'd not hesitate to send that woman to Hell if I ever laid eyes on her again.

If I didn't end up there first.

The man gave a heavy sigh. "I understand this is difficult for you. The adjustment will take some time. But please, give it a chance. My wife … her words are harsh … but she speaks some truth. If you leave now, you will die out there. Alone. And you might be trouble, but you looked to me like a man who wanted to live. Was I wrong? Are you instead a man who wishes to die?"

I almost laughed again, then pushed the heels of my hands against my eyes to stop the swell of self-loathin'. The right one was still sore.

That was the question I'd been askin' myself since Ethelyn and I had run off terrified into the dark, into the woods behind our homestead that night. Pa's blood still warm where it'd splattered across my face.

I'd wondered then if maybe it would have been better to die with our parents. And I'd wondered again when I'd returned from scoutin' out hideaways to find Ethelyn gone. I'd spent so many sleepless nights frettin' about her. Wonderin' if she was dead … or wonderin' if she was wishin' she was dead.

And so many times in the years since then, when I was gone hungry another day, or robbed of what little I had, or shootin' another fella in the face 'cause he was tryin' to rob what little I had. Or any of the days Holt and I had taken from the honest folk, or been chased away from another backwater town by the bullets of lawmen and the threat of bein' hanged.

How often I'd wondered if it'd just be better to die.

And yet, despite everythin', despite my wonderin', I just kept on livin'.

I kept tryin'. I kept fightin'. I kept shootin' and robbin' and lyin'.

"I gotta find my sister," I said, and the words surprised me. I hadn't meant to tell him that. I hadn't meant to answer him at all.

"I see. Well, son, it seems to me you cannot find your sister if you are dead. Hmm?"

I ground my teeth. Yes, damn him, such was the curse of my existence. As long as there were rumors of Ethelyn Delano bein' alive, it seemed I was doomed to keep on livin', too.

As long as she was alive, as long as there was a chance fer me to find her … I had just enough hope to keep on goin'. Just enough hope to think maybe I wasn't a complete failure, that maybe I was worthy of still breathin' … long as I didn't give up on her.

"Well." I heard the man's bootsteps move, and dropped my hands and opened my eyes to look up at him. He set the knife down carefully atop the bureau on the other side of the room. "I trust I will not need that, no?" He came back to me and reached down to hook his hands under my armpits. "Come. Let us get you back into the bed."

He grunted as he hauled me up off the floor, and I braced my good right leg under me to help him. I could have used the leverage to knock him off his feet. Could have lurched over to the bureau and grabbed that knife. Could have left the house right then.

But I didn't.

Instead I let him help me back to the mattress and eased down onto it. Sat back against the pillows he propped up behind me. Let him throw the covers back up over my legs to my waist, coverin' up the brace of metal that had replaced my left one.

My body felt numb, my mind strugglin' to accept any of this. Strugglin' to accept his kindness. His understandin'.

His sympathy.

Maybe I was finally dead, after all.

Maybe this was Hell.

"Please, rest," he said. "I will bring you some broth and water. You have been on a liquid diet for a few days ... you will need to work up to solid foods."

He turned to move for the door.

"How long?" I blurted.

He turned with an eyebrow raised. "I beg your pardon?"

"How long since you found me?"

"Oh. Nearly four days now."

I made a noise of despair, sinkin' back into the pillows.

His brows furrowed. "Is something wrong?"

"Yeah," I husked. "I gotta get to Bravebank. Need to meet someone there. Not sure how long they'll stay."

That expression of disapproval came across his face again. "I'm so sorry. You really should not travel for a few more weeks yet. But I would be happy to take the wagon to town and deliver a message to this person for you, to tell them you are currently … indisposed, but will meet them just as soon as you are well."

I laughed loud and long at that one, makin' him frown.

"Is there something amusing about my offer?"

"Yeah," I gasped, "yeah, sure is. You thinkin' this person is so polite and civilized as to care if I'm indisposed or not. Tell him that and he's just as likely to tail you home and murder us all as he is to spit in yer face at the news."

The good, decent doctor blinked rapidly at this information. "Why ever would you want to meet such a person?"

My amusement died down at last and I shook my head. "You act like I have a choice. I don't."

He was silent at that, as if tryin' to determine what to make of it, or waitin' for me to tell him more. But I'd already told him more than I'd meant to. More than I'd wanted to.

"Well," he said at last. "I will fetch you some food. If you rest up and do as I tell you, you may be able to make it into town sooner."

I said nothin' in reply, starin' out between the lace drapes at the distant clumps of creosote and cacti outside, tryin' to ignore the stranglin' feeling those damned curtains brought to my throat.

He took up the knife on his way outta the room and shut the door softly behind him.

I closed my eyes and leaned my head back against the down pillows, already makin' a plan. It didn't matter what the doctor said; I had to get to

Bravebank just as soon as I could. It'd already been five days since I'd met Nine-Fingered Nan in her hide-out. Who knew if her man was still in Bravebank or not, or, if by some miracle he was still there, how much longer he'd stay.

Every day that passed lessened my chances of findin' him, that much I was sure of.

And without that meetin', there was no deal with Nine-Fingered Nan. And without that deal, there was no hope of gettin' Ethelyn free.

Well, there was a few more things I knew now after talkin' with the good doctor who had chopped off my leg, and I was fairly certain it was enough to get me to Bravebank.

I knew this family had a wagon. That meant they had horses or mules to pull it. I could borrow one of those animals to get me to Bravebank.

I also knew it was likely the doctor had set up shop in Bravebank. There weren't no other towns very close, certainly none less than a day's ride, and this climate didn't lend well to growin' crops or raisin' livestock. The only people livin' out here were either into the mines, or into supplyin' and transportin' those who were into the mines.

Or doctorin' those who were into the mines.

And if this doctor had a shop in Bravebank, he wouldn'ta put up his house too far out of the town limits. So he could drive there and back in a day without wastin' too much daylight.

My heart quickened a bit at this realization, knowin' I couldn't be too far off with such speculations. And all of this meant I was closer to Bravebank than I'd thought. All I had to do was wait for my opportunity to relieve the good doctor of one his fine animals.

And find out where he'd hidden my guns and my clothes.

And figure out how this confounded metal leg worked.

THE CONSEQUENCES OF KINDNESS

I had evil dreams and fitful sleep, there in that proper bed with its cotton sheets.

I tossed and turned and woke up in a cold sweat, swearin' I'd heard my mother scream. There was an orange, flickerin' glow cast across the strange room when I opened my eyes, and for a heartbeat my muscles seized in terror, believin' I was gonna have to relive that nightmare yet again.

Then I caught sight of a shadowy figure to my left, sittin' beside the bed, and I nearly jumped outta my skin again as I realized it was a woman. A real flesh and blood person ... not part of my nightmare. And not just any person, it was the doctor's wife.

The orange glow in the room came from the lantern she had lit and set on the bedside table. She sat in a simple wooden chair which she'd pulled up next to the mattress, still and quiet, watchin' me. And in her lap, she turned a knife over and over in her hands.

Not no choppin' knife this time, neither. A huntin' knife. The kind you'd use to dress an animal carcass.

I bolted upright in the bed, scramblin' back away from her to press myself up into the corner. I eyed the window with those damned lace curtains, wonderin' if I was gonna have to throw myself outta it.

But the woman raised a hand and shook her head. "Shhh. Calm down. I am no murderer."

I glanced to the knife still in her lap. The fat blade glimmered in the lantern light.

She followed my gaze, and smiled softly. "This is only a precaution," she said in her heavy accent. "I came here to give you a warning, *idegen*. What I said earlier today; I meant it. My husband is an idealist. I am a realist. If he wants to waste good metal on you, so be it. But do not think you can take anything else from us, understand? While you are here, we will take care of you … unless you give me reason to doubt my husband's belief in you. Unless you prove to me that *my* impressions of you are correct. In that case…" Her grip on the huntin' knife tightened. "In that case I will not hesitate to defend my family. Do not think our kindness makes us weak. Do not think our kindness makes us stupid. For we are neither."

I studied her face in the flickerin' light, saw the deadly seriousness in her flat stare and set jaw, and swallowed. I knew the look of a person who would kill if they had to.

She had that look.

I gave a nod in acknowledgement. "Ma'am," I said hoarsely, "I don't believe you are either."

Maybe I *had* thought 'em stupid at first … stupid for takin' in a stranger like me, who coulda robbed and killed the lot of 'em as soon as I was on my feet again … but it seemed the good doctor's wife at least had already entertained that possibility, and planned fer it.

Which coulda also been why my belongin's—includin' my guns—were nowhere in sight.

"Good." She stood from the chair. "Then if you

are to be a guest in our home, you will see that you obey the house rules. No swearing, prayers before dinner, and wash on Sundays. Understand?"

I blinked at her, wonderin' if maybe I was still dreamin'. A multitude of replies ran through my mind, most of 'em impolite, but then, she *was* still holdin' that knife. "Yes ma'am," was all I managed.

"Good," she said again. She moved the chair back against the wall and slipped the huntin' knife into the sash at the waist of her simple cotton dress. "Now that we have an understanding, I will leave you to rest. Pleasant dreams."

And with that, she picked up the lantern and left the room, closin' the door behind her.

I exhaled loudly and sagged back into the pillows.

Almost three weeks later, I was still no closer to gettin' to Bravebank.

Though it weren't fer lack of tryin' … it was fer lack of havin' two natural legs. As much as I wanted outta that house—and the urgency burned like my own personal Hell in the center of me every damn day—my body weren't cooperatin'.

The pain in the stump of my thigh and the strangeness of havin' all that metal attached to me had me bed-ridden fer a week, and then when I finally forced myself up onto my feet in the second week, the doctor fussed over me like a broody hen over her nest. I didn't want to listen to his multitude of instructions, but it turned out I had to, if I ever hoped to walk normal again. Or if I hoped not to die from another infection.

There were exercises to do to get used to my new leg, which he insisted I perform every day, and I reluctantly did so, though mostly only 'cause his wife was there, starin' me down through narrowed eyes with a choppin' knife in her hand.

And there was washin' and bandagin' to do of the place where my flesh met the metal, every day at first, then every other day, then every few days. Didn't matter how many times I watched the doctor do it, or how many times I did it myself, I didn't understand it.

I didn't understand how he'd done it. I didn't understand how it was possible.

Felt sick to my stomach every time I looked at it. Part of me wanted to demand he cut off the metal leg, too, and leave me be with my stump.

But I wouldn'ta fared very well out here in the Territories with one leg and a crutch. And payin' off the debt I now owed to Nine-Fingered Nan woulda been a hell of a lot harder, too.

So I kept the metal leg. I kept it and wondered what the doctor imagined I owed him fer it. I kept it and did my best to learn how to use it quick as I could, so I could get outta there and get back to trackin' down Ethelyn. I kept it and tried not to ever look at it. Not unless I really had to.

Now it was goin' on three weeks since I'd first woken up in the good doctor's home, and I was feelin' like my time to go was fast approachin'. I stood outside against his wishes, leanin' heavily on a crutch propped under my left armpit, eyes closed against the bright afternoon sun, breathin' in deep the dry, dusty air. I was in the side yard of the family's house, if it could be called a yard at all, which it could not.

Only dust and rock here, and the surly desert plants that grabbed, scratched and needled you as you tried to pass.

I had been mildly impressed to see a small garden sprouting off the back of the house, which I'd later learned was irrigated by a deep well and some complicated length of plumbin' the doctor had engineered himself, and all powered by a windmill that rose up off the roof of the house.

I opened my eyes and squinted down at the toe of my boot stickin' out the bottom of my left pants' leg. Inside of that boot was a metal foot. Maybe the doctor shouldn'ta been called a doctor at all, but more an engineer. I still couldn't fathom how the false metal leg he'd attached to me could work on its own, either, and he said that's why I was havin' so much trouble controllin' it.

"Walk as if you still had both natural legs," he'd urged me.

But that was hard to do when I couldn't feel the ground under my left foot. All I could feel was the metal where it met the flesh and muscle of my left thigh. I felt it pressin' there, shiftin' and movin' when I swung my leg and took a step, and it was still mighty sore.

And I was still mighty weak. Not nearly myself.

And that wouldn't do if I was gonna be owin' Nine-Fingered Nan.

I heard footsteps aproachin' from behind, light and quick.

It could only be the boy. Radley, he was called.

Probably slipped away from his mother's watchful eye again. She didn't like us talkin' much, and truth be told, I didn't like it much, either. I wasn't so good with kids. I never quite knew how to act around creatures so innocent.

He stopped beside me.

I said nothin'. Just kept studyin' the toe of my boot. At least they'd given my clothes back. All cleaned and pressed, too. And gifted me an old, beat-up hat to replace the one I'd lost. My guns, however … my guns were still missin'.

And I surely still felt naked without those belts around my hips.

"Are you really a gunslinger?" Radley asked abruptly, almost like he could read the thoughts in my head right then. He hardly had an accent at all.

I sighed and took my time to answer, shiftin' my weight experimentally to the metal leg. It held me well enough, but a little shock of pain flared again in my thigh. I winced and transferred my weight back to the crutch. "Who says I'm a gunslinger?" I asked finally.

"Fanni says," he answered simply. "And Mama, too. Well, Mama says you're an outlaw, mostly. She says 'gunslinger' is just a fancy name for 'murderer'."

The corner of my mouth pulled upward at that statement. Good ol' Hanna was more right than she knew about that one.

"Papa doesn't help outlaws, though," the boy went on. "He turns 'em over to the sheriff. So I don't think you're an outlaw. Anyway, Papa said there aren't any posters with your face on 'em hanging in town."

No, there ain't, I thought wryly. *Not here. Not yet.*

"I bet Fanni six penny candies that you weren't a gunslinger. So, are you?"

I turned my head finally to look over at the boy, archin' an eyebrow at him. "Ain't ya a little young to be gamblin'?"

His brows came down to hood his dark blue eyes and his hands balled into fists. "It's only candy, mister."

"Okay, all right." I shrugged. "Take it easy. Just thinkin' yer mama wouldn't approve."

"Mama don't know."

"Of course she don't." I switched my gaze out to the westward horizon, rollin' with the desert heat. I'd discovered where this family kept their wagon and mules easily enough; the barn behind the house was hard to miss. My guns were the only thing left to find.

There was a moment of stony silence between us. "Well?" he prompted. "Are you or aren't you? I wanna tell Fanni who wins the bet!"

I cleared my throat and swiped at the sweat that beaded on my upper lip. "Now why would yer sister —or yer mama—think I was a gunslinger?"

The boy scuffed the toe of his boot into the dirt. "I dunno. Well, I mean, you got two guns. They say a man lookin' to protect himself carries a gun ... and a man lookin' to kill some folk carries two guns."

A snort of amusement escaped me.

"What?" the boy asked suspiciously.

Hanna, the good doctor's wife ... more fulla truth than I gave her credit for. But I surely didn't wanna confirm his mama's worst fears. So I only shook my head and said, "What about the man who travels across a lot of bad land? The man who'd like to reload after twelve shots instead a' six when a buncha bandits come out of the rocks?"

The kid was silent for another minute, presumably thinkin' it over. "I dunno," he said again. "I guess that makes sense."

"And what about you?" I asked, suddenly curious. I turned slightly to face him, my boot and my new metal foot crunchin' in the gritty dirt. "What makes you think I *ain't* a gunslinger?"

He looked up at me, right in the eyes. "On account of your leg, mister."

I frowned. "My leg?"

He nodded. "Sure. You were shot in the leg, bad enough Papa had to take it off and give you a metal one."

"Gunslingers get shot sometimes, too, ya know," I said.

But Radley shook his head. "Nah. Gunslingers shoot folk dead, or get shot dead. I've never heard of a gunslinger who crawled away into the desert after getting shot in the leg. At least, that's never what happens in those books Fanni reads."

My eyes narrowed at the way him sayin' it like that made me sound like a coward. At the way he so casually compared the romanticized tale in a dime novel to my daily Hell of a life. But the rise of anger sputtered out nearly as quick as it came.

He was only a kid. He didn't know. I prayed he'd never know.

It didn't matter what he thought of gunslingers, anyway. Or what his mama or sister thought of gunslingers, neither.

I was no gunslinger either way.

I was just a man lookin' fer the only family I had left. Lookin' fer a way out of the grave I'd been diggin' fer myself since the day Ethelyn had disappeared.

"Well, yer right," I muttered. "I ain't no gunslinger." Maybe if I had been, I'd of got the draw on Nine-Fingered Nan, and she'd be dead now, and Ethelyn'd be free, and I'd still have my leg. I mighta been pretty damn good at shootin' guns, but out here, anythin' short of the bein' the best eventually landed you dead.

Hell, if Nine-Fingered Nan hadn'ta wanted to fuck with me, I'd be dead already. I wouldn't be here now, talkin' to this kid.

"Ha! I knew it!" Radley exclaimed triumphantly, breakin' me outta my broodin'. "I gotta go tell Fanni! She's gonna owe me next time we go to town!"

He turned on his heel to make off for the house, but I called out to him before he could get too far. "Hey, kid!"

He drew up short and turned to face me again, shieldin' his eyes against the sun with his hand. "Yeah?"

I glanced around the yard, and didn't see none of the other family about. But still, I didn't want to take any chances of bein' overheard. I hobbled carefully toward him, leanin' heavy on the crutch, my metal foot half walkin' and half draggin'. I stopped about an arms' length from him, where I could talk quiet. "Look," I said, "you know I ain't no gunslinger. And I ain't no outlaw, neither." Well, that weren't entirely the truth. But it weren't entirely a lie, neither. I weren't an outlaw in this state. Yet. "Yer pa said himself, there ain't no posters of me up."

The boy shrugged. "Yeah."

"And I appreciate what yer family's done fer me and all … but I got business to attend to in Brave-bank. Business that can't wait. Business that requires I go in with my guns. Understand? You wouldn't happen to know where yer ma or pa hid my guns, would ya?"

He only stared up at me from beneath his hand. "I thought you said you weren't an outlaw? Murder's against the law, mister. Unless … are you a lawman?" his voice rose a bit at that last part, as if he were suddenly comin' to a realization. "Is that why you have two guns?"

"No … no," I said, signalin' hastily for him to quiet down. I glanced around again to make sure his mama wouldn't come out and catch this conversation of ours. She mighta used that knife she'd threatened me with if she knew what I was askin' of her youngest. "Not a lawman, kid. But the people I'm supposed to meet … they're bad, bad men, see? I ain't goin' there to murder 'em, but they might try and murder me. And if that happens … well, I need my guns. To defend myself."

He pursed his lips and dropped his hand from his eyes, lookin' around like I had done to see if any of his family was close by.

"Please, kid," I said, and I let some of the desperation clawin' around in my chest into my voice. It was embarassin' to be at the mercy of a ten-year-old boy, but so I was. His sister wouldn't come near me, and neither of his parents were gonna hand me back my weapons till they were good and sure I was healthy and healed and headin' out far away from their homestead, I was sure of it.

"If I got your guns for you, would you leave?" he asked at last.

It wasn't the response I'd been expectin'. But I answered honestly. "Yes. My business is urgent. I've already been here too long."

He looked me up and down then with a scrutinizin' eye I didn't much like. "I'm not sure that's a good idea, mister. Papa says you need to—"

"Yer papa don't understand," I bit off, and then at the widenin' of his eyes, checked myself and exhaled slowly. "I'm sorry. But like I said, my business is urgent. I can't afford to waste any more time. If it makes ya feel any better, I'll come back when it's done. Yeah? Let me go take care of my business, and then I'll come back here and heal up nice just like your pa would want."

Now that ... that was a full-out lie. But I'd gotten pretty good at lyin' in my lifetime. It sounded like the truth.

Radley was silent for a long moment, chewin' at his lip.

I wanted to say more, to push him for an answer quick-like, but it wouldn'ta helped. He had to make the decision for himself. So I waited in the dusty yard, quiet and still on the outside and jumpin' with nerves on the inside, sweat slidin' down my neck.

"Okay," he said finally.

I blew out the breath I'd been holdin'.

"But don't tell no one how you found 'em, okay? Else Mama'll give me a whooping and..." he looked me up and down again, "well, I don't know what she'd do to you."

"I have a pretty good idea," I muttered. "My lips are sealed, kid. You have no idea how much yer helpin' me, here."

He nodded, resolute now that he'd made a decision. "Yeah, sure. I'll get 'em for you tonight. But you'll need to be gone before morning, and get back quick as you can. Otherwise Papa might organize a search party for you. He worries a lot about his patients."

My eyes lifted from Radley to rest on the barn in the back. "I can see that he does," I said, but my mind was already gone, thinkin' ahead to tonight, makin' up my plan to escape.

We had dinner in awkward silence, per usual, with Dr. Balogh—as I'd learned was their family name—attempin' and failin' to make small talk. Then Hanna read to her children from the Good Book by lantern light, and I excused myself into the small spare bedroom and closed the door, unable to bear the sound of those verses.

The Good Book hadn't saved my mama, despite her readin' from it daily.

It hadn't kept our home from burnin' down, neither. Nope, the Good Book itself had burned up with everythin' else … reduced to nothin' more than a pile of ash, indistinguishable from any of the rest of it.

I did not undress for bed this night, but propped my crutch against the wall and eased myself under the sheets fully clothed. I had to grab my false leg under the knee and drag it up onto the mattress, and I winced at the throbbin' in my thigh.

Perhaps the doctor had been right about not wantin' me to travel so soon.

But I didn't really have a choice now, did I?

I settled back against the pillows and waited, watchin' the play of the lantern lit in the corner against the walls and ceilin'.

Despite myself, I must have dozed. I jerked awake at a soft creakin' noise, and looked over toward the door to see the boy tip-toein' in. And, bless his innocent little soul, he had my gun belts in his hands.

I sat up and scrubbed my hands over my face, shakin' off the sleep. The lantern in the corner was burnin' low now, barely givin' off enough light for the boy to see as he crept across the room. He set my belts and my two holsters, complete with both revolvers, on the end of the bed. "Here," he whispered.

"Thank you," I whispered in return. I wished I had somethin' to give him for his help, but all my belongin's—what I hadn't left with Holt back in Grave Gulch, anyway—had been lost to the desert. "I'll bring ya back somethin' nice from town," I offered instead.

I threw back the covers, swung my feet to the floor, and pulled the belts toward me.

"How you gonna get there?" the boy asked, still in a whisper. "I don't think you should walk, not with that leg. And the wagon's too noisy."

"Just gonna borrow one of the mules," I said, bucklin' on my first belt. A part of me questioned the wisdom in tellin' him so much of my plan. But then … he had almost as much to lose in this as I did now. He wouldn't tell no one.

He shook his head. "Oh. Papa won't like that."

"I imagine yer parents won't like any part of this plan, kid."

"He can't drive the wagon with just one mule."

Guilt weaseled its way into my gut, workin' up toward my throat. I tried to swallow it down and buckled on my second belt. Damn this family and their cursed kindness.

What did kindness get 'em, anyway?

Another mouth to feed and a stolen mule, that's what.

And what did their kindness get me?

A whole wagon-load of guilt, damnit.

I shook my head and stood from the bed, reachin' for my crutch. "I'll bring it back," I said. "Won't be long. Promise." I hoped he couldn't see my face in the dyin' lantern light.

I was surely gonna go to Hell fer lyin'.

DEAD MEN MAKE NO DEALS

In the end, I took more than the mule. I took one of their saddles, a pair of their saddlebags, a canteen of water, a mutton steak wrapped in brown paper, a bit of bread and cheese, and the bottle of laudanum the doctor had put on the bedside table for the pain in my thigh. I stuck my crutch in the saddle scabbard made fer a rifle.

Radley was an accomplice to all of it, which didn't make me feel no better. In fact, it made me feel worse, considerin' the fact he thought I was comin' back. At least he didn't see me off. I made him go back inside to bed before I mounted up, partly because then he could honestly claim he hadn't seen me ride off, and partly because I didn't want him to see me try to get that tangle of metal that was now my left leg up over the saddle.

But I did it, finally, after a lotta gruntin' and cursin' and sweatin'.

The mule wasn't too happy about it, neither, swivelin' its ears around and chompin' the bit, dancin' in place.

"Just calm down, ya edgy bastard," I growled as I gathered up the reins. I urged it off at a lope, wantin' to put as much distance between me and the Balogh homestead as quick as possible.

The moon was up, no longer full, but bright enough still to light my way.

Far as I could tell, it was near midnight. And the kid had said Bravebank was only four miles away. I could make it there in no time at this rate.

I set my sights on the path ahead, the non-existent road, and resisted the urge to kick the mule into a full-on gallop. It wouldn't do to go tearin' off into the dark, even if this were a mostly flat piece of arid land. Last thing I needed was for the animal to go down, or to go lame.

And anyway, just ridin' at a lope was makin' my thigh ache bad enough. I ground my teeth against the pain, tryin' to ignore it.

I remembered what the doctor had said, about my body rejectin' the leg if I didn't rest up enough, and whispered a curse that was lost beneath the mule's drummin' hooves.

Maybe I could rest when I was dead.

My heart leapt when I saw the lights of Bravebank.

It was a big enough town to have a few street lamps, and these glowed yellow against the night, throwin' weak circles of light on the ground below as I finally turned down its dusty main road.

Most of the shops were dark at this hour, but down the street a-ways I saw the lighted windows of the sanctuary for any weary traveler: the saloon, the hotel, and the brothel. I dropped the mule into a walk as I approached, the boisterous piano music spillin' from the saloon growin' louder with each step.

There were a few people out on the street, mostly

drunks or saloon girls hopin' to catch a late arrival and steer 'em inside, but I ignored all of 'em as I reined up my mount at the hitchin' post. I fished out the bottle of laudanum right quick and took a little swig, hopin' it would dull the fire that now ate away at my left thigh after my ride.

I couldn't go in there with the crutch. Couldn't risk Nan's man—or anyone else, for that matter—thinkin' I was an easy mark. I swiped suddenly sweaty palms against the grips of my guns. Least I had those back, and plenty of bullets.

That would have to do.

I swung down off the mule real careful, but the shock of pain was still enough to make me suck in a sharp breath. Sweat prickled under my collar. I took a minute to compose myself, leanin' against the animal.

"Long ride, my love?" a woman's voice asked. "Need me to take care a' ya?"

I glanced up to her, saw her leanin' over the hitchin' rail and battin' long lashes at me from above the rim of her fan. Her corset had been pulled tight, her ample bosom nearly spillin' out the top, and her skirt was short. Her long hair was pinned atop her head, spirals of curls fallin' down around her bare shoulders.

I swallowed hard, cursin' the lust that stirred despite everythin'. I wondered if The Stag's girls were actually sportin' women, or if she just wanted to get me inside so I'd spend all my money on drink. "Nah," I husked. "Not now."

She feigned a pout. "Aww. You sure? You look tense. I could help ya relax…"

So maybe she *could* offer more than a drink. But

it didn't much matter. I didn't have the coin or the time for such things. She sauntered in my direction, but I waved her off and shook my head. "Maybe another time." It took a mighty load of concentration to stay standin' without a woman hangin' on my arm, too.

To my relief, she accepted my second refusal with grace, steppin' back to take up her post again at the hitchin' rail. She fanned herself and shrugged. "All right, then. You know where I'll be."

"Sure." I took a breath, and took a step with the metal leg. It hurt. I grimaced and wavered there fer a minute, thinkin' I was about to go down into the dirt. Well, they'd probably think I was just another drunk.

The girl watched me stagger there with a raised brow. "You ain't even gone inside yet," she commented.

I tossed her a glare, but made no retort. It took too much focus to keep my balance. But somehow, miraculously, I made it to the boardwalk, and thanked what shit luck I had that this saloon didn't have no stairs out front. And then I reached the door and drew another deep breath, shovin' the pain down deep as it could go.

I pushed through into the noise and light of the place.

The late hour had not slowed the business of The Stag Saloon, certainly. There were plenty of girls busy makin' the rounds, the bartender was busy pourin', the piano busy playin', and a whole lotta folk busy drinkin' or dealin' cards.

My God, did I want a shot a' whiskey all of a sudden—maybe more than one—but I had no coin fer that, either. I kicked myself for not swipin' a few of those off the good doctor too while I had the chance.

Guess I'd have to do this sober. My eyes swept the floor, lingerin' on the poker tables. Nan had not given me a description of the man I was supposed to meet, nor his name, but I'd figured he'd probably know I was comin'. And my face weren't on any posters in this town, no, and I might not of had a hole in my leg anymore … but the metal one did give me a limp that was painfully obvious no matter how much I tried to hide it.

I limped now, slow and careful, over toward the left wall, plannin' to plant myself there and watch till I identified the fella I was lookin' fer. I leaned back against the wall and crossed my arms, wantin' nothin' more than a chair. But the place was full. There weren't no more chairs available.

So I stood, ignorin' the pain, and watched.

My heart throbbed in my throat, and the very real worry that I'd come weeks too late rubbed at my nerves. Or maybe he'd retired early. Or maybe he was a day gambler.

Or maybe Nan had played me fer a fool entirely, and there was never no man a' hers to meet here.

Anger burned in my ears at the thought, knowin' it was surely possible.

There was so much I didn't know. Too much.

And I'd been so distracted by my dead horse and the bullet in my leg and the revolver pointed at my head and a chance at earnin' Ethelyn's freedom that I hadn't thought to ask more questions.

As if Nan would have answered 'em, anyway. So I stood. And I waited. And I watched.

And the time ticked by on the pendulum clock across the room.

Saloon girls came to see if I were interested in a dance or a chat or a nice, warm bed, but I declined 'em all.

Then they came to see if I would at least buy a drink or some food, but I declined that, too.

I started gettin' a suspicious side-eye from the bartender, so then I told 'em I'd order once the man I was meetin' here showed up. They left me alone for awhile after that.

My leg ached somethin' awful. Sweat gathered under my collar. My skin felt hot, and all I could think of was the doctor, and how mad he'd be if I ended up droppin' dead out here.

Then the laudanum kicked in, and the pain dulled for a bit.

Then the laudanum wore off, and the pain came back, worse than before. A cold sweat broke out all over. Exhaustion pulled at my body, my mind, my eyelids. People came and went in The Stag Saloon, the moon trekked across the sky, and I still stood there, watchin', tryin' my damnedest to stay awake, and to keep from swoonin'.

I needed somethin', anythin', to keep my strength up and dull the fire eatin' away at my thigh. So I started lookin' fer marks, instead of my contact. Plenty of the men here now were blind drunk. They'd never notice a missin' coin purse. Not till they sobered up, and then it'd be too late.

One such man was staggerin' toward the doors now. He tilted, wavered, and stumbled sideways into a table, jostlin' the drinks and elicitin' angry protests from the men seated around that table.

I moved quick as I could manage—which wasn't quick at all—toward the fella and grabbed the back of his vest, haulin' him back upright just as he was shoutin' threats at the seated men. "Okay, mister," I muttered. "Think you've had enough. Time to go."

"Git yer 'andsoffame!" he slurred, swingin' around with a fist, which I easily dodged.

The men at the table he'd stumbled into laughed, which only made the drunk's face get redder.

I ignored his curses and the new threats he was now directin' at me and dragged him toward the doors, cursin' my heavy limp and the eyes he'd drawn toward us. But his fumblin' and staggerin', while nearly knockin' me off balance and onto my ass myself, gave me enough cover to snatch the small purse at his belt in the dimness of the saloon's entrance. I shoved it into my own pocket, then threw him out the door.

He went sailin' and landed with an *oomph*, rollin' out into the dusty street.

Where he pushed himself back to his feet again and turned to face me, hand goin' fer his gun.

The grip of my own weapon was in my hand in an instant, but I didn't even have to draw. The drunk swayed, starin' at me, then his eyes rolled up into his head and he fell face-first into the dirt, out cold.

I released my own gun and turned back to face the interior of the saloon, which had considerably hushed since I'd laid my hands on another patron. I gave those who was lookin' at me now, and that was most of the saloon, a rueful smile and held my hands shoulder-high, shruggin'. I surely didn't want any of 'em to think I was here lookin' fer trouble.

Well, if Nan's man was here and hadn't noticed me yet, he couldn'ta missed me now.

To my relief, it seemed the drunk I'd booted was not a particular favorite here. The other patrons merely blinked at me, then went back to their business. A few of 'em whistled or clapped.

And then everythin' went back to the way it was, and I let out a long, slow breath.

There was an empty chair at a table to my right now, so I limped over there and sat heavily, unable to hide the grimace at the flare of pain in my thigh.

Two old men sat at the table I had joined, with plates of biscuits, beans, and bacon. Miners, judgin' from the state of the grime dug into the creases of their skin and clothes. They had a bottle of whiskey set between 'em, and two glasses. One of the men poured a finger of whiskey into one of the glasses, and pushed it toward me.

I raised an eyebrow.

He nodded at me and swiped at the beans stuck to his grizzled gray beard with the back of his hand. "Ya done us a favor, boy. Tha' Jake, he's a right ol' blowhard, he is. Always in here full as a tick, causin' trouble. Ain't no one like 'em. Go on, drink up. Ya deserve it."

I grunted. Seemed I'd picked the right man to rob and toss. I downed the whiskey and closed my eyes at its burn, willin' it to cool down the burn in my damned leg.

"Jus' you be careful tomorrow, though," the second miner said then, gesturin' at me with a greasy finger. "Jake, he likes ta pick fights. If he remembers ya tomorrow, he'll be lookin' fer ya."

I sighed. Or I'd picked the wrong man to rob and toss.

The first old miner poured me another finger, and chuckled as he did so. "Here. Here's ta hopin' he don't remember ya." He pushed the glass at me again.

I shook my head and threw the whiskey back. "Here's to hopin'," I muttered.

Despite the scene I'd caused, no one approached me to talk business. No one took any particular notice of me.

Folk in The Stag Saloon just kept drinkin' and eatin' and gamblin' and flirtin' with the girls.

I ordered my own whiskey with the coin I'd lifted off the angry drunk, and helped myself to some hard-boiled eggs and cold-cuts off the back table, now that I'd ordered myself some alcohol and satisfied the narrow-nosed bartender, who'd been givin' me a hard glare now and then up till that point.

I sat with the miners till they bade me farewell and retired for the night, then sat with some other folk I ignored. And they ignored me, in turn.

Just the way I liked it.

Gradually, the patrons of the Stag thinned out. They went upstairs to their rooms, or out to their residences or the other hotels, some with a girl on their arm, some alone.

But I stayed.

The sky I could glimpse through the saloon's

front windows above the buildin's across the street began to lighten. My eyes burned. My body wanted nothin' more than to sleep.

That urgent desperation I'd felt when facin' off against Nine-Fingered Nan was back, that feelin' of bein' so very close … and yet not bein' quite close enough.

I'd missed him. I must have missed him.

My heart beat hard in my throat, and I swallowed more whiskey to try and drown it.

Damn it all to Hell, I couldn't let it end like this.

I slammed the glass back hard to the table, but the only one sober enough to disapprove of my recklessness was the bartender himself. I ignored the fresh glare he tossed me, squeezin' shut my achin' eyes. I rubbed at my face with my hands.

How long could I stay here?

Not forever. Not long at all, in truth.

Soon enough the doctor and his family, well, all of 'em except Radley, would find out I'd gone. They'd discover a mule was missin', and I'd told 'em I had business in Bravebank. They'd know where I went. Doctor Balogh would come lookin' fer me here, I was sure of it.

And when he found me … what then?

Would he try and force me to return to his homestead with him?

And if I went back with him, what would his wife think? How would she handle my stompin' all over her family's good will and tenuous trust?

And would they accuse me of stealin' their mule?

I grimaced at the thought. At least I hoped it wouldn't come to that. I was in no state to outrun or fight off any law who might come after me fer such a thing. And I most certainly didn't want to hang over a mule.

I swallowed more whiskey. Surely Radley would tell 'em I was only borrowin' the animal. Maybe it was a lie, but they only had to believe it was the truth long enough fer me to make the deal with Nan's man and get outta town.

Course, that was the catch, weren't it? I couldn't get outta town till I made the deal, and I couldn't make the deal till I found Nan's man. And he was provin' to be harder to find than I'd hoped.

Anxiety crawled all over me like a livin' thing. My skin itched with restlessness and I glanced again out the window.

He's not here. I missed him. I came too late.

But I shook off the thought soon as it went through my head.

No. No. He has to be here ... maybe he's just up-stairs, havin' a good time with one of the girls. He'll be back. He's got to be back eventually...

I kept tellin' myself that. And kept nursin' the whiskey, hopin' the drink would soothe my nerves and numb the pain in my leg.

I couldn't leave now. Not after I'd finally made it here. Not until I was absolutely certain.

And I couldn't stay, neither. Not unless I wanted to face a very disappointed Dr. Balogh, or chance runnin' into an angry, sobered-up Jake, or possibly encounter a lawman come to get me fer rustlin' a mule.

Outside, the sun crept closer and closer to the horizon.

Inside, I did my best to drown all my hopes and fears in whiskey.

"Well, well, well."

I jerked awake and sat up straight, then winced and caught my breath at the shootin' pains that raced up my spine. And my legs were goin' numb. I squinted in the light, liftin' a hand to shield my face, blinkin' hard to clear the blur in my vision.

"Look what the cat dragged in, boys."

I blinked some more, tryin' to find the source of the voice. A silhouette in the shape of a man moved across my field of view, followed by another. And another.

I closed my eyes and rubbed 'em. Moved my toes around in my boots.

No, wait. I couldn't feel my left foot.

My eyes shot open, and I grimaced again in the sudden onslaught of light. A headache stabbed in my temples and I groaned. I supposed I might have tried a little too hard last night to forget my worries—*shit!* And that's when I remembered. That's when I remembered all of what my worries the night before had been.

My hands dropped to my guns—both of 'em—but in the morning silence the sound of five pistols clearin' leather might as well have been loud as a herd of stampedin' cattle.

I froze.

The silence held. No one fired.

I forced myself to breathe slow and deep, though my heart had quickened, and blinked again in the dazzlin' mornin' light. I cursed the cloud of stupid the whiskey had brought down upon my head. The risin' sun had broke above the buildin's across the street, and I'd picked a table dead-set in the middle of its blazin' rays. *Stupid. Stupid, Van! You shoulda stayed sober. And awake.*

"Whew, boy!" the voice said, the tone of mock relief. But I heard a thread of truth in there … the barest of trembles to the man's tenor. "Better watch it, fellas! This one's quick. So they say. This is Lucky Logan's brat. Ain't you?"

I tried to focus on the fella who kept talkin', the one who clearly thought he was the leader. He was at least smart enough to stand directly in front of that damned blindin' sun, so that no matter how hard I squinted, I couldn't make out none of his features. He was only a shiftin' silhouette, a blur of black against the bright.

Well, he thought that made 'em smart, anyway. Sure, I could hardly peel my eyes open to get a look at him, but what I did see of him was outlined real nice against such a shiny background.

"Depends on who's askin'," I said. I kept my hands restin' on my guns, real light. I didn't move 'em, didn't so much as twitch. Those five naked guns hadn't found their five empty holsters yet. And even I didn't like those odds.

But I moved my focus to my hands, then. Away from my achin' back and legs and waterin' eyes and that bastard of a silhouette. Just to my hands. The feel of the metal warmin' beneath my skin. The texture of the grips beneath the slight curl of my fingers.

"I told Nan you were dead," the man said.

My focus shattered at those words, and the world became a blur of light and shadows and pain once more. "What?" I strangled out. All I could think of was Nine-Fingered Nan then, tellin' me Ethelyn would be safe enough till the deal was made … lest I died in the desert.

"I told her you was dead," the man repeated, louder and slower.

"I ain't dead," I snapped.

"Not yet," the man drawled. "But Nan said to watch fer ya weeks ago. Ya didn't show up. Thought for sure that bullet she put in ya killed ya."

"It didn't. And I'm here now." My heart throbbed in my throat, pulsin' wildly. So this was the man Nan had told me to meet. I'd found him at last. Or rather, he'd found me. But if he'd already told Nan I was dead … was it too late? *Please don't let it be too late. Please.*

I lifted my hands from my guns, slow and careful, and set them flat on the table in front of me. "So we gonna make a deal or what?"

He laughed, and then a brief silence followed, and I listened to the poundin' of my own heart in my ears.

"Maybe," he said. His shadow moved around the table, closer, and I heard the click of a hammer bein' pulled back, closer. "But I already told Nan you were dead. And I'd hate to be made a liar."

I shook my head, choosin' my words carefully. "Somethin' tells me Nan wouldn't like it much if anyone killed me but her."

"She'd never know. She thinks she killed you already."

I chanced a glance away from him, away from the sun's glarin' light, first to my right, then to my left, to the rest of his group, tryin' to judge where their loyalties lie. More with him, or more with Nan?

Their expressions were hard, unwaverin', their gun hands steady. I glanced around the rest of the saloon, searchin' to see if there might be any witnesses. There were a few men asleep as I had been, folded over the tables, even a few sprawled on the floor, but no one currently conscious. And the bartender was conspicuously absent.

I sighed, bringin' my eyes back down to my own hands, still flat against the table, and nodded. "All right. What do you want?"

"I want a percent of whatever you get fer Nan."

"Ain't that somethin' you should work out with her?"

He laughed again. "Nah. You just add my percent on top."

I rubbed at my throbbin' temples and closed my eyes against the light. "And what are Nan's terms, then?"

"Ah. Glad to hear yer willin' to be reasonable." I heard his hammer ease off and his weapon slide back into its holster. The scrape of the chair he pulled out was loud to my achin' head and I winced. The chair creaked as he settled down into it, and then there was a thump and the jingle of spurs as he set his boots up on the edge of the table.

The other four men he'd brought with him did not holster their weapons, nor did they sit down. I waited. And listened.

"Well, ya see, Nan's been offered a lot o' money for yer sister," he said.

Revulsion roiled in my gut at the words and I

tensed. So help me, soon as I had Ethelyn back, I was gonna end everyone involved in this…

"So the only way yer gettin' her back is to pay Nan at least what she's been offered already, if not some more just to make it worth her trouble of entertainin' ya in the first place."

Entertainin'? Is that what she called shootin' my horse dead and nearly shootin' me dead?

"How much?" I asked.

"Twenty-five thousand."

I barked laughter, pushin' my chair back away from the table and squintin' at him into the sun. "You're outta yer goddamned mind!"

"And if you wanna stay alive long enough to earn that twenty-five thousand," he said evenly, "you'll add another five thousand fer me and my boys here."

I swore, havin' half a mind to just draw then and there and take my chances in the rain of bullets that would surely follow. But before I could decide one way or another, someone walked into The Stag Saloon.

All eyes turned to him, and he paused just inside the door. He looked toward us. I imagined our little group made quite a sight. But then I blinked again. Even with my sun-dazzled vision, he looked familiar.

"Van?" He sounded surprised.

And I was just as surprised to hear his voice as he must've been to see me here, in this predicament. Or maybe that part wasn't what surprised him. Maybe what surprised him was that I was still alive. "Holt?"

For a heartbeat no one moved, no one said a thing.

My seared vision cleared a bit, and in that

second of clarity I saw on Holt's face what he was gonna do.

Holt was fast—you didn't get to be an old bastard like he was by bein' slow—and two against five were much better odds, but I wasn't tryin' to kill these men, not yet. I was tryin' to make a deal fer my sister's freedom. And you couldn't make a deal with dead men.

I opened my mouth to tell him not to do it, but too late. He drew and fired before any of Nan's men could react. The one standin' nearest to my right jerked and hit the floor in a spray of blood.

Then I hit the floor, too, but on my own accord, just as the inside of The Stag Saloon filled with bullets.

THE BARGAIN AT BRAVEBANK

"Stop!" I yelled, throwin' my hands up over my head as splintered wood showered over me. "Cease fire! Cease fire, damnit!"

My words were drowned by the noise of gunfire, the crack of bullets punchin' into wood and shatterin' glass. I rolled as one of Nan's men pushed the table over and barely dodged it landin' on me. The fella crouched down behind it and I crawled over to another table, pushin' it over and doin' the same. I drew a gun of my own, the undamaged one, and swore some more, cursin' Holt's timin'. If only he coulda given me a few more minutes. Or if only he coulda found me weeks ago, when I was facin' Nan herself.

"Cease fire!" I roared. "Holt! You bastard! I'm tryin' to make a deal!"

One of the guns—the one nearest the saloon entrance—stopped firin'. After a long moment, the others fell silent, too.

My ears rang. Cautiously, I lifted up onto my knees and looked out above the edge of the table. Three of Nan's men were dead on the floor, their blood soakin' into the floorboards. The leader and the one other fella left were still ducked behind the other table, far as I could tell.

I saw Holt pressed up against the doorjamb at the entrance, his revolver still held at the ready, but quiet. From that angle, they'd never get a clear shot at him.

The other patrons passed out across other tables or on the floor hadn't so much as stirred. Which was good fer them, otherwise they mighta ended up dead. I dropped back down behind my cover.

"What kind of deal?" Holt said from the doorway.

"A deal ta buy his sister back," Nan's man called out. "But ya just shot up three of my boys. Nan ain't gonna like that. Good help is awful hard to find these days, ya know."

My fingers clenched hard around the grip of my gun, then I winced as the soreness in my palm turned sharp again and loosened my hold a bit. Somethin' in there still weren't quite right since that day Nan had shot the gun outta my hand. But at least it was healin'. Slowly. "Yeah, well, look at the bright side," I said. "Five thousand split two ways is better than five thousand split five ways, ain't it?"

"Five thousand!?" Holt shouted from the door. "Yer out of yer damned mind, kid! How do you know they even have yer sister? Eh? Did ya even think to ask?"

"Five thousand?" Nan's man repeated, not givin' me time to answer Holt. "Oh no. The price is gone up now. On account of the emotional trauma you's caused me by murderin' half my crew."

I ground my teeth and knocked my head back against the underside of the table I leaned against. I breathed a long string of swear words. "Fine," I spat. "How much?"

"Whaddaya mean, 'How much?'?" Holt demanded from the doorway. "Don't be stupid, Van!"

I ignored him, listenin' for Nan's man's answer instead.

He ignored Holt, too. "Make it a nice, even ten thousand and ya still got yerself a deal."

"Ten thousand!" Holt exploded.

"Deal," I said. I didn't have the faintest idea where I was gonna get my hands on thirty-five thousand dollars … but I was gonna find it, one way or another.

"No deal!" Holt said. "They're playin' ya fer a fool, kid. How do ya know they even have yer sister?"

I shifted to glare at him from over the battered table edge, but he just shook his head in that infuriatingly disapprovin' way of his. He'd never believed my insistences my sister was still alive, not since the day he'd met me.

Nan's man laughed. "Oh, we got her, all right. Purty little thing, she is. Couple of us wanted to keep her fer ourselves, but Nan wanted the money. Oh well. Guess we can buy a whole lot of whores with ten thousand dollars, eh?"

I lurched to my feet and shoved my table to the side. It crashed against a chair as I limped across the floor to their sideways table and lowered my gun over the top of it, straight at the leader's head.

His and the other man's weapon came up quick, hammers cockin'. "Ah ah ah," he warned, "careful, boy. Kill me and I can guarantee ya, there'll be no deal at all."

My heart pulsed in my throat, and my headache pulsed with it, red seepin' in around the edges of my vision. I wanted nothin' more in that moment than to pull the trigger, to freeze that slimy smirk under that black, droopin' handlebar mustache in place so he could show it to the Devil when he woke up in Hell.

"Van…" Holt said uneasily, but I hardly heard him.

There were people shoutin' out in the street. Surely they'd heard our gunfire and were callin' for the sheriff. But I didn't move. Didn't blink. Just stood there with my gun leveled at his head, rage hummin' in my blood.

"Here," Nan's man said, and his free hand slowly lifted to a small pocket in the breast of his shirt. "Ya want proof?" His fingers slipped down inside and fished around, then pulled out a delicate golden chain. "Nan gave me this ta show you. Said you'd know what it was." He extended his arm outward, the chain danglin' from his closed fist.

I risked lookin' away from his face to glance at the necklace. Hangin' from the chain was a small, oval cameo of a white rose.

My breath hissed out between my teeth. I suddenly felt too light. Woozy. My gun hand wavered.

"Van," Holt called again from the doorway. He'd leaned around the frame of it, watchin' us warily. "That don't mean it's yer sister's. Plenty of women got necklaces like—"

"Not like this one," Nan's man interrupted. His dark brown eyes were locked on me, glitterin' with a cruel glee. "There's an engravin' on the back. With a date and a name. Think you'll find it mighty familiar."

My breath came short and ragged as I stared at it.

After so long … sometimes even I had believed she was a ghost.

After so long … to know I had been right all along … to know I had finally found her…

I snatched the necklace from him. My gun hand steadied. "Where is she?" I husked. I remembered what I'd done to Lloyd Renneker to get him to talk. Nan didn't want this one of hers dead? So maybe I wouldn't kill him. Maybe I'd do so much worse….

His long black mustache twitched as he grinned. "Don't ya worry about her none. Nan's keepin' her safe and cozy fer ya. Long as you get us that money, anyway. When ya get it, come find me here again, and I'll tell ya the spot to meet Nan. And get yer sister."

Holt scoffed, and from the corner of my eye I saw him lean out toward the street briefly before duckin' back inside the saloon. "Back here? We done shot up the place!"

Nan's man shook his head once. "Me and the sheriff have an … understandin'. You two, though…" He clucked his tongue in admonishment. "Well I can't speak fer you two. He probably won't take too kindly to yer murder and destruction of property. Guess that ain't my problem though, now, is it?"

The shoutin' outside was gettin' louder.

"Van, we gotta go," Holt said. "Like *now*."

I hesitated. There was still so much yet I wanted to do. I wanted to shoot the bastard at the end of my gun and the other man with him, too. Or I wanted to *hurt* them. Hurt them until they told me where Ethylen was, and the thirty-five thousand be damned.

"Van," Holt said again.

The man at the end of my gun lifted an eyebrow. "Well, boy, what'll it be? Ya wanna get that money and get yer sister back? Or you wanna hang fer murder? I gotta admit, I wouldn't mind watchin' ya swing."

I took another step forward and thumbed my hammer back.

He didn't so much as flinch, starin' me down, his gun still ready too, pointin' at my middle.

More voices from outside filtered through the silence.

"Van, *now*!" Holt barked.

"*Damnit*!" I lowered my pistol and eased the hammer down, then shoved it back into the holster, spinnin' away from Nan's men and hobblin' fast as I could manage toward the door where Holt waited all fidgety like.

"They're gonna see us leavin'," he muttered as I approached.

"We'll just have to make a run fer it," I said. And hope they wouldn't get a good look at our faces, or the good doctor and his family would see mine on a poster in town, after all.

"Yeah, that's right," Nan's man called from where he still crouched behind that table. "Ya better run, boy. Run, boy, run!" He cackled a laugh.

I swore again at my shit luck, wishin' I had the time to do somethin' about his arrogance. But I didn't. So I followed Holt out of the saloon and squinted in the bright mornin' sun.

The mule was there, right where I left him.

I shoved Ethelyn's necklace deep into my pants pocket and struggled up into the saddle from the right side, suckin' in a sharp breath as my left leg went over the cantle. It hurt almost as bad as it had when there'd still been a bullet stuck in it.

"Come on, come on, let's *go!*" Holt urged. He was already kickin' his horse up into a gallop, and I followed suit, grindin' my teeth against the pain in my thigh as it jostled against the mule's side.

"Hey!" someone shouted behind us. "Hey! Stop in the name of the law! Stop, I say!"

But the voice fell behind quick, drowned in the noise of our thunderin' hooves as we hauled ass toward the edge of town.

A rifle cracked, and I ducked low over the mule's neck, Holt and I both jerkin' our mounts quick around the nearest corner. Then there was empty street ahead of us, a wide stretch of dirt road, and I supposed maybe my luck was good enough at least to have us leavin' early enough in the mornin' to give us a clear path outta town.

We raced side by side, Holt and I, the town blurrin' by around us, until we broke out clear into the wild desert and left Bravebank behind in a cloud of dust.

We spent the rest of the day runnin'.

Well, runnin' and then takin' turns doublin' back to make sure we weren't bein' followed. And then coverin' our tracks.

By the time the sun was dippin' low to the horizon, we still hadn't caught any sign of pursuit.

"I think we're clear," Holt said, comin' back from checkin' our trail again.

"Think so," I agreed. Surprisin', considerin' we'd left three dead men in our wake. But maybe the sheriff of Bravebank weren't too fond of Nan's men, either, no matter their **understandin'**.

We looked for a place to camp for the night then, and settled on a little patch of dirt in between some big boulders. It weren't too tight, so we could get out in a hurry if we needed, but the bulk of the rocks would also hide our silhouettes and those of our mounts from any casual passersby. We were still in the valley, the land mostly flat, spotted with scraggly bush, mesquite trees and tall cacti. Two men and two horses woulda stood out pretty clear, even in a dark night.

On account of the fact we didn't want to be found, this spot seemed the best we could manage given the circumstances. We made a cold camp, too. No fire. The blaze woulda been a beacon fer all sorts of unwanted attention from all sorts of vultures.

It wasn't until we'd unsaddled, hobbled our mounts, and rolled out our bedrolls that Holt finally said what I'd known was on his mind all day.

"Ten thousand!" he blurted. "Christ, Van. Thought I raised you smarter than that! This ain't a game of cards, kid. You can't bluff yer way outta this one. Where you gonna get that kind of money? And how do ya know they have yer sister, anyway?"

The fingers of my right hand went to my pocket where I'd tucked the necklace. There was an engravin' on the back, just as Nan's man had said. I'd studied it good and hard while Holt had been off scoutin'. And it *was* mighty familiar. Pa had given it to Ethelyn for her tenth birthday, just weeks before he'd been killed. It was the most expensive thing she'd ever owned, and she'd worn it every day. Even slept in it.

"They have her," I said. "Renneker said so. And I saw it on Nan's face when I offered her money. And ... that bastard in the saloon had her necklace."

Holt rolled his eyes and scoffed. "That ain't proof, kid. Renneker weren't no lieutenant. And with what you did to him, well, any man woulda said anything to end it. Of course Nan ain't gonna say no to money, not if yer stupid enough to offer it to her. And that necklace ... yer sister coulda pawned it off fer a hot meal, fer all you know."

"They have her," I snapped, glarin' at him through the darkenin' twilight. The sun had dropped below the horizon now, and the moon was only a thin crescent creepin' up to take its place, but it was more than enough to see by. I saw his hard, level gaze, silvered by dusk, and his mouth turn down in disagreement. "They have her," I repeated, but more for myself than fer him. He didn't understand.

If Nine-Fingered Nan didn't have her, I'd have to go back to bidin' my time, waitin' fer another clue to follow. And I'd already spent nine years doin' that. This was the best, most solid lead I'd had yet by far.

Whether or not it turned out to be real, I'd never be able to live with myself if I didn't pursue it.

"Fine," Holt spat at last. "Then where you gonna get that kind of money? Nan ain't gonna give her to you without it, and I ain't sure she's gonna give her to you *with* it."

"I'll get it," I grumbled. I didn't think now was exactly the time to tell him I needed thirty-five thousand, not ten thousand, or that I had not the faintest idea how I was gonna get that thirty-five thousand. "And I won't be leavin' there without Ethelyn, one way or another."

Holt grumbled then, and shook his head. "You ain't gonna be leavin' there at all, at this rate. Yer gonna end up dead. You and yer sister both, if they've got her."

I eased down to the dusty ground, my left leg stretched out straight in front of me, and leaned back against my saddle. "Maybe," I admitted. But at least she'd know I hadn't abandoned her. I'd come back fer her, just like I'd promised.

"Hell, I thought you was dead already when you didn't come back to Grave Gulch!" Holt said. "Looked fer you fer weeks. Thought I was seein' a ghost when I walked into that Bravebank saloon."

"Near enough," I said. I fished in my saddle bag for the laudanum. My head was still throbbin' from my overindulgence in whiskey the night before and a day in the sun. My whole body ached from the hard ridin', my thigh on fire again.

I was sweatin', but shiverin' too. I didn't think that was too good. "How'd you manage to find me, anyway?"

He shrugged. "Luck. Like I said, I been searchin' fer you fer weeks. Goin' anywhere people said Nan had business. Bravebank happened to be my next stop. Figured if you wasn't there, least I'd probably be able to rustle up a score of some kind. That sa-loon ... she owns it, ya know."

"I didn't know that." But it made sense, now, lookin' back. Her man bein' there, the bartender gettin' scarce this mornin', the understandin' with the local sheriff....

I took a rather large swig of the medicine.

Holt was watchin' me, his gray brows low over those suspicious blue eyes. "What's that?"

"Medicine," I croaked, and shuddered at the bitterness of it. I corked it and shoved it back into my bag.

"Laudanum?" he asked. "How long you been on that stuff?"

I closed my eyes and leaned my head back on the saddle. "Not long."

He grunted, clearly not believin' me. "I got whiskey. You take that next time instead, ya hear?"

I didn't answer. I didn't think there was any amount of whiskey that could take away the pain I was feelin' right now. Felt like needles stabbin' into my skin where the metal started, hookin' the flesh, burnin'. The pain went down deep into the muscle, to the bone where it'd been sawed off. It throbbed. And sometimes I swore I could still feel my natural leg there down below, but of course that was a lie. An ugly lie my mind told my body, a phantom hope that was shattered over and over again every time I tried to move it.

The doctor had said the metal leg had advantages. Like some medicines built into it to help me heal. I didn't understand any of it, but I was hopin' now that was true. I was gonna need all the help I could get, 'specially judgin' from the way I was feelin' right now.

Maybe I shoulda asked the kid to grab me the schematic of the leg along with my guns. The doctor had mentioned he was gonna give me such a thing when it was time fer me to be on my way. Along with even more instructions. But I hadn't waited around fer those, and now I was kinda wishin' I had.

"What happened to yer horse?" Holt asked abruptly.

A pang of regret hit me. I'd really liked that horse. "Shot dead."

I heard him sigh. "Nan?"

"Yeah."

"And yer limp? That curtesy of the ol' hag, too?"

I smiled. Smiled like a mad person and opened my eyes, sittin' up. "Yeah. More than that, too." I rolled up my left pant leg to expose the metal rods that made up my lower leg now and the gears that made up my knee.

Holt stepped backward at the sight of it and spat a string of curses, his hand droppin' down to his gun like maybe he thought I was some kind of abomination.

Maybe I was.

Then he looked back to my face, his eyes wide and face paler than I'd ever seen it. "What in the Devil is that?" he hissed.

"My new leg." I covered it up again and resumed my reclined position on my saddle.

"Wha ... what ... *how?*"

I shook my head and shrugged. "I dunno. Nan shot my horse, then shot me in the leg. She woulda killed me outright then, but I made a deal she liked, and she let me live. Fer a little while longer, at least. I tried to make it to Bravebank. Couldn't. I woulda died in the desert, but this doctor found me. This doctor ... he ain't from around here. He said my leg was dead, so he sawed it off. Then … gave me this one. Said it has *ad-vantages*."

Holt still stared, mouth open, hand restin' on his gun. "*Advantages?*"

"Yeah. That's what he said. I ain't found no ad-vantages to it yet, though. All it is, is trouble. And pain."

A long silence stretched into the night. I waited for him to comprehend, if he could. I wasn't sure I did, still. And I'd had the damn thing for weeks now.

"Is it … is it Old World tech?" he asked slowly.

"I think so."

"And he just … he just gave it to you? Fer free?"

"Like I said, he ain't from around here." Though he'd probably at least expected me to repay him and his family with kindness and respect. I hadn't even done that much. My eyes shifted to the mule, standin' quiet and tired to my right. I wondered if Radley suspected I wasn't comin' back yet. I won-dered if he regretted givin' me back my guns yet.

I wondered if there were posters of my face up in Bravebank yet.

I closed my eyes against the wash of guilt. I'd make it right, someday. After I got Ethelyn back, I'd atone for all my sins. It was a promise I'd made my-self a long time ago.

It helped me sleep at night.

Holt muttered more curses. "Christ, kid. I told ya. I told ya! Never shoulda started down this road. Yer gonna get yerself killed."

That was a very real possibility, sure. No arguin' that.

So I didn't argue.

Instead I reached back and pulled my hat down over my face, the hat that had come from the doctor, too, easin' into the warm embrace of the laudanum as it finally soaked into my blood and took the edge off the hurt.

Maybe this road only led to my death … or maybe it finally led me to Ethelyn.

Either way, I supposed I'd be atonin' fer my sins one way or another soon enough.

Hoofbeats woke me, fast and loud.

I sat up with gun in hand still blinkin', groggy from the opium. Damnit, I'd taken too much of that, too. It took a minute to remember where I was, what had happened, and by that time Holt was already crouched up against one of the boulders, guns drawn.

Our mounts were still in place, still hobbled, though both of 'em now had their heads up and ears pricked in the direction of the oncoming hooves, keen on seein' who of their kind might be approachin'.

I scrambled to join Holt behind the nearest boulder, wincin' as I dragged that confounded metal leg behind me. "Who is it? Can you see?"

He peeked beyond the edge of the rock, then shook his head. "Nah."

"The law?"

He gave me a look that said I should know better. "The law wouldn't come chargin' in here like a herd a' terrified cattle. They'd come in slow and quiet, try an' catch us asleep."

I frowned, concern tightenin' in my belly. "Who, then? And how'd they find us?"

"I don't know. And I don't know that they're after us, yet. They might not know we're here."

"Sounds like they're headed right for us," I whispered.

"Maybe. Just stay quiet. Don't fire till we know fer sure, understand?"

I nodded, but he didn't have to tell me. Gun shots were louder than thunder out here. They'd draw more trouble than a fire even, in the end.

I glanced to the mule again. He looked awfully eager about these new arrivals. I hoped he wouldn't try and run off to join 'em with those hobbles still on, or I'd be out another mount. I also hoped he wouldn't call out to 'em. *Stay quiet*, I urged him silently. *Please don't—*

He opened his mouth and let out a terrible warblin' sound, some bastard cross between a bray and a whinny that properly reflected his unnatural heritage.

I flinched.

Beside me, Holt swore a blue streak. "Goddamnit, Van—"

"I didn't have a choice," I hissed. "It was the mule or walk!"

I wasn't sure the riders out there in the dark had heard it, anyway, not over the sound of so many gallopin' hooves. Who was stupid enough to race through the desert like that in the night, makin' so much noise?

Either stupid ... or good enough and mean enough they don't have to care.

My mouth went dry at the thought. I pulled my second gun from its holster, the damaged one. I didn't wanna have to use it and risk it explodin' in my hand, but maybe just the presence of it would be enough.

We waited.

They came straight for us, all right. Maybe they'd heard the mule call out, maybe they hadn't. But they came straight for the boulders without slowin' down, and even if they couldn't see us, there weren't no way they didn't see those loomin' rocks. They veered around 'em at the last second, and fer a heartbeat I thought they'd ride on by.

But they didn't.

They circled round.

And round and round.

The damn mule gave another bastardized whinny, and if they hadn't heard it before, they'd heard it now. I couldn't tell how many there were, but they sure outnumbered us.

Their circlin' kicked up a lot of dust that thickened the air and clouded the once-clear moonlight. I squinted my eyes against it and coughed, and next to me, Holt readied a few quick-change cylinders.

"Van Delano!" one of 'em shouted, a woman, and my stomach clenched.

Through the dim, murky moonlight, Holt looked to me sharply.

"We know you're in there! And that no good ol' cur Haggerty too! Ain't no one passes through Nan's land without her knowin'."

I looked to Holt. The expression on his face then couldn'ta been more clear:

You gone and got us both killed, kid.

"She knows about yer mess in Bravebank, too," the woman shouted. "You killed three of her men, Delano. She really ain't happy about that. That weren't part of the deal!"

This time I glared at Holt, well sure he knew exactly what I meant: *I* told *you not to shoot those men!*

He grunted in reply and shoved the pre-loaded cylinders back into his belt.

I didn't bother to shout back that it hadn't been me who'd killed those men at all. It didn't matter to Nan who had pulled the trigger. It only mattered that I had been there, and the one who had murdered her men was an associate of mine. That was enough.

"Such things got consequences, Delano! Nan ain't gonna stand fer that! From now on, you get an itchin' to kill someone, you kill someone Nan wants dead, ya hear? In fact, from now on, till yer debt is paid up, you don't so much as spit 'less Nan tells ya to, understand?"

I ignored Holt's look this time, though I could feel his stare burn hot as a brand into the side of my face. But I didn't need his reprimandin'. I'd known what I was gettin' myself into the day I'd ridden away from Grave Gulch to confront Nan the first time.

"We'll be watchin' you, Delano. Don't think we won't be. Nan's got eyes and ears all over this country. Ain't nowhere far enough you can run now."

"I ain't runnin'!" I barked, then coughed again from all the dust.

The bastards out there were still circlin'.

Like vultures.

"Glad to hear it," the woman said. She, at least, was stationary, planted on the other side of the rock Holt and I crouched behind. "In that case, you just keep yerself outta trouble till Nan calls upon you, got it? And remember … you lay a finger on any more of her men … the deal's off. And more than that, we'll be comin' fer yer head."

I said nothin'. I didn't need to.

An object sailed through the swirlin' dust and thumped to the rocky ground near our boots. Nan's men—and at least one woman—wheeled their horses and took off with a few partin' yells.

Holt and I didn't move, not even as the whoopin' and hollerin' and hoofbeats faded.

It wasn't until the night had fallen silent again, and my damn mule let out another lonely whinny, that Holt shoved his revolvers back into their holsters and swore again. Loudly.

I did the same. Well, I holstered my guns. And I swore, but my swearin' was silent. I threw an arm over my nose and mouth to breathe through the dusty air and reached out to pick up the thing they'd thrown at us. It was a square of burlap tied with twine.

I checked on Holt, but he'd wandered back over to his bedroll and was rummagin' around in his saddlebags, still mutterin' and grumblin' and shakin' his head.

I untied the twine, and realized then that my

fingers were wet. Frownin', I held them up to the dusty moonlight.

Blood.

My breath hitched. I stared down at the folded burlap, and pulled back the layers with tremblin' hands. Fold by fold, the dread crawled up my throat to choke me, until my breath was harsh and ragged, and then stopped, and I couldn't breathe at all.

Fingers. Three fingers.

A woman's three fingers.

Some kind of noise escaped me.

There was a note tucked in alongside the fingers, marred with blood, the ink smeared. I plucked it out and blinked hard, tryin' to clear the black spots dancin' in my vision. I read the words without seein' 'em, then read 'em over and over again until their meanin' finally sunk in.

"Careful, boy. There's plenty more where this came from."

My hands shook violently. I dropped the bloody bundle back to the dirt.

"Van?"

I looked up to see Holt standin' near. His eyes went to the burlap square. The severed fingers. "Holy Mother," he breathed.

I hardly heard him. There was a rushin' in my ears soundin' like a freight train. "I … I ain't…" I stopped and swallowed. "I ain't gonna be her errand boy."

Holt cleared his throat. "Van—"

"I'm gettin' Ethelyn back. *Right. Now.*"

"Van, ya heard what they just said! If you try an—"

"I'll get Nan the damn money," I growled. "I'll get the money and I'll buy her back outright. And then I'm gonna even the score." I pushed myself to my feet, the rage singin' hot through my limbs. "I'm gonna put a bullet right between the eyes of that old hag."

"Van, I know yer upset—"

I shoved past him and limped to my own bedroll; started gettin' my stuff ready to ride.

He followed me. "Kid, don't do this again. Last time you stormed off in a rage Nan killed yer horse and nearly killed you. Remember? It weren't even that long ago! You got a metal leg now, fer Chrissakes! You need to stop and cool down, *think*!"

"I'm thinkin'," I spat. And I was. I was thinkin' of all the ways I was gonna lay the hurt on ol' Nine-Fingered Nan, and any of her cronies who got in my way.

"And where you gonna get that kind a' money, anyway? Ten thousand is gonna take time, you gotta plan—"

"It ain't ten thousand," I said. "It's thirty-five thousand."

"Thirty-five … *thirty-five thousand*?! Van Jensen Delano, you have certifiably lost yer goddamn mind! No. No way. Where you gonna find that kinda currency?"

I already knew. I'd already decided. I'd done a lotta bad things in my life, had a lotta sins to atone fer, but there were still a few things I hadn't done. There was still a line I'd refused to cross.

Until now.

"I'm gonna rob a bank," I said.

A BLESSING OR A CURSE

That got Holt's attention.

He'd been itchin' to rob a bank fer years, sayin' we could stop sleepin' in the dirt and livin' day to day if we just got one big score.

'Cept he always forgot he'd told me once that he and Pa and the others they'd run with when they were young and stupid had robbed a bank.

More than one, in fact.

And it seemed to me, from the stories Holt told, one score was never enough, no matter how big. There would always be "just one more job" on the horizon. And no matter how much you robbed, no matter how far you ran, you just couldn't reach that horizon.

You didn't stop till you took a long drop on a short rope ... or till you took a shotgun blast to the face from some old acquaintance who didn't appreciate the fact you'd tried to go straight.

"A ... a bank?" Holt repeated.

"That's right." I shoved thoughts of Pa outta my mind. There wasn't nothin' I could do fer him anymore. But Ethelyn ... I still had a chance to save Ethelyn. I buckled up my saddlebags and hefted my saddle, limpin' over to the mule, who nickered at me. I scowled at him. He'd caused enough trouble fer me already. "Ain't that what you always wanted?"

"Well ... yeah."

At least the man was bein' honest.

"But Van … not like this. We hit a bank now and all that money'll go to Nan."

I shook my head. "I'm only usin' the money to get the meetin'. Then I'm gonna kill her. And then we can keep the money fer all I care. Long as I have my sister." I tossed the blanket onto the mule's back, then the saddle, and cinched it up.

"Ya can't spend money when yer dead, kid. And havin' yer sister back won't matter if yer dead, neither."

I whirled to face him. "And what else am I supposed to do?" I demanded. "Keep livin' like this? Give up on her? Leave her to be sold off to some slaver overseas?" I waved at the piece of burlap still on the ground and the three severed fingers, turnin' gray now. "Look what Nan did! I ain't leavin' Ethelyn with that monster a day longer than I have to. So you can do what you want. But I'm gonna go rob a bank and get myself thirty-five thousand dollars. And if I happen to get more than that, I'll keep it, sure. Unless I'm dead, in which case, you just keep it all fer yerself. That's what you want most of all anyway, ain't it?"

Holt's expression soured, but he stayed silent. He just stood there starin' at me, hands planted on his hips right above the grips of his guns.

I turned away from him then, undoin' the hobbles and puttin' on the bridle. Then I rolled up my bed mat in a hurry and tied it to the back of my saddle with more force than necessary. I hauled myself up onto the back of that mule with effort and settled my seat, glarin' down at Holt, who still hadn't said a word.

"Well?" I prompted. "You comin' or what?"

He frowned and sighed heavily. Then scuffed the toe of one boot into the dirt. "Which bank?"

"I dunno yet," I snapped.

"You honestly think you could pull off a bank job of that size all by yer lonesome?"

I kept his level stare, but swallowed. "If I had to." Truth be told, I didn't want to have to. But I was also too angry at the moment to admit that.

He grunted in response and shook his head. "Christ, kid. Fine. Wait up a minute, I'll saddle up."

"Yeah well hurry up," I growled. "I want that money by sundown tomorrow."

Holt let out a noise that made it clear he didn't think there was a chance in Hell we'd have that money by sundown tomorrow. "Wish you woulda had this kinda enthusiasm for robbin' a bank a long time ago," he muttered as he threw the saddle on his black gelding. "Maybe if you had, we wouldn't be where we are now."

"Yeah, you're right. We'd be hanged already."

He tossed a glare at me over his shoulder. "And if you try and rush this job, kid, we'll end up hanged now. Fer sure."

"I ain't gonna rush it."

"Sounds to me like you are." He bridled his horse, checked his saddlebags, and mounted up, gatherin' the reins as he pulled the gelding around to face me. "Robbin' banks takes careful plannin'. Took us weeks sometimes to set everythin' up, and there was lots of us."

"We're gonna do it with two," I said, and I pulled my own mount around and gave him a kick, sendin' him out between the boulders and into the cool desert night at a lope.

Holt caught up to me and matched the mule's pace.

"And we got from here to Blessing to plan it."

"Blessing, huh? That where you wanna pull this job?"

"Yeah." I'd just decided that, too. But it made sense. It was north of where Nine-Fingered Nan had her strongest influence, and was one of the richest towns in the territory, owin' to the massive cache of Old World metal some miners had found buried there awhile back. Thus the town's name. Some considered such a stash to be a blessin'.

Others, namely those enslaved by the metal merchants and made to go down into the ruins to gather the stuff, and those who often got murdered so someone else could steal their share of the stuff, considered it to be a curse.

But the town of Blessing had a bank. And the bank of Blessing held a lot of rich people's money. It'd take the rest of the night and a good part of tomorrow to get there, but if any town within a day's ride would have the thirty-five thousand I needed, it'd be that one.

Holt was quiet a minute as he contemplated. "Makes sense, I guess," he finally agreed. "But the security there is gonna be tough. Those metal barons don't like partin' with their coin. Not even to give it to a bank. It'll be locked up tight and guarded well."

"Yeah," I said again. I knew that, too. "That's why I have you. You said you'd done this kinda thing before. So come on. What's yer plan?"

Holt laughed then and shook his head, adjustin'

his hat as we rode along under the moon, weavin' through the brush and cacti. "I can't make a plan till I see the place, kid. And anyway, this is yer rodeo. Or maybe yer funeral. You should take point on this one."

I grunted. He was probably right. But all I could think of then was those three severed fingers, and the necklace still tucked in my pocket, and Ethelyn still in the clutches of the monster Nine-Fingered Nan and her demon minions.

Disfigured … and who knew what else.

I kicked the mule on faster, ignorin' the pain that was steadily buildin' again in my left thigh and the rocks that littered the path ahead, threatenin' to trip up my mule. To Hell with the pain. To Hell with the metal leg. To Hell with Holt and his doubts, and to Hell with Nan and her threats.

I was gonna get the money. And I was gonna meet with Nan. And I was gonna get Ethelyn back and kill Nan and as many of her people as I could, and then we were gonna run, Ethelyn and I.

Together. Far, far away. Maybe even all the way to the East Republic. And start over again.

The town of Blessing was gonna be my blessing, all right.

And I was gonna be its curse.

We plodded into Blessing in the afternoon the next day, hot and sore and tired, and hungry and thirsty, too. Holt was proper mad by then, 'cause I hadn't let us stop to rest or eat anythin' outside of what was absolutely necessary to not kill the horses.

After all, I surely didn't want to be stuck in the middle of the desert with no horse again.

I'd told him he could stop and rest and do whatever he liked if he wanted, but I was gonna get to Blessing before nightfall the next day.

He'd thought about stoppin' without me, I could tell, but in the end he'd kept up, though with great reluctance and a whole lotta curses. Most of 'em aimed at me.

I'd ignored him and rode on, thinkin' only of that money.

Thinkin' of how in the hell I was gonna get that money.

But by afternoon, when we finally made the turn and went under the archway of patchwork metal that marked the town's main entrance, my thoughts were all runnin' together, and I wasn't really thinkin' much at all anymore, 'cept for about how much I wanted some food and drink. And sleep.

The mule's hooves were draggin' now, his head sunk low and ears droopin'. He was lathered up and breathin' hard, and I felt a little bad for pushin' him so much.

But we were here now.

I'd let him rest up and cool down, get him some good quality feed. He deserved that much.

And me and Holt, we deserved somethin' too, while we were makin' up this plan fer the robbery. I urged the mule up the main street toward the nearest saloon and took note of the townsfolk starin' … and those who didn't stare. Blessing was a busy place, sure enough.

The street was wide, but crowded enough to make it slow goin' even if we weren't spent and tired. Horses and carts and loaded wagons of all kinds clogged the way, and foot traffic, too. And here and there on the street corners perched a lawman or two, their stars rough-hewn and hammered outta rusted scrap.

Well, there weren't really no *official* lawmen out here in the Western Territories, but each town generally had its version of 'em, fer better or worse. Whether or not the so-called lawmen upheld the law or just took advantage of it, though, was always a gamble.

I studied these particular lawmen of Blessing as we passed 'em by, but didn't look too long. Lookin' too long at anyone in these parts was a good way to get yerself a bullet in the gut.

They watched Holt and I hard enough in return, fer certain, which didn't bode well fer the chances of our robbery bein' a success. I cursed my shit luck again as the saloon came into view. Of course. The town with all the money had the lawdogs who actually wanted to uphold the law.

But then ... maybe I could find a way to convince them to look the other way. This town liked money, after all. Maybe these lawmen wanted more of it.

I stopped the mule outside of the saloon; the wooden one. Down the street a ways I saw another one, but that one was made outta metal, gleamin' in the sun like some sort of unnatural jewel. My left thigh flared, as if the metal attached to it could sense its long-lost cousin down the road.

I scowled at both of 'em. I'd never liked much

made outta metal. Not much except my guns and the lead they fired. In my experience, metal was meant to kill.

Not to make a roof over your head.

Or a leg for walkin'.

The people comin' outta the metal saloon looked different, too. Their clothes were fancier and less full of dirt, and the chains of pocket watches glinted on their breasts. And the women on the arms of such men didn't look like prostitutes, neither. They were all dressed up in frills and lace and bustles. There were lawmen posted at the door of that one, too, rifles already in their hands as if they were expectin' some kind of trouble.

Holt was lookin' at it too as he pulled his gelding up next to me. "Now what do you suppose that is?"

I tore my eyes away from the thing and shrugged. "I dunno. A place we don't belong, fer sure."

"I'd say."

I took a breath and eased myself down outta the saddle, keepin' myself upright mostly by my grip on the mule's stiff mane. I closed my eyes and took a minute again to gather myself.

"Come on, kid," Holt said, suddenly at my elbow. "You look like death. Let's get you some whiskey."

I nodded mutely and pulled the crutch from the rifle scabbard. It didn't matter now what people thought of it; I had Holt to back me up. And anyway, after such a long ride, I wouldn'ta been able to walk straight—or at all—without it if my life depended on it.

I glanced around at the busy street again, and at

the lawmen at the nearest corner, and hoped my life wouldn't depend on it.

We tied our mounts at the hitchin' post and walked on in.

Well, Holt walked. I limped and hobbled, every bone achin'.

We found a place at the bar with only a few curious looks our way. Most folk didn't seem to care, though. Not about my limp and my crutch, nor about the state of ourselves, sweaty and dusty from the long hours in the saddle.

To my surprise, the barkeeper was a woman. Tall and slender, her complexion a warm, mellow brown, she slid our way with a grace like no other barkeep I'd ever seen. Not surprisin', since she was the only woman barkeep I'd ever seen.

"What'll it be, boys?"

"Whiskey," Holt answered, diggin' in his pockets for some coin.

"Hrmm." She looked at him, then at me, her dark eyes sweepin' me up and down, then glancin' to the crutch I'd leaned up against the bar's edge. I tensed on my stool, but she only inclined her head in my direction. "I can see that one needs the medicinal variety. But what about you?" She swung her gaze back to Holt. "You paying for the same, or you just wanna get drunk quick?"

Holt glanced at me, then sighed. "Just give me the same." He fished out more coin and tossed it to the counter.

She nodded and swept the money away with one hand, the other hand procurin' two shot glasses, which she set in front of us. Then she was pourin', and I found myself mesmerized by the preciseness of it, how she spilled not a drop.

But maybe that was just the exhaustion and the pain workin'.

"You boys gonna stay long?" she asked, pushin' the full glasses toward us. "Need rooms for the night? I got some."

I shifted on my stool. So she was the barkeep and the saloon keeper, too.

"Depends on how much," Holt said. He brought the glass up to his nose and sniffed, and his thick gray brows lifted.

I glanced down to my own full glass. Holt was mighty picky about his whiskey. This musta been good stuff, indeed. I'd have to enjoy it, then. Wouldn't be able to afford any more of it.

The woman watched him, her mouth quirked in amusement. "Half dollar a night, each."

Holt pursed his lips, paused, then swallowed back his drink.

"We'll take two," I answered for him. My hopes of havin' the thirty-five thousand by sundown had been checked by the sheer number of people in this town.

And the sheer number of lawmen in this town.

Holt was right, damn him. This was gonna take more careful plannin' than I'd wanted. Better to hole up for the night, get some rest, and have a place where we could discuss a strategy without no other nosey eyes and ears around us.

And anyway, we needed our mounts fresh for the job, too, so they could get us outta here real quick once it was all done.

I reached into the pouch on my belt and gave

her the coin myself this time. Ol' drunk Jake's money was comin' in handy, all right.

She swept that away too and smiled at me. "How about baths? Or girls? Though I have to insist, if you want any of my girls, you're gonna have to bathe first. We have standards here, you know. Maybe not as high as the Iron Jewel's standards, but we do have 'em." She gave a nod as if to motion down the street, and with a name like *Iron Jewel*, I guessed she probably meant that metal monstrosity of a saloon that squatted down the road.

Self-consciously, I looked down at myself. I supposed I probably did look a mess, and Holt weren't much better. But he always had some scraggly mess of beard on his chin, and dirt rubbed into all the creases of his skin. Me, I usually preferred to be clean-shaven and mostly washed. A consequence of growin' up with a roof over my head and a wash basin at my disposal, I suppose.

Though neither myself nor my clothes had had a good cleanin' since the Sunday before I'd left Dr. Balogh's homestead.

I cleared my throat and swallowed my whiskey, then closed my eyes to appreciate it. It was the good stuff, all right.

"We're all right fer now," Holt said.

"If you say so," the woman said. "But if you change your minds, you know where to find me." She smiled again. "Feel free to help yourselves to the spread at the back." She nodded toward the back of the central room, where a long table was set with a bigger variety of food than I'd ever seen, too.

Seemed Blessing was full of surprises.

My stomach growled.

"If you want anything special, you come see me. I got a chef who can make almost anything from any region. You get a hankering for anything specific, I can get it made for you."

"For a price," Holt muttered.

Her smile widened to show white teeth. "Of course, darling. Everything comes at a price in Blessing. But it's the same everywhere else too, really, ain't it?"

"I guess."

"Most certainly it is. Now, I'll have Ginger make up your rooms for you. They'll be upstairs, numbers five and six. You boys make yourselves at home here in the meantime, but don't cause no trouble." She folded her hands on the bartop then and leaned forward, as if she were gonna tell us a secret.

I leaned toward her instinctively, catchin' a whiff of her perfume.

"They call me Seven Knives Sally around here," she told us, lookin' at us each long and hard. "I bet you can guess why that is. And I bet you can also guess why I'm still running this place, despite the fact there's a mighty lot of greedy bastards out there who'd love to take it from me."

Her gaze shifted over my shoulder, and I twisted on my stool with my hand halfway to my gun, expectin' to find someone unfriendly comin' up behind me. But there was no one.

In fact, now that I took the time to look around this place a little better, I noticed it was clean and well-kept, and the patronage less rowdy and raucous than what could be found in most other saloons I'd visited.

I turned back to Seven Knives Sally and lifted an eyebrow. "Awful nice place you have here," I said.

"Yes," she agreed. "And I plan to keep that way. So you two will be causing no trouble, ain't that right?"

"Of course, ma'am," Holt said, all sugar, tippin' his hat to her. "Wouldn't dream of it."

"Glad we have an understanding," Sally said. She started to slide away, to help the next set of thirsty customers down at the end of the bar.

"Wait," I spoke up, stoppin' her in mid-step, "we're needin' a place to stable our horses. Someplace good."

She flashed me that white smile again. "Why of course. Best horse care is Abbott's Livery. Head north two blocks, then west three blocks and you'll run right into it. Tell him I sent you."

And then she left us.

Holt watched after her, then exhaled a long breath and shook his head. "Whew-boy!" He gazed down into his empty whiskey glass. "I'm kinda startin' to like this town."

I scowled at him. "Well don't. We ain't stayin' long."

"Right." He eased off his stool. "You stay here. I'll bring ya some food, see if we can't get the color back in yer face."

He headed off toward the back table, and I glanced to my reflection in the large oval mirror behind the bar. It was etched with gilded, flowin' letters that spelled out the name of this place—Seven Knives, right enough—but between all the shiny flourishes I could see myself.

And he was right. And so was Seven Knives Sally.

I looked like death.

The sun was settin', and I was stretched out on a bed in the upstairs of the Seven Knives saloon. It was a nice bed, too. I leaned back into the pillows, feelin' the effects of a full stomach, that whiskey—it was somethin' special, all right—and the laudanum I'd sipped soon as Holt had left.

He'd gone to take our mounts to the stable and to do some scoutin' of the town, he'd said. We'd learned the bank weren't too far from the Seven Knives, just a few blocks north. Holt had insisted on walkin' by it, maybe goin' inside it, checkin' to see the specifics of its layout and security.

At first I'd wanted to go with him, but he'd insisted I stay here and rest up, get my strength back, 'cause we were surely gonna need every bit of our wits to pull off this job.

Now, as I marinated in the brief comfort provided by the food and whiskey and opium, I saw the wisdom in that decision. My thigh was finally startin' to feel a little better, and the rest of me, too.

I'd stopped shiverin' and sweatin'. And sure, got some color back, too.

The room was decent; the wallpaper only a little faded and a little ripped in places, only one bed post missin'. Seven Knives Sally had a nice place, indeed.

I looked down to my left boot. The foot I couldn't feel. With my pants and the shoe, you couldn't tell that leg weren't natural. It looked completely normal from the outside. I stared at that boot and tried to move that foot.

I could hear the gears and pistons of the metal leg movin' and turnin'. And my boot twitched.

I tried to bend my left knee. Well, it weren't really *mine* no more. It was the machine's knee. But I tried to bend it, anyway.

There was more whirrin'. And then the leg jerked.

I rolled my eyes and sighed, leanin' my head back against the pillows. *Just walk normal*, Dr. Balogh had said. Sure. That was workin' out real fine, all right.

A soft knock sounded at the door and I bolted upright, hand goin' to my gun. "Who is it?"

"It's Ginger, love. May I come in?"

Ginger. The older woman Seven Knives Sally employed to keep the place tidy. I swept a gaze around the room to be sure nothin' incriminatin' had been left out in the open—but then, we hadn't robbed the bank yet—and I had precious little to my name anymore. "Sure," I said warily.

I still couldn't fathom why Ginger'd be payin' me a social call.

I kept my right hand near my holster as she swept open the door and paraded into the room, a wooden tray balanced on one hand. She came straight to the bedside and set something down on the night table.

Another shot glass of whiskey.

I lifted my eyes to her in question. "I didn't order—"

"Oh I know, love." She turned and smiled at me

over her shoulder, givin' me a wink. "It's on the house. Sally says so herself." She lowered her voice, though it was still a great deal louder than a whisper. "I think she might fancy you." Her round figure sashayed toward the door, but drew up short just before passin' through it. "Oh, and I'm supposed to ask if you want us to call a doctor? We know a real good one."

"No. No, I don't need a doctor."

She lifted one sculpted, painted eyebrow and tilted her head to the side. A few of her graying curls fell against her face. "You sure, now?" She looked to the crutch I had propped up against the wall and then at my left leg. "You get shot? That can fester, you know. Better to get it looked at then die later from infection! I should know. My cousin Louisa, her good friend—"

"I'm fine," I blurted. Then, seein' her aghast expression at bein' so rudely interrupted, sighed. "I already got it looked at by a doctor. It's fixed up." *In a matter of speakin', anyway.* "Just gotta heal now. It takes some time."

Her expression softened. "I understand. Well, glad to hear it. We don't like folk dyin' under our roof, if you know what I mean."

I didn't.

She gave me a nod. "G'night, mister. Remember, you change your mind about a bath or some women —or men, mind you, we gots those, too—just go downstairs and tell me or Sally, yeah?"

"I'll remember."

"Good." And with that, she slipped out and shut the door behind her.

I looked down to the whiskey on the night table.

Damn. Maybe at another time in my life I woulda gone downstairs right away and shown Sally some appreciation for her kindness. Woulda at least gone down to see if Ginger was right … find out if Sally really did fancy me.

But not now. Not this time.

There were too many other things needin' my attention right now.

Like the Bank of Blessing.

And thirty-five thousand dollars.

And Ethelyn.

The sight of those three severed fingers flashed into my mind again and I squeezed my eyes shut, rubbin' at 'em like maybe I could scrub that memory away. Then I groaned and opened my eyes again.

I took the whiskey and pushed myself off the bed, limpin' carefully to the window. I opened it to let in the fresh air, relishin' the fact this air weren't full of dust like all the towns further south.

The sun had sunk low, and the buildin's on the street below threw out long shadows over all the people still bustlin' about, goin' about their business.

I wondered if this town ever really slept.

My eyes went north, toward the so-called Iron Jewel, and I sipped at the whiskey, savorin' it this time. Just beyond that somewhere was the bank.

I was feelin' pretty confident now that by the time Holt came back this evenin', he would have some kind of a plan in place.

We'd have the money by this time tomorrow and be outta here, well on our way back to Bravebank to arrange the meetin' with Nan.

And get Ethelyn back.

I was about to turn away from the window and

get back to the comfort of the bed when a commotion broke out on the street below. I stepped over again to see what was goin' on.

A group of lawmen on horseback were clearin' the streets, trottin' up fast and nearly runnin' over a few folk. Shouts of offense and indignation welled in their wake, but they drew up short in front of the Seven Knives, right below my window. They milled about restlessly, scannin' the crowds nearby, who were quickly dispersin'.

My right hand drifted down to my gun, restin' easy.

The group below looked almost like a posse. And I didn't much like posses. Especially when they were comin' after me. I wasn't sure who this group was after, exactly, but they were surely after someone. I didn't think they could be after me or Holt, but it was always better to be safe than dead.

I eased my pistol a little out of the holster, quietly and carefully pullin' the hammer back.

"Where is she?" one of the men in the posse bellowed, his voice echoin' out across the street. "I know one of you saw where she went! Failure to aid us is a crime, you remember that! Speak up now or face the justice of the law!"

Oh. *She.* I eased the hammer down again and settled my gun back into leather.

Wait. She?

"*Where is she*?" the lawman demanded again. But now there was hardly anyone left in the street to hear him. They'd all scattered at the sign of trouble.

The doors to the Seven Knives opened, and I saw Sally herself exit the saloon and calmly walk down the front steps to face the group of lawmen.

They all turned their horses to face her. In turn, she put her hands on her hips and shook her head. "Now, now, gentlemen," she scolded. "Pray tell, why must you make such a ruckus in front of my saloon?"

"We're looking for a slave that run off," the lawman snapped. "One of Baron Whittaker's. Young woman. Red hair. About your height. You seen her?"

Sally crossed her arms. "I have not. But I will certainly alert the sheriff's office if I do."

My hand tightened again around the grip of my pistol, and a sour taste rose in the back of my mouth. Slavers. Like the ones who'd caught up to Ethelyn. I'd kill 'em all myself if I could.

But killin' all those lawmen down below wouldn't be smart. Not now. Not yet.

There was a heartbeat of silence, and I could tell the lawman didn't believe Sally hadn't seen the woman they were after. "We tracked her here," he said finally. "She's around here somewhere. Probably trying to hide in one of these buildings, I imagine. Maybe trying to hide in your saloon."

Sally shrugged. "Maybe. Why don't you put up a poster of her with a nice reward?"

"We already did," the man snarled.

"Well then I imagine the best thing to do would be to wait. Give it some time. There's a lot of people in this town, mister. Someone's bound to find her."

"We ain't got time," the lawman said. "Baron Whittaker wants her back. Now."

The door to my room flung open behind me and I spun, gun drawn. But it weren't no thief or bounty hunter comin' after me, it was a woman. She slammed the door shut again behind her, latched it, and turned, then froze at the sight of me and my revolver, eyes going wide.

I blinked, takin' in the sight of her dirt-streaked trousers and blouse, her skinny frame, the red hair a mess and fallin' down over her shoulders and face. It was *her*. The escaped slave.

Through the open window I heard Sally say, "Seems to me Baron Whittaker could stand to learn some patience."

"I have money," the woman in front of me blurted. Then she squeezed her eyes shut and shook her head, snapped them open again. "I mean … my family has money. Help me escape. They'll pay you twice as much as Whittaker would."

I lifted my eyebrows. I didn't even know how much this Baron Whittaker was offerin' fer her return. It didn't much matter. I wouldn'ta taken her back to him, anyway.

But the offer of money didn't sound too bad, neither.

"Search these buildings!" the lawman roared to his men below. "Every single one of them. Every single room. Find that girl!"

Shit.

Across the room, her dark blue eyes grew impossibly wider.

And that's when I realized there was only one way out of this.

PROPER MANNERS

"Take off yer clothes," I ordered.

"I beg your pardon! *What* did you just say to me?"

I'd never heard a woman sound so offended. I limped to the wardrobe, throwin' it open. Course there weren't nothin' suitable for a woman in there, but I weren't lookin' for clothes. I was lookin' for somethin' else, and prayin' Sally kept some of it stocked in her rooms as a service. Usually the nicer places did, and Sally had a nicer place. "Take off yer clothes," I repeated. "You want those lawdogs to find you or not? We ain't got much time. Wash yer face in the basin, strip, and get in the bed."

She let out a little laugh, high and airy.

I heard some of the posse stompin' around downstairs, and my heartbeat quickened. I pulled open the wardrobe drawer, rummagin' through shavin' supplies and—finally! Boot polish. I pulled it out.

"You think I'm going to bestow my *charms* upon you just because I asked you to help me escape? No way, mister. No way." She'd backed up against the door, hands clutched to her breast, shakin' her head.

I stared at her fer a minute, then grasped her meanin' and realized my instructions had sounded all wrong. "No," I said. "No, lady, I ain't tryin' to take advantage of you. I'm tryin' to help you escape!

But they're gonna recognize you unless we change up yer appearance, you follow? We can make it look like yer one of Sally's girls, but we gotta act fast."

Comprehension dawned on her face.

I heard some of the posse stompin' up the stairs now. We were *really* runnin' outta time. "Quick!" I snapped. "I'm gonna smear some of this in yer hair to cover up the red, yeah?" I held up the boot polish.

She grimaced in disgust, but nodded.

I got to work on her hair best I could as she splashed water on her face, scrubbin' off the dirt. Then I scrubbed the polish off my hands best I could and threw the dirty basin water out the room's side window. By the time I'd done that and replaced the basin, she'd taken off her dusty clothes and shoved them beneath the sheets at the end of the bed, and crawled under the covers herself.

I heard heavy bootsteps comin' down the hall.

I tossed my hat to one of the bed posts and pulled my shirt up over my head, havin' no time to mess with the buttons, throwin' it to the floor.

She watched me with terrified eyes as I un-buckled my gunbelts and let 'em thump to the floor, but within easy arm's reach of the bed. Better to be safe than dead.

She didn't fully trust that I wouldn't take advantage of her, that much was plain on her face. I stepped out of my boots, hearin' doors bein' busted in now and the loud protests of the other rooms' occupants.

"You try anything, mister, and I'll yell," she whispered as I moved toward her. "I'll tell the law who I am and tell Whittaker what you did and he'll—"

"I ain't gonna try anythin'," I hissed back. "I ain't even takin' off my pants!" And I wasn't. For more reason than to prove to her my honest intentions. I also didn't want her to see my metal leg. I slipped under the sheets, avertin' my gaze from her nakedness, and rolled over on top of her just as our door got kicked in.

I scowled and swore, feignin' anger at the interruption, and twisted half-around to glare at the two men who'd barged in. "Hey! Ya mind? Can't ya see I'm a little busy?"

"Shut it, you," one of 'em growled. "We're looking for an escaped slave." He stepped into the room and opened the wardrobe, then looked behind it.

"Well they ain't in here," I said, lowerin' down over the girl as the second of 'em came closer to the bed, then bent down to look under it. "Pretty sure we woulda noticed." I hoped they wouldn't look at her too close. The polish in her hair was rubbin' off on the pillow. Her naked breasts pressed into my chest and I felt her rapid breathin', the poundin' of her heart.

I swallowed. Maybe this hadn't been the best idea. It'd been a long time since I'd been in bed with a woman. I cleared my throat and refocused my attention on the two lawmen. "You boys about done? I'd like to get on with it…"

They were makin' a show of checkin' the room, lookin' behind the single chair and wash basin stand, even though it were obvious there was no one hidin' there.

"Oh, no, take yer time," the girl drawled, surprisin' me. She'd made her voice higher and inflected a southern accent. She lifted one hand to stroke my cheek and smiled up at me, puttin' on a show. "I charge by the hour, after all."

Despite the fact she weren't no real whore and I'd never really hired her, my frown was a real one.

It made one of the lawmen chuckle and one of 'em scoff. To my relief, they both headed toward the door. One turned back just before leavin'. "You see a skinny redhead girl with the Whittaker brand, you tell the sheriff. One thousand dollars to you if you bring her in yourself. Got it?"

I nodded. "Sure thing, officer."

He touched the brim of his hat, eyes slidin' toward the lady.

I held my breath.

"Enjoy," he said, and then he stepped out and pulled the door shut behind him.

Of course, it didn't latch no more, seein' as they'd busted it. But it stayed mostly closed, only a thin crack lookin' out into the hallway. Then I heard 'em thump back downstairs. My room was the last room in the hall.

I breathed out a long, slow breath.

The woman planted her hands against my chest and gave me a shove that knocked me clean outta the bed. I went sprawlin' to the floor, takin' most the sheets with me, and hit with a grunt on my left hip and elbow, wincin' as pain shocked through my leg.

She yanked the sheets back toward her to cover up her nakedness, scootin' me a foot or so along the floor. She was damn strong for bein' so skinny. "Ow," I complained, rollin' free of the twisted sheets and crawlin' toward my discarded shirt. "No need fer that. I was gettin' up."

She didn't answer, already diggin' around in the bed in search of her own clothes. "I have to get out of here," she muttered.

"That wouldn't be too smart," I said.

She lowered the sheets from over her head, and I saw she already had her shirt back on. It was streaked with black shoe polish now, her black-streaked hair an awful mess, and her dark blue eyes blazin'. "Excuse me?"

I shrugged into my own shirt and then used the edge of the bed as leverage to push myself to my feet. "They're still out there. They'll be searchin' this block fer awhile. Best to stay here. Maybe fer the night."

She gave me a look.

I chuckled at her resolute suspicion and shook my head, pickin' up my gun belts to buckle 'em back on. "Look, lady, if I was gonna take advantage of you, I woulda done it just then. You asked me to help you escape. You want help or not?"

Her expression softened, and I saw the unmistakable fire of hope light in her eyes. It twisted my stomach.

Hope.

The killer of souls.

But I suppose hope had also been what hadn't let me give up on Ethelyn, even after all this time. And now I had a chance to save her. Hope had gotten me this far, so maybe it weren't all bad.

I looked away from her to grab my hat and pushed it back onto my head.

"If you take me back to my family," she said breathlessly, "they'll pay you handsomely."

"How much?" Maybe takin' this woman back where she belonged would be easier than robbin' a bank. I hobbled to the open window and shut it, drawin' the shades. The posse might've already searched this room, but no need to take unnecessary risks.

"Ten thousand, at least."

I sucked a breath through my teeth. Well, that was sure somethin'. But not enough. Not nearly enough. "Where is this family of yers?"

"The East Republic. Pennsylvania."

I swore and turned to face her. "Pennsylvania!? That's a whole country away!"

The burnin' fire came back to her eyes, her full lips thinnin' into a hard line. "Yes. And I was dragged all that way by dirty bandits who sold me to Baron Whittaker! Take me back to my parents and they'll pay you well, I promise."

I swore some more and paced the room, or at least, paced as well as I could with my lame leg. I rubbed a hand over my mouth, stubble scratchin' at my palm. As an afterthought, I grabbed the wooden chair set in the corner and used it to push the door closed and hold it there. Releasin' a heavy sigh, I shook my head. "I'm sorry. I … I can't."

She lurched off the bed and threw back the sheets, fully dressed now. "You … *can't*? What do you mean you *can't*?"

"I can't go that far. I'm sorry. I have someone near here who needs me, soon. I can't take the time to escort you all the way to the other side of the country. Maybe if yer parents were closer I could … but no. Not that far."

Her mouth opened, but her words seemed lost. She stared at me for a long minute, and I saw emotions play across her face, everythin' from fury to terror to hopelessness, and then comin' back around to anger. "So everything you just said about helping me escape was a lie, then?" Her voice trembled now, and tears shone in her eyes.

I let out an exasperated breath and eased down into the chair I'd pushed up against the door. Guilt tightened in my chest again. I'd done a lot of stuff I shouldn't have in my search for Ethelyn ... and *not* done a lot of stuff I probably should have, too. "No. I helped you avoid those lawmen, didn't I? I just can't take you cross country. I have ... other people who need me here right now."

She made a show of lookin' around the empty room. "Really? And where are these people?"

I met her angry gaze evenly. "Kidnapped. Enslaved. Just like you." I fished around in my pocket and pulled out Ethelyn's necklace, holdin' it out so she could see. "My sister."

Her stiff stance sagged a little and she blinked rapidly, the tears streakin' down her cheeks.

"Nine-Fingered Nan has her," I said, though I wasn't sure exactly why I was tellin' her more. Surely she didn't want to hear about mine or my sister's problems. She had plenty of her own. "I'm going to buy her back."

She swallowed visibly. "The bastards who took me," she said quietly. "They were Nine-Fingered Nan's crew."

I straightened on my chair at this news. Nine-Fingered Nan's gang ... all the way in Pennsylvania? I remembered what her woman had yelled at me just the night before. About how there was nowhere far enough away I could run to now. Maybe that was truer than I had been willin' to accept. *Shit.*

"And she sold me to Baron Whittaker," the girl finished. She sat down abruptly on the edge of the bed. She wasn't angry now. Just exhausted. Sad. Hopeless.

Hope.

That soul killer.

I watched her and swallowed hard, thinkin' of how Ethelyn must be feelin' pretty much the same right now. Only probably worse, if Nan had really knifed off three of her fingers. The thought made me sick.

"He wanted me to be a part of his harem," the girl currently sittin' on my bed continued, and the words made my stomach lurch again. She stared across the room at the wardrobe, eyes unfocused. "But I fought him so hard he decided he'd try and break me first. Thought he'd show me how much worse life could be so I'd beg him to come back. He sent me down into the mines with the others." Her blue gaze slid back to me, hardenin'. "Six months I've been in the mines. Collecting scrap for twelve hours a day, barely eating, barely sleeping, and I'd rather do that till I die than share his bed."

Then she dropped her eyes to her hands, folded in her lap. "But ... this isn't the first time I've escaped ... and if he catches me again ... well. I don't want to think about it."

I sighed and dropped my head into my hands, then rubbed at my face again. I couldn't help her. Not like she wanted. But the thought of doin' nothin' turned my stomach more than even the horrors this poor girl and my own sister had experienced.

Doin' nothin' was out of the question. "How many slaves does Baron Whittaker have?"

She frowned at the question. "Nearly a hundred. Why?"

I let out a low whistle. That was a lot. "All of 'em itchin' fer freedom as much as you?"

"Many of them. Some of the older ones have given up. Some of the older ones are even loyal to the bastard."

I nodded. That happened sometimes. "I still can't take you back to yer parents. But there might be somethin' else I can do."

She looked at me in question, but didn't let herself hope this time. Not fully.

I rose from the chair and lit the room's lamps, then went to the side window and pulled the shades there, too. I faced her, then, and considered what I was about to do.

Holt was gonna be mad. Again.

"What if we give Baron Whittaker a lot of other things to think about besides gettin' you back? That would give you time to clear the area, get a big head start toward Pennsylvania."

She swiped at the tears on her cheeks and sniffed. "What do you mean?"

I hooked my thumbs into my belts, thinkin'. "What if we set 'em all free? All Whittaker's slaves. And set his house on fire. And … he keep his money at the bank?"

She tilted her head to the side. "Yes. Most of it…"

"And we rob the bank. I take what I need to get my sister … you take what you need to fund yer trip back to yer parents."

She stared at me as if I'd gone mad. Maybe I had. But I was bettin' she weren't gonna go runnin' off to tell the law my plans, seein' as she was wanted by the law herself. And truth be told, we could use another hand for that job, if she was up fer it.

"Well?" I prompted.

Her mouth opened. Then shut. She stood from the bed, but then hesitated. "I … I don't know. What you're proposing … if we're caught … they'll hang us for sure."

"Is that any worse than what Whittaker will do to you if he catches you again?"

Her eyes dropped to the floor. "No."

"Would you rather go back to him and live out the rest of your life in his bed? Or the mines?"

Those dark blue eyes flicked up to meet mine again. This time her voice was hard, resolute. "No."

I spread my hands. "Then why not make his life hell for a bit? Don't he deserve it after what he's done to you and all those others?"

"Yes." She straightened, throwin' back her shoulders and liftin' her chin, and through the black shoe polish smeared in her hair and the dusty state of her clothes, I saw clearly for the first time the young woman she must have been, before all this tragedy befell her. A young woman of proper breedin', most like, with manners and money and everythin'.

The adjustment to life out here as a slave musta been rougher on her even than most.

"All right," she said. "Let's do it."

I smiled. Holt hadn't even come back yet with his scoutin' report or his plan, but I was already well on my way to makin' my own. A hundred escaped slaves and a baron's house on fire would make mighty good cover for a bank robbery. "Good. Well then, Miss, if we're gonna be workin' together, I suppose I should properly introduce myself." I tipped my hat to her. "Name's Van. Van Delano. Pleasure to make your acquaintance."

She arched one eyebrow. "I'm sure it is, considering you've already seen me without my clothes on."

Heat rose to my cheeks. I cleared my throat. "For what it's worth, Miss, I never looked. I would never ... I mean I only made the suggestion to keep you—"

"I know," she cut me off, wavin' away my words. "And I suppose it worked. So ... thank you, I guess. But never again, understand?"

"Of course not."

She gave a little nod, another gesture reminiscent of the few ladies of high society I'd ever seen in my life, and stepped forward, holdin' out a hand. "Charlotte," she said. "Charlotte Harrison. Pleased to meet you, Mr. Delano."

I momentarily panicked at her formal tone, havin' not the slightest idea about proper manners. But I'd seen a gentleman or two kiss the hand of a lady before, so I did the same now, takin' her hand in mine and brushin' my lips against her knuckles and hopin' that's what she'd been expectin'.

Seemed it had been, 'cause when I straightened she was lookin' at me with both surprise and somethin' like pleasure.

I stepped back then and exhaled a quiet breath, feelin' awkward and my face burnin' worse than before.

To Hell with all these manners. I needed to get back to things I knew. Things like shootin' and robbin' and settin' things on fire. I cleared my throat again and limped to my half-glass of whiskey. I scooped it up and offered it out to her. "To the end of Baron Whittaker," I said.

She eyed the glass fer a second, then took it. Half her mouth quirked into a humorless smile, and her fair features hardened. It was a look I knew well.

It was the look of anticipated revenge.

"To the end of Baron Whittaker," she said, and threw back the rest of the drink.

It was then someone knocked on the door.

SMOKE AND FIRE

Charlotte gasped and spun to face it, droppin' the whiskey glass, which thankfully didn't shatter as it hit the floorboards, only thumped, bounced, and rolled underneath the bed.

I drew my gun and stepped in front of her, shovin' her behind me and aimin' at the door. "Who is it?" I called.

"Who ya think it is?" Holt grumbled from the other side. "It's me, Holt! What the hell happened here? The place is a mess!"

I exhaled in relief, holsterin' my pistol. "It's my partner, Holt," I said to Charlotte, and went to move the chair. "He's all right. No friend of slavers, that's fer sure." Or the law, but I wasn't entirely certain how much of that to tell Charlotte just yet. Generally the folk of the East Republic tended to frown upon livin' a life outside the law even more so than the folk of the Western Territories did.

I stepped aside to let Holt in and then shut the door quick again behind him, movin' the chair back into place.

"Fer Chrissakes, Van," Holt complained, stompin' into the room, "I leave fer a few hours and the place we're at gets—" He stopped and drew up short, his eyes finally fallin' on Charlotte. "Oh. Errr. Hey, if you have company, we can talk about this later." He turned toward me, stickin' out one of his thick fingers and shakin' it in my face. "But she better be one of the cheap ones, Van, cuz we ain't got much more coin to be wastin' on—"

I slapped his finger outta my face. "She ain't a whore, Holt."

His bushy gray eyebrows furrowed. "Eh?"

"She ain't a whore."

He turned to look her over up and down. "Well then what the blazes is she doin' in here?"

"She, uh … she needs our help."

Holt rounded on me again, givin' me that look. That disapprovin' look. That look that said, *Van, we have enough problems to worry about right now without tryin' to help out strangers, too.*

And that was true enough.

'Cept in this case, her cause could help out our cause.

And anyway, maybe a part of me felt like doin' some good fer Charlotte would make up fer what I'd done to the Balogh family by stealin' their mule.

"Van—"

"It'll keep the law busy while we rob the bank."

His eyes widened and he motioned fer me to quiet down. He glanced at Charlotte, clearly uneasy with her bein' included in this discussion.

"She knows," I said. "And she's in."

His lips thinned into a hard line. He tried to bluster some protests.

Charlotte crossed her arms. "I know how to shoot a gun," she said, as if that were the only criteria needed to convince Holt of her trustworthiness and usefulness.

Well, she weren't too far off.

He grumbled some more and shook his head,

stickin' his thumbs in his belt. Then he sighed, and shrugged. "Fine. Fine. You wanna drag a nice lady into this mess, and she's crazy enough to jump into it, fine."

"I'm in a big enough mess myself already, mister," Charlotte said. "Adding a little bit more now surely won't make any difference. And anyway," she looked to me over Holt's shoulder, "like your friend told me, I think this might be the best way to both get what we want."

"I hope so, missus. I surely hope so." Holt sighed again. "Well then. I suppose we're gonna do this. Shall we make a plan?"

We did.

Long into the night we talked, and spent more of our dwindlin' coin on some drink and a meal fer Charlotte. And some more drinks fer us, too.

Holt told us what he'd found out about the Bank of Blessing. It weren't too different than most other banks in the Territories, 'cept with a few extra armed guards. But it had a teller same as the others, and from what he'd been able to see from the lobby, safes like all the others.

But the teller hadn't seemed timid or shy. Wasn't likely we'd be able to bribe or threaten him into helpin'. So we'd have to deal with the safes directly.

Holt laid out a few sticks of dynamite on the bed, and I shook my head.

"Not very subtle. They'll hear us robbin' that bank fer miles."

Holt snorted. "Thought you said we had some-thin' in line to occupy the law?"

"We do. But the sound of dynamite might make 'em look back toward the bank awful quick."

"You got an ear fer openin' safes, then?"

I scratched at my chin and shook my head. A regular lock I could pick, sure. But not those combination safes. All those little clicks sounded the same to me.

"Then I guess we'll wait till the law is good and distracted, and then we'll have to get outta that bank when the job is done right quick, too."

"Yeah…"

Charlotte was silent. She looked nervous, her pale face even paler now.

"It's all right," I told her. "We'll get you a fast horse." I surely didn't know it was gonna be all right, and we'd have to *steal* her a fast horse, but there was nothin' much else to be said.

This had to work. It *had* to. Ethelyn's freedom depended on it.

And now, Charlotte's too.

She gave me a nod in return, but I could tell she weren't convinced.

Hell, I don't think any of us were. But we were doin' it, anyway.

"All right," Holt said. "Tomorrow we find the girl a horse. Tomorrow night, you two get to the baron's manor and light it up, get those slaves free. Meanwhile, I'll be waitin' on the bank to close up, get inside all quiet like. When you two are done at the manor, *hustle* it back to the bank, understand? I don't want to have to hold it all by my lonesome long. I won't blast anythin' till you two show up …

'less you get yerselves killed beforehand. In that case, I'm takin' all the money myself and high-tailin' it outta town. Got it?"

Charlotte and I nodded in unison.

"Give us an hour," I said. "An hour after you hear the fire alert go out … we'll be there. Unless we're dead." I glanced to her. "But I don't plan to be dead."

She met my eyes. "Me neither."

"All right, then, it's a plan." Holt pushed himself standin' from where he'd been sittin' at the edge of the bed, and the springs squeaked. "Now you two be careful at that manor, ya hear? I heard a few things about Baron Whittaker while out today, and none of 'em were particularly pleasant."

"I know my way around that place," Charlotte said. "Trust me, the last thing I want is to be found by any of his men. We'll be careful."

Holt gave her a grave nod. "Let's all get some rest. We're gonna need it." He looked at me one last time, and I knew what he was thinkin'.

This is your show, kid. Or maybe yer funeral.

"Good night," was all he said aloud. He tipped his hat to Charlotte as he made for the door. "Miss."

Then he was gone, and I stood from my seat on the bed too and slipped my boots back on. We'd rented a third room from Sally, and I was gonna take that one so Charlotte could have this one. I bid her good night as well, and left her alone on the bed, huggin' herself, as I slipped out into the hall and shut the damaged door best as I could behind me.

She was gonna move the chair under the knob once we were gone to secure it. That's what we'd agreed. I hoped she'd remember.

I considered our strange meetin' and mutual goals as I shuffled down the hall to my own room. I also hoped all this would go accordin' to plan.

Most of all, though, I hoped she wouldn't try and sneak off on us durin' the middle of the night.

I didn't sleep well, and was up with the sun the next mornin'. To my relief, Charlotte hadn't run off. We took breakfast in her room, not wantin' to risk any greedy folk downstairs recognizin' her. Those lawmen who had so courteously searched the saloon's rooms had left a poster of her face up on the wall right next to the bar.

Sally was still put out by the damage done to her property, but there weren't much she could do about it 'sides complain and apologize to her patrons. Which she did. Profusely.

I assured her we had experienced worse, and slept in worse, and to not trouble herself over concern fer our comfort. Then I took our plates of food and rushed back upstairs.

Sally gave me a funny look as I left with three plates instead of two, but didn't ask no questions, fer which I was grateful.

The three of us ate quick and light, not much in the mood fer food.

Nerves were already gettin' to me.

Sure, Holt and I had done plenty of robbin' and stealin' since I'd first met up with him eight years ago, but nothin' on this scale. And maybe he'd done somethin' like this before, sure, but it had been a long time ago.

Back before I was born.

Back when he was a lot younger and quicker, and still ran with my pa. Back when my pa still ran with Paul Johnson, better known in most parts now as Kill 'Em All Paul. Back when they'd had a much bigger crew than just two. Back when the Territories were even wilder and more lawless than they were now.

We didn't talk much, and after we'd eaten what we could, we spent the rest of the day makin' the last few preparations and gettin' the rest of our needed supplies. Holt and I did, anyway.

Charlotte didn't like havin' to stay hidden away in the room, but she didn't want to be recognized by the law or anyone else wantin' that thousand dollars, neither, so she reluctantly stayed behind.

We managed to bribe one of Sally's girls into givin' us an extra pair of women's clothes, at least, so she could change and get herself cleaned up a bit while we were out.

Holt picked up more dynamite and I got myself a good huntin' knife to replace the one I hadn't got back from those bastards who'd robbed me when I was passed out half-dead in the desert. I'd have preferred throwin' knives, to be honest, like the kind I was pretty sure had given Sally her name, but I was no good at throwin' knives. Those took a skill I had yet to figure out.

And I surely couldn't afford to be missin' any throws tonight.

We also went on the lookout fer a fast horse for Charlotte, but didn't have any luck.

There were plenty of horses in Blessing, all right. Plenty of mighty fine steeds. But there weren't many good opportunities fer stealin' any of 'em. Especially given the fact we wouldn't be leavin' town till nightfall.

It was too much of a risk the animal would be reported stolen and found again before we were gone.

So we left it. She'd have to ride double with either me or Holt. Not ideal.

Not ideal at all.

"Wish you woulda just left it," Holt grumbled as we made our way back through the crowded streets toward the Seven Knives. "Don't know why you always gotta do this kinda thing. I've told ya once and I've told ya a million times, ya gotta start *thinkin'* 'fore you go rushin' off into things."

I shook my head. "I didn't rush into anythin'." I'd had nothin' to do with Charlotte burstin' into my room, certainly. "And anyway, I don't know why yer complainin'. Torchin' Baron Whittaker's place gives us good cover. Without it … we'd almost be sittin' ducks."

Holt spit from the side of his mouth. "Maybe. But we could torch the baron's place well enough without the girl."

"Maybe," I echoed. "But we wouldn'ta even known about him if not fer her. And anyway, I'd rather have her there to show me around. Don't wanna be wanderin' around blind in a place like that. Not if the baron is really as *wonderfully pleasant* as you heard he was."

Holt grunted. "I guess. But now we got another body to worry about. She'll slow us down."

I rolled my eyes. "She don't weigh that much. It'll be fine."

"Whatever you say, kid."

Dusk came slow.

Or so it seemed.

By the time we were ready to head out, I felt as anxious as one of those ol' seasoned quarter mile race horses, pawin' and chompin' at the bit at the startin' line, ready to explode onto the track.

Holt headed off toward the Bank of Blessing on his black gelding, leadin' my mule behind him.

Charlotte and I went the opposite direction, toward Baron Whittaker's manor, arm in arm. Fer now, we played the part of a young couple in love, meanderin' along and window shoppin'. I'd had a wash and a shave, myself, and Charlotte looked different all right, all shined up and with her hair pinned atop her head. She'd borrowed a clean green blouse and dark brown skirt from one of Sally's girls, and a lace parasol, too. The parasol threw patterned shadows across her freckled face, and I hoped her change of clothes and a bit of cover fer her head would make her less obviously the wanted, escaped slave she was.

Just in case, we made sure to pass wide around those law officers stationed at some corners. But fer the general public, our idea seemed to be workin'.

Fer now.

We kept on mosyin' along, and the sun kept settin'. The crowds were thinnin' out now though, finally, now that it was almost dark. Along the main streets, a few street lights had been lit. Eventually, the buildin's of the town became fewer and further between. Ahead, the dirt street turned to cobblestone, and it seemed the town itself just stopped. There was a large stretch of empty land carpeted by lush green grass, and then a massive residence at the top of a small hill, all lit up with electricity. The cobblestone road led right up to its expansive porch and front door. It was surrounded on all sides by a makeshift metal fence, lookin' like it had been patched together with pieces from the Old World ruins itself. The front gate of that patchwork fence had two men standin' on either side of it, armed with rifles.

I frowned at the looks of it.

"That's it," Charlotte whispered to me. "The baron's manor."

I could feel her tremblin' through the arm she had entwined in mine. I wasn't sure if she was tremblin' from fear … or rage. "Come on," I whispered back. We ducked into the next alley, a narrow space between a tailor's shop and a gunsmith's. "The bank'll be closin' up soon. We need to light that place up."

"Going around back is best," Charlotte said. Her fingers were clenched around the parasol handle so tightly now her knuckles were white. "That's where the slave barns are, anyway. They'll have some guards, of course, but I think the dynamite will distract them."

"I'd think so." I opened the small satchel hooked to my belt, checkin' on the sticks of explosive. They were still there, right where they were supposed to be. The matches I'd put in Jake's coin pouch on the other side of my belt. "All right. Let's do this. You ready?"

She stared at me with wide eyes, then swallowed. Her breathin' was fast and shallow, but she nodded.

"Okay. Stay close. I'm gonna try not to shoot anyone on account of the noise. Least, not till there's some other noise to cover it up. But no guarantees. Still … if things go south … you just run. Understand? Just get out of here and don't look back. Head fer yer family. Got it?"

Again the wordless nod.

"Okay. Here we go."

Charlotte closed the parasol and pulled the long, slender knife that had been cleverly hidden in the handle. Those prostitutes had to be as resourceful as anyone, I figured. She set the rest of the parasol against the shop's wall, and then we both moved out from the shadow of the alley, stickin' to other shadows, instead.

We crouched and moved as fast as we could, which wasn't too fast on account of my leg. I'd left the crutch holstered in my saddle scabbard, and as such, the best I could manage was a lurchin', fast walk.

Interestingly, Charlotte never asked any questions about my limp. Not before, and not now, despite the fact it slowed us down somethin' awful.

At least it wasn't hurtin' quite so much anymore. And it seemed maybe even the metal foot was sorta goin' where I wanted it to go.

But there was no time to properly test it. We had to keep movin'.

So we did. Excruciatingly slowly, it seemed, bein' real careful to stay far enough away from the house that no one gazin' out the windows might spot us. There were a few perimeter guards, but we stayed far away from them, too. We reached the back at last, where there was another gate in the fence, this one guarded, too.

Only the two of 'em, though, and they weren't payin' much attention.

I pulled my left pistol and held it out toward Charlotte, butt-first.

She only stared at it.

"Just in case," I said, and nodded toward the gun. "Try not to shoot on account of the noise, like I said. But if you gotta, you gotta."

She took it gingerly, then tucked it into the waistband of her skirt, next to the knife from the parasol.

I took out two sticks of dynamite, then, and handed one to her. Then divvied up the matches. "One should do it. But make it a good throw. Soon as this first one goes off, you make a run fer the house. I'll go straight to the slave barns, like we talked about. When yer done, meet me there. Got it?"

"Got it." Her words were hardly a whisper.

"All right." I lit a match, then lit the fuse to my dynamite. I stood, took aim for a nice open spot in the baron's extensive back yard, and hurled the thing with all my might.

I covered my ears and braced myself, and Charlotte did the same.

A long, silent minute passed.

Then ... *BOOM!*

I flinched despite myself, my heart nearly leapin' outta my chest. Charlotte, too, cringed away from the blast, duckin' her head as a few clumps of grass and dirt rained down around us.

The two guards by the fence fair near jumped outta their boots, squawkin' and shriekin' and fallin' all over themselves as they scrabbled fer their rifles and turned in the direction of the explosion.

Charlotte and I both moved fer the gate, then.

She went through it, and I went right up behind the nearest guard and slit his throat with my new huntin' knife. His partner didn't even notice … till I did the same to him. I side-stepped the fallin' body and grimaced, wipin' the blade on my pants leg before sheathin' it again. I woulda rather shot a man any day over bleedin' him out like that, but in this case I surely didn't want all of Baron Whittaker's loyal men pin-pointin' my location from my gunshots.

I kept in a crouch and moved across the back yard through the shadows. There were shouts comin' from inside and around the house now, women soundin' scared and men yellin' fer someone to go out and see what the hell was goin' on.

It sounded like a lot of them. A lot of people in that house.

I wondered if it had really been a good idea to send Charlotte up—

BOOM!

The second explosion nearly knocked me flat. Instinctively I covered my head with my arms and threw myself back against the side of the nearest buildin'. A hole opened up in the back of the house, the wall fallin' inward on itself with a tumble of plaster and wood and shattered glass.

I blinked. That had been a good throw, all right.

Now there was a lot of screamin' and wailin'.

BOOM!

I ducked and swore, ears ringin' good now. A second blast to the house had never been a part of the plan. Where had she even got more dynamite?

I felt absently at the satchel on my belt, but I hadn't really counted the number of sticks. Maybe I shoulda.

I looked up to see the wood timbers of the house, the wooden furniture with its highly flammable lacquer, and the curtains all on fire. That second blast had opened a crater inside the house, and apparently upset a candle or an oil lamp or somethin', 'cause the flames were spreadin' fast now.

Well, that's just what we'd wanted, all right.

Charlotte had sure taken care of the house, so I refocused on my own job. Turned around to see the barn I was leanin' against was probably one of the slave barns. I heard runnin' footsteps comin' in the grass and pressed myself up against the wall again just as several more men with rifles rushed past.

But they weren't payin' no attention to me. They were all gapin' at the house.

I turned quick around the corner of the barn and went to the doors, still standin' open. Maybe that's where the men with the rifles had just come from. I ducked inside and took a quick look around the dim interior.

A lot of confused, wide eyes stared at me.

This was one of the slave barns, all right. Looked like they were all bedded down fer the night on mounds of straw, a lot of 'em crowded into a single, wide open space. A few had pillows or blankets, but that was all the belongin's I could see.

Which was good, 'cause I was about to burn it all down.

"Go!" I hissed at them, wavin' toward the door. "Go! You're free! Quick!"

They looked to each other, then back to me.

And didn't move.

"Go, damnit!" I drew my gun, and that got their attention. I waved it at 'em. "Go! Get out that door and run! Go, go!"

A few of the ones nearest to me scrambled away from my weapon as I advanced on 'em, and I acted like I might shoot 'em if they didn't run.

That they seemed to listen to, that and watchin' some of their fellows go, because soon they were all jumpin' up and runnin', pourin' out into the night. I chased 'em out of the barn and made sure they all kept runnin', over the fence and through the gate and across that carpet of grass. Then I marched back into the barn, took down a few of the lanterns from the walls, and smashed 'em into the straw.

It caught fire quick.

I limped outta that barn and headed fer the next one.

Rifle fire barked behind me and I ducked again, throwin' myself into the nearest shadow.

There was shoutin' everywhere now, and it took me a minute to figure out where the rifle shots were comin' from.

Behind me.

I turned. Some of the guards who'd been starin' at the house had now realized that some of the baron's slaves were escapin'. They were aimin' into the dark, takin' shots at the fleein' people.

My hand tightened around my gun, still in my

hand. "Shit!" I hissed. I could get a few of 'em, sure. And then the rest of 'em would turn right around and see me, and those odds weren't good.

I stood for a second in indecision, heart hammerin' in my throat.

They took a few more shots. Some of the slaves dropped mid-run. Some were dead. Some were wounded, addin' their cries to the rest now fillin' up the night.

My revolver lifted and I clenched my teeth. Braced myself.

My finger wrapped around the trigger, but still I hesitated.

I couldn't help Ethelyn if I was dead.

The flames in the barn next to me roared up, lightin' up the night. The men with the rifles saw it and turned, and I jumped around the side of it hopin' they hadn't seen me. My metal leg tripped me up and I hit the ground with a grunt, then bellycrawled a few feet before gettin' back up and hobblin' to the side of the next barn, thankful the light of the fire hadn't reached its shadow yet.

"Fire!" one of the men yelled. "Fire! Get the fire wagon! Get the fire wagon *now*!"

That was our signal to get out of there and head toward the bank. But I had three more barns to burn. And I hadn't seen Charlotte yet.

I swore under my breath as I reached the second barn. "Come on, come on, girl. Where are you?" A part of me wanted to go to the house and find her. *No. Just stick to the plan, Delano. Stick to the plan.*

So I kicked open the door to the second barn with my good foot, ready to shoot if I had to.

Only terrified eyes met mine. No guns. Just like

the last barn, it seemed any guards there might have been had run off to investigate the explosions and the fire. Better fer me.

I had to run these slaves out same as the first group, only this time I was swearin' all the while. Charlotte shoulda been here by now.

Somethin's wrong.

I smashed some lanterns into the straw again and limped toward the third barn. We still had to get back across town to the bank…

Somethin's wrong…

A barrage of gunfire erupted from inside the house, bringin' me up short just as I was about to kick in this next set of doors. I looked toward the back of the ruined manor and increased the intensity of my curses. That was most definitely *not* a part of the plan, neither.

The sporadic bursts of gunfire from the house were abruptly drowned in the roar of somethin' else, somethin' that was unmistakably a gun, but like nothin' I'd ever heard before.

It was firin' at an inhuman rate.

Dread settled like an anvil in my stomach.

I almost didn't notice all the people runnin' all over around me … from Baron Whittaker's guards and staff tryin' to organize a water brigade to put out the house and the barns, to the slaves I'd just freed dartin' their way through the chaos to freedom, to more guards now mounted and tryin' to chase 'em down.

And no one else seemed to notice me, neither, standin' there in the middle of it, gawkin' at the house.

Some people came out of the manor, then, from

the side doors and some even climbin' over the rubble, lookin' wild-eyed and scared. Men and women both, well dressed and covered with a fine layer of white dust. They ran, too, joinin' the mess of it all, quickly lost in the flurry of bodies and horses and smoke and fire.

The roar of the strange gun fell silent.

There were no other shots that came after.

I swallowed hard in a dry mouth. Took in a deep breath of air choked with acrid smoke, then coughed. And then I tore myself away from starin' at that ruined house and went back to the barn. One more. I was gonna free one more barn fulla slaves, and set it afire, and then it was time to go.

Even if I had to leave without her.

She's probably dead already. Damnit, Charlotte. Why didn't you just stick to the plan?

I shouldered through the third set of barn doors, expectin' no resistance.

And came face to face with three rifles. I froze.

The man nearest to me eyed me up and down and spit onto the straw-covered floor. "Who the fuck are you?"

I glanced over his shoulder to the slaves in this barn, lookin' much the same as all the others. Dirty. Bedraggled. Their clothes tattered, faces gaunt, and eyes wide and fearful. I brought my gaze back to the three men pointin' their guns at me. And said the first thing that came to mind. "Fire! Didn't ya hear? The other barns are on fire! The house, too!"

They looked to each other. Then at me.

"The fire wagon'll take care of it," one of 'em said.

"And you didn't answer us," another of 'em said. "Who the fuck are you?"

I opened my mouth to answer. But I wasn't sure what to say. They surely showed no signs of concern over the fire, nor any inclination to leave this barn. My gun was still in my hand, the weight of it temptin' me to shoot 'em all down.

But three against one … at point-blank range … I wasn't sure I was that fast.

Turned out it didn't matter, anyway.

Pain exploded through my head at just that moment, and all the chaos of the night got swallowed into blackness.

THE WONDERFULLY PLEASANT BARON WHITTAKER

I came back to consciousness slowly.

My head ached somethin' terrible, especially around my right temple. The pain was sharp and pulsin' there, and judgin' by the wetness spread down that side of my face, I guessed I'd been hit pretty hard.

Hit by who or what didn't matter.

All that mattered was that I was pretty sure I was fucked.

I tried to open my eyes. Managed to pry 'em open a crack, but all I saw was darkness and a dim orange glow. I blinked and groaned. My skull felt like it was gonna split open.

I tried to shift my arms, but they were stuck. Slowly, I moved my awareness to the rest of my body and away from my throbbin' head. Pulled on my arms again.

They were tied. Tied at the wrists behind my back, around the back of a chair. A wooden chair, by the feel of it. And a damned uncomfortable one at that.

I tested my feet next, already knowin' what I would find, and not bein' disappointed. My ankles were tied, too, presumably to the legs of the chair.

Even my metal leg, which I could only guess was tied same as my natural leg, since I couldn't feel no rope around that ankle. But the thing didn't jerk out uncontrollably when I tried to move it, either.

My boots were missin'.

Yep, I was pretty fucked.

I sighed and forced myself to lift my head. The movement sent shocks of pain stabbin' into my eyes and I grimaced, but kept my head up. I squinted through blurred vision and a smoky haze to see a man standin' in front of me. He was dressed fancy in a suit, which looked odd considerin' he was standin' in the middle of the ruins of one the burned-down barns. A bit of ash or maybe plaster powder from the house explosion dusted his shoulders. His graying hair had only a single piece fallen loose from the rigorous hold of his pomade, and it fell across a stern brow above a pair of severe eyebrows.

He must have been Baron Whittaker.

And he was glarin' at me like any wealthy man who'd had his house blown up and slaves freed and barns burned might.

There were six other men with him, three on each side of him, all givin' me murderous looks. They held weapons of various types: rifles, revolvers, crowbars, knives. But what I found most concernin' were the other, unarmed people present.

They were kneelin' in front of the baron's six men with their hands on their heads, eight of 'em, and from their clothes and their physical state I knew they had to be some of the slaves. Recaptured, maybe. Or maybe these hadn't even had the chance to run in the first place.

I swallowed. I was fucked, all right. Really, really fucked.

I glanced to either side of my lone chair, set in the middle of the burned out hulk of one of the barns. The other barn I'd set on fire had also mostly burned down, but the third was still standin'. Looked like all the flames were out now, though, and there was no sign of the fire wagon. The moon had moved to the other side of the sky.

Looked like I'd been out fer awhile.

Well hell. Holt woulda had the money already, then, and been long gone away from Blessing. And Charlotte … least I didn't see her kneelin' in the ashes there in front of me.

Maybe she'd escaped.

Or maybe she was already dead.

Either way, I was on my own here. On my own and facin' down a very pissed off Baron Whittaker. I cleared my throat. "Looks like you had a bad night," I croaked.

Without hesitation, one of his men stepped forward and cracked the butt of his rifle into my face.

It hurt. A lot. But I swallowed back the cry, not wantin' to give him the satisfaction.

The man stepped back, and I made myself look up again, glarin' through waterin' eyes. The left side of my face was throbbin' too, now, and that eye would probably swell up closed 'fore too long.

Baron Whittaker held up a hand. "Easy there, boys. I want him to be conscious for what comes next." He spoke quietly, each word carefully pronunciated. Then he took one step forward, his shiny shoes swiftly coated in ash as he did so. He directed his next question at me. "Where is she?"

My heart quickened. So maybe she wasn't dead. "Who?"

He smiled. "The girl. The redhead."

I scoffed and shook my head. "Mister, you know how many redheaded women I know? Yer gonna have to be more specific."

His smile thinned. "Her name is Charlotte. She ran away from me yesterday, and yet I know she was here tonight. She nearly killed me in my own house. Now, it seems, she has vanished, leaving only you."

"Sounds like a smart girl," I said.

Now his smile vanished, just like Charlotte seemed to have done. "Did she put you up to this? She give you some sad story to pull at your heart strings and convince you to come here and risk your life? And for what?" He turned slightly to glare down at the kneelin' slaves, his lip curlin' in a sneer. "For these poor wretches?"

I said nothin'. Sayin' nothin' was usually best in these types of situations.

Baron Whittaker held out a hand toward his men, palm up. One of 'em handed over a revolver. The baron pointed it toward the head of the nearest slave.

I tensed. It took everythin' I had to stay quiet, to seem like I didn't care. But inside, my heart thundered in my temples, puttin' my head in a vice of pain.

"You one of those freedom fighters, then?" Baron Whittaker asked. "Come to set these poor souls free? Well, I can help you with that." He fired.

I yelled, tryin' to come up outta the chair. But the ropes held me fast, and I only succeeded at nearly tippin' myself over.

Baron Whittaker looked at me, one eyebrow raised. "Oh. So you do care. Perhaps we are getting closer to the truth, then." He aimed at the head of the next slave, a woman, who was now tremblin' and cryin'. All of 'em were.

I stared at him, strainin' against the ropes, breath comin' fast and hard.

"Well," he said, voice maddeningly calm, like those people didn't matter to him at all. "Let me show you what you have done for these people." He fired again, and the second slave in the line of eight fell backward with a bullet hole between her eyes, a cloud of ash risin' up around her like a shroud when she landed.

He took aim at the third.

"Stop!" I shouted. "Stop, please!"

He drew back the pistol and turned to face me. "Where is she?" he asked again.

"I don't know."

He shot the third slave without even lookin'.

"Stop, goddamnit!" I pulled hard at my wrists, the rope rubbin' the skin raw, but I'd been tied tight. Not that it'd do me much good to get my hands free, anyway, as they'd taken my gun belts. But I couldn't stand to just sit there and watch this. I had to get free. I had to do *somethin'*.

Course, ***doin' somethin'*** was what had landed me —and the poor sods now dyin' and kneelin' in the ash—in this spot to begin with.

Maybe I shouldn'ta agreed to help Charlotte at all. Maybe I shoulda just left her to chance escapin' the law and the baron on her own. Maybe Holt had been right all along.

"We split up," I blurted. And I was glad I didn't know where she had gone, then. I had a feelin' this Baron Whittaker woulda been able to tell if I were lyin'. And if I'd known where she'd gone, I'd have to lie, now. As it was, I could be honest. "We split up and I don't know where she went. She was supposed to meet me back here at the barns, but she didn't. I thought she was dead."

The baron tilted his head to the side fractionally. His blue eyes narrowed, and I could tell he was weighin' my words, decidin' whether or not he believed me.

I kept my eyes locked with his, both to sell the truth of my words and to keep my gaze from slippin' to the five slaves still alive. I couldn't look at 'em. Couldn't stand the thought of them dyin' just so the baron could get at me. If I looked at 'em, he would see that.

And I couldn't let him see that.

"What does it matter, anyway?" I went on at his continued silence. "You have me. This was my idea, not hers. I talked her into it. She wanted to just run … I convinced her to come back here and show me the way in."

My voice caught. Because it was true. It *had* been my idea. I'd used her and her desperate situation, risked her life, all to cause a distraction so we could get our money.

My money. For Ethelyn.

And now here I was. Guess I'd be atonin' fer my sins sooner than I'd thought.

Baron Whittaker lowered the hand that held the gun. "Why?" was all he said.

I kept my gaze away from the cryin' slaves only with difficulty, and swallowed again. That, I didn't want to tell him. The truth, whether about Ethelyn or Charlotte, he'd only use against me, and there weren't no suitable lie he wouldn't see through in a second. I shoulda learned more about the wealthy barons of Blessing. Maybe then I coulda claimed to have been sent to sabotage him by a rival or some such.

But as it were, I knew nothin' about Baron Whittaker's rivals. So I said nothin'.

He nodded, as if my silence itself were some kind of answer. "I see. Let me give you a piece of advice, young man. The next time you decide to go after one of the barons of Blessing … you be sure you kill him. First thing. And you raze his house and everything he has to the ground. You should probably be sure to kill the rest of his family, too." He gestured to one of his men who held a crowbar, and the man walked around behind me.

I braced myself for a blow, but none came.

The baron made a show of openin' the cylinder of his revolver and reloading the three empty chambers. "You see," he went on, clickin' the full cylinder closed again, "we don't forgive. And we don't forget. You leave us alive, and we're going to be sure we get back what you took from us."

I worked on the ropes around my wrists, but all I managed was to send them into a fire of pain, too.

"So let's see. What have you cost me tonight?" Baron Whittaker paced slowly along the line of five slaves, some of whom had started to quietly beg him for mercy. Some of whom threw themselves at his feet, grovelin'.

It made me sick to watch. I tried to get up outta the chair again, but it only rocked at my efforts.

The baron paid me no mind, pacin' back and forth between me and the slaves, gun in hand. "You've cost me a lot of money, certainly. A lot of trouble. And a good night's rest. But I can tell from the looks of you that you don't come from money. So I won't bother demanding monetary retribution. Nor can your one body replace the number of slaves I've lost tonight." He stopped pacin' and turned on his heel to face me. "So, I shall take it in blood, Mr. Freedom Fighter. And I think it will take a good long while to make all of this up to me." He lifted his hands, pistol and all, and waved around at the smokin' destruction that surrounded us.

I gave a little laugh despite myself. "That's … that's very melodramatic of you, Baron."

He smiled at me again, that thin, humorless smile. "Perhaps I do have a weakness for theater," he conceded. "I always do like to put on a good show." Then his smile went away with chilling abruptness. "Which is why they are going to watch what happens to people who try and steal my property," he nodded toward the slaves, "and then you are going to watch them die."

The man with the crowbar reemerged from behind me, and the end of his crowbar was now glowin' orange. There musta been some embers still smolderin' somewhere.

"Hey hey hey, *wait*," I said, eyin' the crowbar as the man stepped close to me. Heat shimmered off it and I pressed myself back further into the chair. "They don't need to die. They had nothin' to do with any of this!"

"Oh, I know," the baron said. His voice was gentle, sympathetic. Terrifyin'. "Do you think I enjoy destroying perfectly good slaves? Of course not." He shook his head. "It's a loss to me as well, in more ways than one. But *you* did this. You condemned them to death as soon as you barged onto my property and tried to spirit them away. As soon as you encouraged them to betray their master, and as soon as they decided to attempt such a thing. Their deaths are *your* fault, Mr. Freedom Fighter. And the others will learn from their mistakes. From *your* mistake."

He waved his man forward.

I opened my mouth to argue further, but then the end of that glowin' crowbar pressed into my right bicep with a hiss, and all my words were lost in a blaze of white-hot pain. My scream echoed up outta that ruined barn, up into the night, up to the glitterin' stars that watched us all with their cold, impassive stare.

The crowbar drew back, then bit again. And again.

I lost track of how many times that bastard branded me with that pry bar. The pain all ran together, lightin' up the whole of my right arm like they'd put it in the fire itself. I struggled against the ropes, tried to pull away from it, tried to escape its relentless advance.

Tipped myself over once and got a face full of ash, only to be pulled upright again by unseen hands.

Then the fresh pain stopped.

I waited, braced for it to come again, hunched in the chair and gaspin', my face wet with traitorous tears. My right arm still screamed, waves of pain runnin' from shoulder to fingers.

"Ah," Baron Whittaker said in his calm, quiet voice, "don't worry, Mr. Freedom Fighter. We're only just beginning. Soon we will move to more … *sensitive* … areas."

I peeled my eyes open to give him what glare I could muster, blinkin' through a blur of tears and ash and agony.

He was smilin' again, but a real smile this time, truly enjoyin' my sufferin'.

I wanted to kill him, then, even more than I'd wanted to kill him before. I wanted to kill him fer what he was doin' to me, and fer what he'd done to the people enslaved to him, and fer what he'd done to Charlotte.

Unfortunately, it seemed unlikely I'd get the chance.

"But first," he said, and waved at another of his men with a crowbar, who advanced on me.

I wondered why these men seemed to have such a fascination with pry bars. But I shouldn't have. I got my answer in the next second, when he drew it back two-handed and then smashed it with all his might into my left knee.

If it woulda been my right knee, the blow woulda surely shattered my kneecap, and I woulda been sent into a world of hurt that made the brandin' seem trivial, indeed.

But it was my left knee, instead, made up now of metal and gears, and the pry bar bounced off it with a clang, makin' me jump in surprise and the man weildin' it stagger backward.

He lowered the crowbar and stared at me.

I stared back. And I thought of what Dr. Balogh had said about the metal leg havin' *advantages*. I'm sure this wasn't what he'd meant. But I was thankful fer not havin' a shattered kneecap just then, certainly. Though I also had the impression that Baron Whittaker findin' out about my metal leg wouldn't lead to anythin' more pleasant in the end, anyway.

"What was that?" the baron asked.

"I dunno," his man with the non-heated crowbar answered. He stepped forward again and tapped on my shin experimentally with the end of the bar. It made a little *tink tink tink* sound.

Unmistakably metal against metal, even through the fabric of my pants.

Shit.

"What the Devil…?" Baron Whittaker handed off his revolver and took one of the big huntin' knives instead. He came up to me himself now, and I wished more than ever I could get even just one of my limbs free from the damned ropes.

But I couldn't.

I kept tryin' anyway, even as he stabbed the knife down hard into my leg, right above the knee. Least he hadn't tried it in my thigh, where I still had flesh and bone.

The knife's edge jarred off the metal pipin' of my leg.

The baron looked at my knee fer a minute, then looked up at me.

I said nothin', but I could feel my heart throbbin' in every part of me they'd hurt. I didn't know what he'd do when he saw my leg. The town of Blessing was famous for its Old World ruins.

Baron Whittaker was wealthy 'cause of his expeditions into those ruins.

Was my metal leg Old World tech? And workin' Old World tech, at that?

I didn't know. I didn't even know if Dr. Balogh knew, really.

But it sure seemed similar. And people had killed fer a lot less when it came to Old World tech.

Baron Whittaker returned his attention to my leg, slidin' the knife blade into the hole it'd made in my pants, then cuttin' down all the way to my ankle. He tore the pants leg open, and there was my metal leg, all right, gleamin' dully in the light of the moon.

"Well, well, well," he mused, standin' back to study it, "would you look at that?"

The man who'd hit me with the crowbar muttered and signed himself.

The one with the heated crowbar only stared, seemin' to have forgotten to re-heat his tool, because the end of it was no longer glowin'. Course, that was just fine with me.

The baron's four other men glanced at each other, some swearin' and some prayin' under their breath.

And the five slaves still left alive somehow looked even more terrified. They huddled together in a bunch, their eyes so wide I could see the whites, even in the dimness of the night.

Baron Whittaker clucked his tongue. "Now where oh where did you get that, Mr. Freedom Fighter? You steal it?"

I barked a laugh. "It don't even work," I rasped. "It might look fancy, but it's just a crutch. A crutch made outta metal in the shape of a leg. That's all."

"Where did you get it?"

I shook my head. "Doesn't matter."

"Oh, it matters." Baron Whittaker grabbed a fistful of my hair and pulled my head back so I had to look up at him. "You see, I don't know of anyone in the Territories who can do such work. And that's a problem. Because I make it my business to know everyone who has such talents. It's not fair their gifts be *wasted* on people such as yourself, you see."

I grinned at him through the blood and tears. "Well shit, Baron. Life ain't fair though, is it?" I worked up a nice bit of phlegm and spit at him. It landed on the front of his fancy suit.

He released his grip on my hair and pulled a handkerchief from the front pocket of that fancy suit. He wiped the hand he'd just had in my hair, then wiped up the wad of spit from his jacket. Then he tossed the silken square into the ashes and sighed. "All right. You just let me know when you're ready to talk. I can wait. As I said, we're only just beginning."

He left me, exchangin' his knife for a gun again and goin' to stand behind the cluster of five slaves this time. He clasped his hands in front of him, the pistol pointin' at the ground, I was happy to see, instead of at anyone's heads.

I let out a breath. I'd expected that to go worse.

But then I saw the fella with the heated crowbar come up beside me, and the damn thing was glowin' again.

Fuck me. I wondered how long Baron Whittaker would find torturin' me entertainin'. I wondered how long he'd wait fer me to tell him all about Dr. Balogh. I wondered how long I'd be able to stay quiet, or if eventually he'd break me.

And I wondered what he'd do to the good doctor if he found him.

I didn't want Baron Whittaker to find Dr. Balogh and his family. I'd already stolen their mule. I didn't want to get them killed, too.

I'd gotten enough people killed already.

The red-hot crowbar pressed into my inner left thigh this time and I started and yelped, then clenched my teeth against the scream. Hands caught the back of my chair and steadied it as I almost tipped again.

He held the shimmerin' metal to my skin longer this time, probably tryin' to get some noise outta me, but I swallowed it back with every ounce of my willpower till he gave up, pullin' it away.

I dared to breathe again, suckin' in air in harsh, ragged gulps. Fresh tears wet my cheeks. I could stop the screamin', sometimes, but I couldn't stop those. Nausea rolled in my gut, and my whole body was shakin'.

Somewhere in the distance, across the silence of the night, I heard a horse whinny.

"Looks like he's got regular flesh there, Mr. Whittaker," said the man holdin' the hot crowbar.

"Good." The baron's cold blue eyes shifted to me. "And what about your other leg, Mr. Freedom Fighter? Is it metal, too? Or just flesh and bone?"

"Only one way to find out," said the fella with the second crowbar. He walked around to my right side, kickin' casually at the piles of ash in his way as he did so.

I swore I could hear hooves in the grass, comin' from somewhere. But maybe it was just my throbbin' heart, rushin' blood through my achin' head, tickin' down the final hours of my life.

The man with the second crowbar positioned himself to take a nice hard swing at my right knee.

This one wasn't gonna bounce off metal.

This one was gonna hurt like hell.

I sucked in a breath and closed my eyes, bracin' myself.

Another whinny, loud and piercin', and close.

I snapped my eyes open and looked.

A horse galloped by us, no rider and no saddle, whinnyin' again. An answerin' whinny sounded from a little ways away, across the baron's yard. And then a few more horses came gallopin' by, followin' the first.

We all stared after 'em, not one of us understandin'.

Baron Whittaker rounded on his six men, currently all gathered around me in my lone chair. "Those are *my* horses! How did they get out?"

The men looked to each other, but it seemed none of them had any answers.

"You said all the escaped slaves had been recovered, yes?" the baron asked.

"Well, most of them, sir," one with a rifle answered. He had no hat, and his brown hair was long and greasy. "Some of them were shot while escaping. And a few we couldn't find. But John's already talked to the sheriff's office—"

Baron Whittaker's face reddened, his fists clenchin', even the one around the gun still in his hand. "Maddox, Russell, you go get those damn horses and put them back where they belong. The rest of us will stay here and deal with this thieving bastard. Got it?"

Two of the six—unfortunately neither of the men currently holdin' crowbars—nodded and ran off into the darkness.

They were just passin' by the third slave barn, the only one left standin', when it exploded.

The blast sent wood shrapnel and both men flyin'. They landed amid a rain of wooden splinters, and neither of 'em got up again.

I hoped they were dead.

It was then I realized there didn't seem to be anyone else inside the barn that had exploded. There weren't no screamin' and wailin', no bodies.

Baron Whittaker seemed to realize this at the same time. "What in the Devil is going on here?" he shouted. "I thought you men told me the perimeter was clear!"

"It—it was, sir," one with a knife said.

The baron swore. So he wasn't so much better than the rest of us, after all. Funny how all that money and learnin' didn't seem to matter much in the face of danger. "Does that seem *clear* to you?!" He jabbed a finger toward the third barn, now only a heap of broken timbers. Then gestured toward me, toward the slaves huddled before him. "Get them inside! All of them! And one of you go tell McCormick to double—no, *triple*—security out here! I will not stand for—"

The sound of more hooves cut him off.

He turned with a scowl, clearly expectin' another of his horses runnin' free.

And it was another of his horses, I suppose, but this one wasn't runnin' aimlessly. This one had a saddle and a rider.

A rider carryin' a very big gun. A gun that looked more like a cannon.

Baron Whittaker's mouth fell open, makin' a nice, round O.

Hell, my expression probably looked somethin' of the same, because that's when the rider came close enough fer me to recognize her.

Charlotte.

She opened fire.

BEHOLD A PALE HORSE

The cannon of a gun she carried roared and spit fire, and I realized it made the same sound I'd heard earlier, comin' from inside the house. The gun that had silenced all the other guns.

Her horse threw up its head and pinned its ears at the flash and the noise, wild-eyed and jumpy, but she drove it onward with her heels, her finger never comin' off the trigger.

Baron Whittaker was just bringin' his pistol up toward her when a wild spray of slugs punched into his chest and sent him sprawlin' into the ash. Blood splattered across his slaves. They shrieked and flattened themselves against the ground.

The baron's four men around me scrambled fer their guns, too. Only one of 'em had his ready, the one with the rifle. He'd just sighted down the length of it when she mowed him down, and I shoved myself over sideways just as the storm of bullets filled the air where I'd just been.

The three remainin' men dropped heavily all around me, big, gapin' holes punched through 'em. I coughed in the cloud of ash they stirred up.

Heard the hoofbeats circle around, then come to a stop.

I lifted my head and looked through the haze to see Charlotte had dismounted, looped the reins of her nervous horse over a charred two-by-four still stuck in the ground, and was now stridin' in my direction, the cannon still gripped in both hands.

I couldn't rightly tell by the look on her face if she meant to rescue me … or kill me, too. I opened my mouth to ask, but the words got stuck.

She ignored me fer the moment and propped the giant gun back against one shoulder, then bent down to retrieve the heated crowbar, still glowin' a faint orange on one end.

Fer a second I was afraid she planned to use it on me again, but then she turned away and went to the baron's body.

No … he weren't dead yet.

I could see him twitchin', hear the rattle of his breath as he gasped fer air.

Charlotte marched right over to his side, standin' over him with the cannon-gun in one hand and the hot crowbar in the other, her skirt and blouse streaked again with dirt and soot, her wavy red locks, once neatly pinned atop her head, now in disarray and fallin' down around her shoulders.

"Y-you…" the baron gurgled.

"Me," she said. And then she jammed that hot crowbar up between his legs, right into his goods.

I grimaced.

The baron screamed, high and terrible.

The nervous horse whickered and rolled its eyes, dancin' in place.

Charlotte jabbed the crowbar at his face then, into his eye.

His shriekin' raised the hairs on my arms. And yet, it was the kind of justice a man like him deserved.

She took his other eye, too, lettin' him scream

and blubber and choke and rattle, hands weakly flailin', tryin' to find her, or tryin' to find his gun. Then she threw the crowbar away and drew my pistol from the sash at her waist. Her face was hard and expressionless and pale in the moonlight as she aimed. And pulled the trigger.

His screamin' abruptly stopped, his body goin' still, and the sudden silence rang in my ears.

She stood there fer a minute, lookin' down at him. A tendril of smoke trailed from the barrel of my gun. Then she tucked it back into her sash, and looked down to the five slaves still flattened against the ground there, all of 'em now gapin' at her with open mouths.

"Go," she said quietly. "Get out of here. You're free now. Go back to your families."

They didn't move.

She didn't prod them. She looked toward me, instead. Then carefully stepped around them to make her way back to my sideways chair. She picked up my gun belts from where they'd been tossed into the ash and buckled them around her own waist, though they were too big and slipped down low around her hips. She grabbed up my boots next, then pulled the parasol knife and crouched, sawin' through the ropes that bound me.

One by one, my limbs fell free, and I rolled away from the chair and onto my back, starin' up at the stars, gaspin' myself. My head still felt as if it might split in two, my right arm as if it were on fire, and the branded spot on my thigh was worst of all. My left eye had swollen up, all right, leavin' me with half a view.

Charlotte's face eclipsed that half a view of the stars.

At least it seemed she had no intention of killin' me. I didn't think. "What…" I winced, my throat raw from screamin'. "What took you so long?"

"I was freeing the others," she said. "And taking care of some of the perimeter security. How did you know I would come back for you?"

"I didn't."

She leaned down to help me sit, and I winced again at the movement. "You thought I would leave you here? For the baron?"

I prodded gingerly at the swollen places on my right temple and left eye. My fingers came away sticky with blood. "That woulda been the smart thing to do."

She hissed a noise of dismissal. "No. I've seen enough people suffer at his hands. And anyway … you helped me back at the Seven Knives. It was the least I could do to return the favor."

"Except this was my idea," I mumbled. "I coulda got us both killed."

"Could have," she agreed. "But didn't."

"Close enough."

"Hardly. You'll be all right." She gave a little grunt as she helped me to my feet and steadied me as I swayed. She set my boots upright for me and held me as I shoved my feet down into 'em, nearly swoonin' from the pain. "I'm sorry. But you made a very good distraction. I had to be sure I got as many out as I could."

She used her massive rifle like a walkin' stick on one side and wrapped her other arm around me, helpin' me limp toward the horse.

"Was that your plan all along, then? Use me as a distraction?" I felt a fool. I felt used. And yet there was a kind of justice in that, too, weren't there? After all, I'd arranged this whole business as a distraction fer the bank robbery in the first place. The irony of it almost made me laugh despite the pain. *Who used who, I wonder?*

"No," Charlotte insisted, and she even sounded a little offended. "My only plan was … well, our plan. The plan we made at the Seven Knives. But when I got here … once I was inside … my plans changed. I only wanted to kill Baron Whittaker. But he got away from me in the house. I came back out to meet you at the barns, like we said, but by then they'd found you and knocked you out cold. So I improvised.

"I got them all out, Van. All the slaves except those five." She looked over her shoulder to them, and they seemed to be recoverin' a bit from their shock now, sittin' up and talkin' in whispers, pointin' and gesturin' first toward Charlotte and then out at the land beyond the fence. "Well, and except for some of the house staff. But they'd run when the dynamite blew out the house wall. And anyway, most of them were loyal to the baron."

I only managed a grunt, concentratin' too hard on not blackin' out.

"And I found myself a fast horse."

It looked fast, sure enough, but it also looked awful hot, nostrils flarin' and eyes rollin', pawin' at the dirt. It was a tall, sleek blue roan with a mane and tail black as night. And Baron Whittaker's brand on its left hip.

We'd have to fix that right quick, or we wouldn't

get far at all. Not after the sun rose on all the death and destruction we'd rained down on this place tonight.

"Gottta get outta here," I muttered.

Charlotte scoffed. "What do you think we're doing? Here, let me mount up first, then I can give you a hand up."

I clutched a fistful of mane to keep myself standin' as she let go of me, then clumsily scrambled up into the saddle. That damn cannon-gun of hers was heavy and unwieldy, and she had nowhere to holster it, neither on herself nor on the horse.

"Leave it," I said.

She looked down at me in surprise. "I beg your pardon?"

"That gun. Leave it. Too big. It'll just slow us down."

She laid it over the front of the saddle with one hand and reached her other hand down toward me. "I will do no such thing. As far as I know, this is the only gun of its kind in the Territories. Baron Whittaker never shut up about it. And as you saw, it's quite useful. I'll be keeping it, thank you very much. Now, are you coming or not?"

I eyed her and that ridiculous gun, sittin' proud upon that tall horse, and thought suddenly of one of the verses from the Good Book Mama had sometimes read to us. The one about the pale horse and the rider that was Death.

Well, with that horse and that gun, Charlotte could be Death fer a lot of people, certainly. And bring Hell followin' after her, all right.

I steeled myself for new pain as I gripped her

forearm with my left hand and managed to stick my metal foot in the left stirrup.

"On the count of three," she said. "One, two, *three*!" She pulled and I mustered a hop off my right foot, barely managin' to get myself over the back of the horse without either blackin' out or slidin' right off the other side.

I clutched the back of the saddle as the horse danced around.

Charlotte spoke soothin' words to it, though I wasn't sure they did much good.

"Hold on to me," she instructed.

"I'll take us both down if I fall off," I warned.

"Just do it."

I did so reluctantly, slidin' my arms around her slender waist. The feel of her was strangely comfortin', and I had a sudden impulse to lean into her, to rest my head on her shoulder and close my eyes.

But I didn't.

That wouldn'ta been appropriate.

She kicked the horse up into a canter and the comfortin' thoughts all went away with the sharp reminders of all my pain. I sucked in a breath and ground my teeth against it.

"Hold on," she called back to me. "Stay with me. We'll get someplace safe."

Someplace safe. As if that existed anywhere in the Western Territories. And after hearin' Charlotte's story, I wasn't sure even the East Republic was so safe anymore.

But safe didn't much matter, anyway. All that mattered was that money.

"Grave Gulch," I managed to choke out. "Get to Grave Gulch."

Holt woulda left Blessing without us by now, sure, but our fallback meetin' place had always been Grave Gulch. He'd wait there a month before movin' on. That had always been our agreement if things ever went to Hell on a job: go back to Grave Gulch. Wait a month. If the other of us didn't show up by then, we were most likely dead.

"Grave Gulch," Charlotte mused. "That's a pretty far ride."

"Yeah."

"I haven't been here that long, but even *I've* heard the stories about those who live in Grave Gulch. You sure it's the best place to go right now? In your condition?"

"Yeah. We got a camp there. It's fine."

A long stretch of silence, broken only by the horse's quick hooves on grass, followed my statement. I could tell Charlotte didn't like that idea none. But it was as close as I had to a home. As close as I had to somewhere safe. And Holt was as close as I had to any kind of family anymore.

"All right," she finally said, reluctant. But she turned the horse in the right direction.

Of course, there was a chance Holt had taken that money from the Bank of Blessing and decided to strike off on his own without waitin' fer me. He coulda decided to keep it all fer himself.

That kinda money woulda been a mighty strong temptation fer anyone, much less a man like Holt Haggerty, who'd never spent a day of his life on the right side of the law.

My stomach turned at the thought.

If Holt had taken off with the money ... well. I didn't want to have to track him down. I didn't want to have to try and take back that money. I didn't want to have to kill him. Not after everythin' he'd done fer me these past eight years.

But then … maybe he was already dead. Maybe he hadn't pulled off the bank job at all. Maybe the law had gunned him down, and I'd be the one waitin' at Grave Gulch with no money at all, a massive debt still owed to Nine-Fingered Nan, and a lot more scars.

"Hold on," Charlotte reminded me, and her soft voice jolted me back to the present.

I realized my hold on her had been slippin', that my vision had dimmed. I fought back to consciousness, tightened my hold around her waist.

"I'll head toward Grave Gulch," she said. "But we're going to have to camp a few times between here and there. I don't suppose you have any supplies stashed anywhere?"

Supplies. All my stuff was packed on my mule. And Holt had taken the mule. "No," I said.

She said nothin' in reply. She was probably regrettin' her decision to rescue me. Probably wonderin' how we were supposed to make a few days' ride with one horse and no supplies and me in my current state, hardly able to keep myself upright on the back of that pale horse.

I was wonderin' the same thing.

I drifted in and out of awareness as we rode, the rhythm of the horse's hooves lullin' me into a semiconscious state. Any time I'd dip too deep into the welcomin' darkness and start to slip, Charlotte's warnin' would snap me back awake, just in time to grab hold of her again and right myself.

The situation was disturbin'ly familiar, really. It hadn't been all that long ago I'd been atop that vulture Clint's horse, ridin' toward Bravebank with a bullet in my leg and a fever in my blood. Only I hadn't had anyone else with me at the time to wake me up when I passed out.

I'd only come to later, sprawled out on the ground, minus my canteens and minus my horse.

Wasn't sure I was all that much better off currently … but at least I had Charlotte fer the moment. And at least she was on my side.

Fer the moment.

She brought us to a stop in the late mornin' beneath a thick grove of trees. We were several miles south of Blessing now, and these kinda trees wouldn't be commonplace anymore after a few more hours of ridin'. But fer now I was thankful fer their shade, and fer the softness of the grass as I eased off the horse and collapsed down into it.

Charlotte dug around in the saddlebags, then came to my side with her arms fulla stuff. She knelt down next to me. "Take off your clothes."

I turned my head to look at her. "What?"

She set down the stuff in her arms, arrangin' it in a neat semi-circle on the grass. "Take off your clothes," she repeated. There was a hint of humor there in the way the corners of her mouth quirked, the glint in her dark blue eyes. But then she sobered. "I need to treat those burns. You're not the first person I've seen the baron do this to. If we don't get them taken care of they could get infected.

So." She gestured with her hands. "Come on. Off with it."

I grunted and complied. Or tried to. It was hard to work my right hand with that arm still blazin' in pain. The fingers were swollen, even though that hellish crowbar had never gone past my elbow.

Charlotte watched me fumble at my shirt buttons fer a minute, then sighed and reached forward to help me.

I eyed her. "I hope you don't think I'm going to bestow my *charms* upon you just 'cause you helped me escape?"

Her fingers paused on the buttons, mouth twistin' into a wry smile as she looked at me. "Hah. Very clever, Mr. Delano. Maybe I would, if I thought you had any *charms* to bestow in the first place."

I gave a rough chuckle and shook my head. "Fair point."

She finished with the buttons and helped me shrug outta the shirt, sweat-soaked and stained with ash and charred in several spots along the right arm. "There we go. Now, just hold still."

That was easy enough to do. Mostly. 'Cept fer the few times I'd wince or flinch as she cleaned the blistered skin and gently spread a salve over it, then wrapped it with clean bandages. "Where'd you get all that?" I asked, tiltin' my chin toward all the stuff.

We didn't have no campin' supplies, no food, but it looked like she'd managed to bring a whole doctor's medicine cabinet along with her.

She tied off the bandage on my arm and moved to investigatin' my face, holdin' my chin in one hand while carefully wipin' at the dried blood with a damp cloth. "Mm? Oh." She took a deep breath and let it out slowly. A heavy sadness fell over her face and she shook her head. "I knew what he was going to do to you soon as I saw they'd found you. I made a trip back inside the house to get these before it all burned down. Everyone had cleared out of it after the dynamite, anyway."

"You didn't get any food, though?"

She rolled her eyes. "No. But I did grab a few other valuables, too, while I was there."

That piqued my interest. "Like what? And how much?"

"Enough to pay for supplies, if I can find a place to sell them."

I would have liked to have known more about the stuff she'd grabbed from the baron's house, but then she pulled out a spool of stitchin' thread and one of those ugly hooked needles and my attention went to keepin' quiet while she sewed up the gash on my head.

By the time she was ready to fix up the burn on my thigh, I was plum wore out.

And I was grateful she didn't require me to shuck off my pants entirely while she doctored that burn, too. Instead, she just ripped 'em a little more, and I tried to think of other things while she cleaned and applied ointment to that one, both 'cause of the deep, burnin' pain that still radiated from there … and 'cause of the nearness of her hands to my groin.

I suddenly became quite aware of the sight I musta been. A sorry one, indeed.

She finished wrappin' the thigh burn and tugged the two halves of my torn pants leg back together, back over the burn and the bandage, back over the unnatural seam where flesh met metal, back over the rest of the metal contraption that made up the rest of my leg.

Her eyes lingered on it, even after it was covered. "Well, I didn't get any thread for mending clothing," she said, "but I'll add that to the list of supplies I'll try and buy. We'll get those sewn up so they'll be good as new."

Still her eyes didn't leave my leg.

I wanted to say somethin' about it, but I wasn't sure exactly what. I opened my mouth to fill the widenin' silence, but then she turned her face to me abruptly and I closed it.

"Where *did* you get it?" she asked.

I swallowed, shrugged. "Some foreign doctor. I didn't ask fer it. I was unconscious when he … when he took my leg. And then when I woke up I had this one." I twitched the metal foot, then startled as the toes actually moved like I'd intended. Maybe, after all this time, I was finally startin' to understand the thing.

"It's a dangerous thing to have," Charlotte said softly.

I nodded toward her cannon-gun, the fat barrel propped up against a nearby tree. "So is that."

She followed my gaze and smiled. "Except I don't need that thing to walk."

"Well, half the time I don't need this thing to walk, either," I grumbled. "It mostly don't work, just like I told the baron."

Her smile faded. "He would have cut it off you, eventually."

I grimaced at the thought, but had no doubt it was true. I reached out and took her hand, surprisin' myself as much as her. But there was somethin' that needed said. "Thank you. Fer comin' back fer me. And fer doctorin' me up. You shouldn't have … but thank you."

Color rose to her cheeks, tryin' to cover up the freckles there. "Like I said, it was the least I could do. I appreciate you not handing me over to the law as soon as you saw me. A thousand dollars would have swayed a lot of people."

I shook my head.

"And thank *you* for giving me the opportunity to end Baron Whittaker," she said then, her voice turnin' hard. "I never could have done it without you. Those slaves wouldn't be free without you, either." She squeezed my hand. "I'm just sorry for what you had to go through to achieve it."

My mouth was dry and I tried to wet my cracked lips. All I could think of was those three slaves Baron Whittaker had gunned down. And the others shot down with rifles as they'd fled into the night, too.

And everythin' else I had done and hadn't done in all my years of searchin' fer Ethelyn.

I deserved worse, in truth.

But I was close now. So close. Closer than I'd ever been.

Long as Holt had managed to get that money.

I pulled my hand from hers and cleared my throat.

She blinked and looked away, then began to gather up all her stolen medical supplies.

The thought occurred to me then that those supplies were worth quite a bit of money by themselves.

Maybe we weren't so bad off on this journey after all. If she could find anywhere to sell them.

I wanted nothin' more at that moment than to close my eyes and sleep, right there in the grass where I lay. But we weren't far enough away from Blessing yet to rest comfortable, so I swallowed down a few gulps from the single waterskin Charlotte had taken, and struggled up behind her onto the stolen horse again.

We rode on.

We stopped again in the late afternoon, mostly 'cause I couldn't seem to stay on the damn horse. Exhaustion took me soon as I settled back against a young birch. I was vaguely aware of Charlotte headin' down toward the bank of the river we'd been loosely followin', but then slipped gladly into blackness.

I started awake some time later and groaned as consciousness brought back the dull ache of pain, everywhere. Especially in my head. Night had fallen, and I blinked in the glow of a nearby fire. I squinted, fuzzy shapes and colors slowly resolvin' into things familiar.

Charlotte crouched there by the fire, warmin' somethin' in a small pan. She noticed I was awake and came over, bringin' me more water, some jerky and beans, and whiskey.

I drug myself up sittin', thinkin' I'd never seen anythin' more wonderful in my life. "You found a place to sell the baron's stuff," I croaked.

She smiled. Nodded. "Well, traded, more like. But yes. I found a place."

We made little conversation as I ate, for which I was grateful. My head was poundin' too hard fer words to come easy. I ate quickly and gladly accepted the bedroll Charlotte offered me … only after assurin' myself she had her own.

I eased my battered body onto the thin woolen roll, and slept again.

We rode once more at dawn's first light. At my urgin', Charlotte kept our pace steady, but not too fast. I didn't want to lose the horse. And carryin' two instead of one was burden enough.

Hour by hour we rode.

She stitched up my pant leg when we stopped to rest that afternoon under the thin shade of a mesquite. And went scoutin' off around our camp with her ridiculous cannon-gun, leavin' me to fret over every minute of her absence, my hand always waitin' on the pistol in the belts she'd now returned to me.

But she came back soon enough and claimed she hadn't seen no one followin' our trail.

Still, when we headed out again, we kept off the roads.

The landscape had changed over the course of the day into what I'd known for so long now: clumps of creosote and mesquite, cacti, and those red rocks. Gone were the trees and lush grass carpet of the north.

We made cold camp that night.

And carried on the next dawn. Little by little, the pain in my burns eased to somethin' tolerable.

My headache calmed, too. I got some of my strength back.

And then at last, mid-morning, appearin' upright as we rounded a bend, was a human skeleton.

The horse threw up its head and snorted.

Charlotte let out a gasp and reined it in sharply.

"It's okay," I said. "Just markin' the edge of the town. We're close."

Charlotte said nothin', her eyes fixed on the bleached bones, hung as if the person was still alive and standin'. You almost couldn't see the sticks that held 'em up, not till you got good and close, anyway. It made fer a rather alarmin' effect. Which was, of course, the intention.

The horse whickered and pawed at the dirt.

"It's fine," I said. "Go on, it ain't gonna hurt you. They've been dead a long time."

Charlotte hesitated a moment more, then reluctantly pressed her heels to the horse's side. It went wide around the skeleton, eyein' the thing the whole time, same as Charlotte.

I couldn't help but feel amused by their mutual suspicion. Regardless of the stories about this town, I'd lived here a long time, and never yet had the dead risen to haunt me.

No, they did that plenty well already from my dreams.

We headed in toward Grave Gulch at a trot, leavin' the silent skeleton with its baleful, hollow eyes to its eternal watch behind us.

DISAGREEMENT IN GRAVE GULCH

I instructed Charlotte to ride around the town proper and head up into the hills behind it. Our "home", such as it were, was a small cave hollowed out in one of the pale bluffs there. It was nearly midday by the time we finally closed in on it, and up ahead I saw Holt's black geldin' and my mule tethered to some low brush outside the mouth of the entrance.

The mule perked up his ears at our approach and nickered.

Soundin' the alarm again, the bastard.

But I didn't even care this time. The relief at seein' our mounts there and waitin' far outweighed any annoyance at the mule's overly social nature. If the horses were here, that meant Holt was here.

And he was, sure enough.

He came barrelin' outta the cave with both pistols drawn and ready, squintin' in the sun despite his hat.

"Hold up," I said quickly as Charlotte brought the horse to a stop and dropped a hand toward the giant gun across her lap. "It's us, Holt. It's me."

His eyes widened, his mouth droppin' open. He slid his guns back into place and outstretched his arms. "Ho-lee *shit*, Van! Thought fer sure you were dead this time."

"Me too."

He scrambled forward to help Charlotte down from the horse. She surely didn't need it, but accepted his hand, anyway, usin' it to help steady herself as she drug that cannon-gun down with her.

Holt let out a low whistle at the sight of it. "My, oh my. Never seen anythin' like that before."

"No one has," she said, layin' it back over one shoulder. "I don't think." She turned toward me and offered her free hand up, as if to help me down.

Holt laid a hand on her shoulder and gently nudged her backward. "Here, let me do that, Miss." She obliged, and instead Holt stepped up to take my arm as I slid off rather ungracefully, wincin' the whole time. "Well, well," he said. "Don't you look like you took a trip to Hell itself."

"Almost did," I said.

He clapped me on the shoulder and I grimaced. "Shit, kid. You musta got some of yer pa's luck, all right. Ain't seen no one else but you and him come through so many scrapes in one piece."

I shot him a glare. "He didn't come through that last one in one piece, though, did he?"

They may have called my pa Lucky Logan fer most his life, but in the end he'd still died same as everyone else. That was the problem with luck.

It always ran out.

The smile faded from Holt's face and he cleared his throat. "No, I guess not."

Charlotte looked from one of us to the other, watchin' in silence.

"Well," I prompted, not wantin' to talk about pa anymore. That familiar tightness was already closin' in around my throat. I focused instead on the present. On the urgent matter at hand. On those who were still livin'. "We did our part. Blew up the baron's house, burned his barns, freed his slaves. You get that money?"

Holt looked at me fer a minute, then burst out laughin'.

I wasn't sure exactly what kind of answer that was, so I waited fer him to finish bein' amused, impatient. Charlotte glanced to me in confusion, but I only shrugged.

Holt walked between us, back toward the mouth of the cave, still laughin', and shook his head. "Whew, boy!" he finally gasped. "You did yer part! Ha! Oh, that's rich, all right. That's rich."

I followed after him, wincin' as I limped along. Anger at his dismissal stirred in my belly, but I tried to ignore it. "Holt," I said flatly. "I woulda been there if I coulda been."

He turned to face me, his clear blue gaze sharp. "Sure." He crouched at the edge of the small fire he had goin' at the cave's entrance and poked at it with a stick. "But you weren't."

It was my turn to laugh, half disbelief, half anger. I turned to show him the burns along my right sleeve. "You think this was an accident? No, it weren't. Holt, I was gettin' treated to Baron Whittaker's famous hospitality. I got to see his kinda manners up close and personal."

"It's true," Charlotte said, steppin' up beside me. She still held that massive rifle, cradled in both arms. "Van was captured. I managed to get him free … but we were delayed."

"Clearly," Holt muttered.

"You know I woulda followed the plan if I could have," I said, steppin' closer to the fire.

"Right." Holt tossed his stick into it and stood. "Except we had a plan before, Van, a perfectly good plan." He glanced toward Charlotte and tipped his hat to her. "I am sorry fer yer situation, Miss, I really am." He turned back to me, all the softness fer Charlotte goin' hard again. "But we shouldn'ta brought her into this. We shoulda stuck with the plan we had. Yer the one who wanted to complicate all of it by actin' the hero, and look where it landed ya! Nearly dead! Both of ya coulda ended up dead!" He waved at me and Charlotte both, but then focused his frustration back on me. "Meanwhile, there I am at the Bank of Blessing, tryin' to pull off a robbery all by my lonesome! I told ya it wasn't an easy job, Van. I told ya we needed more people! 'It'll be fine,' ya said. Freein' the slaves'll be a good distraction, ya said. Sure. Horseshit! *Horseshit*, Van!"

He spun away from me and paced angrily back and forth in front of the cave. Took off his hat and swiped at the sweat on his forehead.

I only watched him, feelin' more guilt now than anger. And worry. A deep, gnawin' worry that he hadn't gotten the money at all. That it'd all gone wrong, just 'cause I'd wanted to act the hero, so he said.

But it wasn't about actin' a hero. I glanced to Charlotte.

Was it?

I wet my lips and swallowed, bracin' fer the worst. "You didn't get the money?"

He shoved his hat back on his head and rounded on me. "Yes, I got the blasted money!"

My heart soared. I exhaled a gust of relief.

"But not nearly as much as I coulda got if you'd

have been there, too. And I had to shoot more people than I would have liked. And it still weren't no Sunday stroll, no matter what distraction yer antics at the baron's house mighta generated."

The relief was a better salve against the aches and pains in my body than even Charlotte's ointment. My shoulders slumped and I closed my eyes, breathin' in and out, deep and slow, into the reprieve.

"Thank you," I whispered. *Ethelyn, not long now. I'll be there soon.*

"Don't thank me yet," Holt grumbled. "'Cause, kid, I'm sorry … but I'm keepin' it."

My eyes opened, starin' straight at him. "*What?*"

He stood there in front of me, legs splayed and hands planted on his hips, just above his gun grips. "I said, I'm keepin' it."

Anger blazed hot and full. "Like hell you are." My hand dropped fer my pistol, but he'd known it was comin' and had his drawn before mine cleared leather.

"*Don't!*" he barked, the word echoin' out over the hills.

I froze, fingers still wrapped around my pistol grip, the gun halfway outta the holster, the burns under the bandages screamin' as my muscles flexed and stretched the blistered skin. I stood there waitin', teeth clenched and breathin' hard, glarin' across the flat six feet or so that separated us.

From the corner of my eye I saw Charlotte slowly back away from me, step by step, huggin' that big gun to her chest.

I couldn't quite decide then if I wanted her to use it to mow down Holt or not.

"Don't," he repeated, this time in a whisper. He held his gun level at his hip, but it was aimed at my chest. "I don't want to shoot you, kid, but so help me … you draw against me and I *will* shoot you dead. Understand?"

I said nothin' fer a long time, heart racin' and rage buzzin' in my ears, rekindlin' my headache. He couldn't do this to me. He couldn't. Not when I was finally so close. Not after all these years. He knew how much findin' Ethelyn meant to me. He *knew*.

I let go of my gun. Let it nestle back down into the holster. Slowly lifted my hands. "Don't do this, Holt. Please."

"It's fer yer own good," he said. "Now take off yer belts and throw 'em over here. Nice and easy."

I glanced to Charlotte. She was still inchin' away, closer to her stolen fast horse. Holt didn't seem to care if she was gonna leave or stay. He was focused on me.

So I focused back on him. "You can have whatever's left," I reminded him. "That was always the agreement. Just give me the thirty-five thousand—"

"See, that's the problem," he said. "Like I said, since you weren't there, I couldn't get as much money as I'd hoped. And boy, was there a lot of money in that bank." He whistled and shook his head. "But I had to leave most of it behind, all because you wanted to go play Good Samaritan." He shrugged. "Which is fine, sure, but now, if I give you that thirty-five thousand, that don't leave so much fer me. And considerin' I was the one who did all the work to get the money in the first place—"

"*All* the work?" I scoffed. "Holt, if it hadn't been

fer us you woulda had the law all over yer ass soon as you showed that teller yer gun!"

He gave a nod. "Maybe. But ya put me in a real bad spot leavin' me to do that robbery alone, Van. And I told ya … I tried to tell ya we shoulda picked somethin' else to occupy the law. But you insisted. Well, ya risked yer life, her life, my life with this one, and like I said, you were damned lucky to get out of this one this time. We all were. But I'm tired of this. I'm tired of watchin' you run head-first into tryin' to get yerself killed, and stickin' my neck out along with ya, and all fer chasin' a ghost!"

I stepped forward at that, but he lifted the gun in warnin' and I stopped again. "Ethelyn is **alive**," I hissed. "How many times I gotta tell you that? How much proof you gotta see before you believe it?"

"Nine-Fingered Nan is fuckin' with you, Van." He tapped at his own temple with a finger. "She's fuckin' with you! Jerkin' ya around like a puppet on strings, and yer playin' right into her hands! She's gonna take this money from ya and then she's gonna **kill you**. You understand? Even if she does have yer sister, there ain't no way she's gonna hand her over. She's gonna take the money and then whether she has yer sister or not, kill you! You forget … I was there fer a lot of the times she tried to kill yer pa. She hated him probably more than she hated anyone else, and that woman hates a lotta people. She ain't gonna let you walk away, Van. Why can't you understand that?"

"She had my sister's necklace," I husked.

"Which coulda been pawned off to who-knows-where a long time ago," he countered.

"And the fingers?"

"Coulda come from any poor woman they'd got ahold of."

I swallowed, shook my head. "If there's a chance she has Ethelyn, I have to take it. If there's a chance she'll honor her deal, I gotta try. Holt, please. You know I have to do this. It's all that matters to me."

He grunted. "Yeah, and that's why I have to do this. This obsession of yers ain't healthy. I've watched it go on long enough. Now, do as I said and throw over yer gun belts."

"Holt. Please. Please don't do this."

"*Now*, Van."

I swore. Unbuckled my belts. "Holt, goddamnit, you take that money and I swear … I *swear* I'll come after you and take it back."

He sighed and shook his head. I saw the disappointment etched in the lines of his face. "No you won't. I'm gonna make this easy on you, kid. Just come with me. Come with me and we'll take that money and go far away, put this whole mess with Nine-Fingered Nan far behind us. Live out the rest of our lives in luxury."

"You know I can't do that."

"Damnit, Van! Yes, you can. You *can* do that! It's as easy as puttin' down yer gun and ridin' off east with me! We'll even give the girl some cash, just like you wanted, so she can get home, too. Hell, we could escort her back!"

That gave me pause. I glanced to Charlotte again, saw her standin' near her horse, but still watchin' both of us. She'd positioned herself in the middle of us, so that all together we made up the three points of a triangle. I wondered if she was waitin' to see who won this argument … or if she was tryin' to pick a side.

With that gun of hers, whichever side she chose would be the winner.

I turned back to Holt. "I'm going to free my sister. With or without you."

His lips pressed into a thin line. "Yer gonna ignore the livin' fer a chance to save the dead?"

"*She ain't dead!*" The words bounced around the rocks.

Holt sighed again. "Fine. You wanna walk into that hell, that's yer choice. But I ain't gonna sit around and watch you. Throw over yer belts."

I did so, with more force than necessary.

They thumped into the dirt at his feet and he stooped to pick 'em up, loopin' 'em over his shoulder. His pale blue eyes locked on mine. "Don't come after me, kid. 'Less it's to apologize. Let me be clear: I see you comin' at me with a gun in yer hand, and you'll be just one more foolhardy idiot I gotta gun down. Got it?"

"Don't worry, you won't see me comin'."

A little smile curled his lips. "Sure."

Again that dismissal. The fire in my gut raged anew, but he still had his pistol trained on my chest, and his eyes never left my face.

That was somethin' he'd taught me early. A person's face would tell you what they were plannin' to do. Get good at readin' people's faces, and you could predict their actions. You could throw a punch before they did. You could draw before they did. You could shoot before they did.

But you couldn't watch two faces at once.

A heavy whine from Charlotte's direction heralded the warm up of her big gun.

Holt and I both looked at her in surprise.

She was aimin' at him. I guess she'd picked her side.

And I saw in his face the instinctive reaction. He reached fer his second gun.

He wouldn't escape her storm of bullets. But then, she wouldn't escape his shot, either.

I realized in that one breathless second I didn't want either of 'em to die.

SWEET GOODBYES

I launched myself across the six feet of ground between me and Holt and slammed into him, takin' us both down into the hard-packed dirt. He grunted as I landed on top of him. "Don't shoot!" I yelled.

But there were already bullets whizzin' by overhead and punchin' into the rock of the bluff behind us. Shards of stone and bullets both flung off the sheer wall in all directions, stingin' where they grazed skin. "Don't shoot! Stop! Don't shoot!"

My words were nearly swallowed by the roar of that massive rifle.

Holt scowled somethin' terrible, then tried to bring the butt of his right gun into my temple. I managed to partially block the blow, but the edge of the grip still smacked into my face hard enough to send a white flash across my vision. The cut where the rifle butt had smashed into my eye only two days ago was still fresh and swollen and I ground my teeth as a sharp pain flared.

I wrestled with him in the dirt, grabbin' fer his guns and my guns both.

The roar of Charlotte's rifle wound down and stopped, and so did the rain of stingin' shrapnel.

Holt bashed his left gun into the burns on my arm and I gave a cry, my grip on his wrists loosenin'. He lurched sideways and threw me into the dirt, then rolled over the top of me and sat on my chest.

I looked down the gullet of his two twin guns, and couldn't rightly tell if he meant to shoot me or not. "I just … I just saved yer life!" I spat out, gaspin' under his weight.

He opened his mouth to say somethin' in return, but Charlotte loomed behind him and brought her giant rifle down hard across the back of his head.

He slumped sideways, both guns droppin' from his hands. Out cold.

I shoved him off me with a growl and rolled to my hands and knees, then struggled to my feet. Swayed and staggered as all the pain of all that movin' finally registered with my senses.

Charlotte grabbed my elbow to steady me. She looked from me to Holt's unconscious form, pale and wild-eyed. Her horse was the same, dancin' around again. That big gun of hers had even un-nerved my mule and Holt's geldin'. They were all watchin' us with the whites of their eyes showin', their ears flickin' all directions.

"Why didn't you let me shoot him?" she asked, breathless.

I looked down at him, too, and muttered a curse. I bent stiffly to pull my gun belts outta the dust, shook 'em out, and put 'em back where they belonged around my hips. "He's … he's a friend." *A friend who might have shot me.*

She frowned at me, creases formin' on her forehead. "He said he was going to shoot you."

"He wouldn't have." But I took his guns, too, and stuck 'em into my own belt. *He wouldn't have. Not after everythin' we've been through together. Not after eight years of watchin' out fer me, all that talk of pa bein' his best friend.…*

"He sounded serious to me," Charlotte said softly.

"Well, he's surely gonna be serious mad when he wakes up. We'll need to tie him. So he can't follow us. Then find that money."

Charlotte only watched me as I limped into the cave and went to some of the supply crates stacked along the walls. "But what if … what if Nine-Fingered Nan does kill you?" she asked.

It was a reasonable question. I didn't look up as I rummaged in search of some rope. "Then I guess he was right all along."

"But won't he starve if you leave him tied up here? If you don't come back to free him, I mean. Wouldn't it be better to just shoot him?"

I did look up at her then, quirking an eyebrow and then wincin' as it pulled at the bruise around my left eye. "No. I can't … I can't shoot him."

"But you said—"

"I know." I found what I was lookin' for and slammed the lid of the crate shut again. "I know what I said. But he's been my partner fer eight years now. Saved my hide more times than I can count. Found me when I was cold and starvin' as a kid … gave me food and shelter." *Taught me how to rob and kill. Taught me how to survive.* I scowled and shook my head, walkin' over to his prone form. "He's a right ol' bastard, but I can't shoot him. Not even fer wantin' to take that money." I rolled him onto his stomach and pulled his wrists behind his back, bindin' 'em together, tryin' to ignore the headache wantin' to split my skull. "I'll leave him a way to get free in case I don't come back. And leave him a trail to follow fer his part of the money. That should keep him busy fer awhile. Long enough to let me get to Ethelyn before he comes after me to murder me fer this."

The rifle lowered in Charlotte's hands. "So ... he *would* shoot you, then?"

"Naw." I tied his ankles next. "Maybe. Possibly. I dunno. I wouldn't put it past him to put a bullet in me fer this. Nothin' mortal ... just a flesh wound to make his feelin's on the matter apparent."

Charlotte blinked, clearly not understandin'.

"It don't matter," I assured her. "All that matters is I get my sister. I can deal with whatever he brings my way later." I finished the last knot and stood. "Thank you." It seemed all I did these days was thank her. "Fer helpin' me there." In case he woulda shot me.

At the very least, he woulda taken all that money from Blessing and left me back at needin' to find thirty-five thousand dollars.

She swallowed and nodded. Tucked a strand of wavy red locks behind her ear. "Sorry I almost killed your friend. I think."

A smile twitched at my mouth. "Well, like I said, he *is* a bastard."

Her gaze drifted down to him, then to her horse. "If there's a chance Nine-Fingered Nan still has your sister ... you need to go to her." She nodded resolutely, as if she had to convince me. Or herself. "You're right. You can't just leave her with that monster."

I nodded, too. I didn't need no convincin'. "I know."

Her eyes found mine again. "You'll go to her now?"

"Almost. Need to set things up fer Holt here. And see to that brand on yer stolen horse. And see you safely off toward home. Then I'll go to Brave-bank to arrange the meetin' to buy back my sister."

She nodded again. "Thank you. For all you've done in helping me get free. And the others, too."

"It weren't nothin'." That weren't exactly true. But I hadn't really had a choice in this one. I'd done a lotta stuff over the years I weren't proud of, things that woulda made Mama roll over in her grave if she knew. But leavin' Charlotte on her own back in Blessing to face the law, or worse, Baron Whittaker, woulda been unforgiveable, even fer me.

I grazed the stitches in my right temple with my fingertips. "Think I owe you a little more, truth be told. Fer gettin' me outta there and doctorin' me up so good."

She smiled. "Well. Maybe you can repay me by not getting yourself killed by Nine-Fingered Nan."

I grunted and shook my head. "That … I can make no guarantees."

It was nearly evenin' by the time I was ready to send Charlotte off.

We'd dragged Holt inside the cave, left a knife fer him within reach, found the money and taken our part of it, hid his part of it with a note of cryptic instructions on how to find it again, and modified Baron Whittaker's brand on Charlotte's horse.

I felt sorry for the poor beast. Gettin' branded were a particular form of painful.

But it were necessary if we hoped to get very far without bein' too much noticed. I didn't think the authorities of Blessing would have expanded their search this far south yet, but it was only a matter of time.

The Barons of Blessing had a lot of reach, all right, and I didn't think the murder of one of 'em would be forgotten all that easily.

Charlotte needed to head east soon as she could.

And I needed to head west.

There weren't no stagecoaches or trains that left outta Grave Gulch, considerin' no sane person travelled there by choice, so we'd headed up northwest a bit to the town of Peridot. It was small, but on account of Grave Gulch not havin' a coach stop, at least had that, and a saloon, and a general store. Weren't too bad of a town, really. Certainly one of the quietest and cleanest around these parts, and next to a mesa that got carpeted in gold poppies in the spring.

I kinda wished it were spring now.

Woulda been a pretty send off.

As it were, we only had the scrub brush and cacti and dust surroundin' us as the sun sank further into the west.

We'd arranged a ride fer her on the last coach outta town fer the night. It'd stop over the border in Redemption, Lesser Texas just after dark, and she'd stay the night there, then head out east on the first train in the morning. She'd cleaned up in Peridot, bought a new pair of clothes from the store, and looked again like a completely different woman from the one I'd seen kill Baron Whittaker.

This Charlotte Harrison, I imagined, looked like the one she had been back in Pennsylvania. She had a proper dress now, deep purple, the bodice huggin' her top half, the high collar fastened with a cameo brooch, and a ruffled hem on the skirt. Her new boots even had little heels on 'em, and she had a black handbag now, too, where she'd tucked away the money she'd need fer the rest of her journey.

We stood a ways from the stagecoach headquarters, sayin' our goodbyes.

Or tryin' to.

I was havin' a hard time findin' the words.

She cleared her throat and blessedly broke the silence. "I want you to keep the horse. And the gun."

I instinctively looked back over my shoulder, where the blue roan and Holt's geldin' were tied. I'd left Dr. Balogh's mule in Grave Gulch, not knowin' whether or not it mighta been reported as stolen in Bravebank. We'd rigged a makeshift scabbard for that ridiculous cannon-gun off her saddle, and it hung bulky off to one side.

She musta seen the protest formin' on my face. "I have no use for either. The horse will only make my journey home more expensive, as I'd have to pay for its place on the train, and we have plenty of horses on my family estate. And the gun..." She sighed. "It's too obvious. I don't want to draw any more attention to myself than absolutely necessary. I'm sure you understand."

I did. But I didn't like the thought of her goin' on such a long journey unarmed. I pulled one of my pistols—both of 'em undamaged now, as I'd lifted one of our spares from camp to replace the one of mine Nan had shot—and held it out to her. "Then take this, at least."

She looked at it fer a long minute, hesitatin'.

"Look, if you woulda had one of these on you when Nan's men hit yer coach in the first place, you never woulda ended up out here, sold to Baron Whittaker."

She glanced up at me, held my stare. "All right." She took the gun, her fingers brushin' mine.

My breath hitched, and I cleared my throat to cover it. "Will you … uh, will you send me a letter when you get home, let me know you made it safe?" I asked.

She smiled and slipped the pistol into her hand-bag, then withdrew a folded piece of paper from it. "I was going to ask you the same thing. Will you write me? Once you deal with Nine-Fingered Nan and get your sister back? It would mean a lot to me to know you're both safe." She held the piece of paper out toward me. "This is the address you can send it to."

I took the paper and turned it over in my fingers. Swallowed. Gave a nod. Wondered why my mouth suddenly felt so dry.

"Where should I send my letter to you?" she prompted.

"Oh." I hadn't thought that far ahead. Hadn't written anything down on a convenient note. *Stupid.* "Just … address it to me … Van Delano, and send it to the Grave Gulch post office."

Her eyebrows lifted. "They have a post office?"

I shrugged. "Worshippers of the dead still get mail, it seems."

"And you go *into* the town to check your mail?"

"Like I said … the stories aren't all entirely accurate."

Her smile widened. "If you say so. Okay. I'll send something there once I'm home."

"Thank you. I'm … I'm sorry I couldn't take you back myself."

She shook her head, reachin' out to put a hand on my arm. "Your sister needs you more. You've already done more than enough for me."

"Last call!" the coach driver yelled, startlin' us both. "Last call fer those headin' to Redemption, Lesser Texas! All aboard!"

"You'd better go." I put my hand over hers, still on my arm, and squeezed. "And please, be careful. Be ready to use that gun if need be."

"I will. And again, thank you. For everything."

I touched the brim of my hat. "It was the least I could do, Miss."

She rolled her eyes at my formality and leaned up to kiss my cheek. "You be careful yourself, Mister."

Then she turned, her hand slipped from under mine, and she went to board the stagecoach with the others. I watched her, heart in my throat.

But she would be fine. The coach had two shotgun riders and a team of six mules. It'd make good time and be well-protected. And Charlotte had my gun now, besides. She'd be on the first train in the mornin', steamin' toward the east.

She'd make it.

She'd be all right.

She was free now … and Ethelyn weren't free yet.

And if Nine-Fingered Nan had her claws reachin' out all the way to Pennsylvania ... well, I planned to deal with her, too. Soon. Soon I'd cut the head off the beast, and the rest of it wouldn't live too long without her.

Charlotte took the offered hand of the stagecoach driver and climbed the step to duck inside. But she paused in the doorway and looked back to me.

I met her eyes one last time, and it seemed in that one last moment I relived the whole of our brief, whirlwind acquaintanceship. I hoped she would write.

I hoped I would see her again. Somehow.

I tipped my hat to her.

She sent me one last smile and then climbed inside, and I couldn't see her anymore.

But I waited there and watched till the rest of the passengers got on board, and they closed up the coach, and the driver and his protectors settled themselves in their places, and the driver twitched the reins.

"Gee-up!" he yelled, and slapped the reins again.

The mules jerked into motion, the stagecoach wheels creakin' as it gained speed and headed outta town. Eastward.

I watched till its retreatin' cloud of dust faded, then sighed and turned back to the horses. I stuck Charlotte's note with her address down deep into my belt pouch, the one I'd lifted off drunk Jake. I drug myself up atop the blue roan, then winced as the saddle chafed the burn on my thigh. It woulda been nice if I coulda waited till those were healed up more before meetin' with Nan … but Ethelyn couldn't wait that long.

Neither could I, in truth, not with an angry Holt soon to be comin' after me.

So I ponied his geldin' from the roan, and we headed off toward the settin' sun. Westward.

Toward Bravebank.

MORE STUBBORN THAN IMPATIENT

I traveled till the sun went down that night, made camp, and was up again with the sun the next mornin'. Took me a little more than another half day of ridin' to reach Bravebank, and I entered town in the afternoon feelin' anxious.

The blue roan twitched her ears and nickered. I patted her neck and shook my head. "Easy, girl." I tried to relax, as much fer her sake as my own. Didn't need her gettin' skittish now. Holt's geldin' plodded along behind, not carin' in the least about what was happenin', or about what might happen.

But no one gave me any trouble as I headed down the main street toward The Stag Saloon. No one seemed to look at me over-long or give me a second glance. Still, I made sure to study the walls of the buildin's I passed, just to see if I saw mine or Holt's face lookin' back at me from any of the posters hung up there.

I didn't see anyone recognizable, least of all my own self.

I exhaled a long breath. I'd fully expected the bastard I'd made a deal with here to have given a full description of me to the town's sheriff. Just to make my life more difficult. But I guess that ten thousand dollars he'd demanded of me was more than the sheriff could offer in reward fer my head.

Well, that was fine by me. He could have his ten thousand dollars.

Long as it kept my face off a poster.

Long as I got Ethelyn.

I tied the horses to the hitchin' post outside the Stag. It was easier to dismount this time … the leg seemed to be cooperatin' more these days. Now it was just those damned burns protestin' my every movement.

I made sure I had the money stashed right where I'd left it in my saddlebags, threw 'em over my shoulder, checked my single remainin' pistol, and pulled the massive rifle stolen from Baron Whittaker from its sheath, wincin' as the raw skin on my right arm started screamin' under the bandages again.

My arm didn't like draggin' around the weight of that gun.

It *was* too obvious of a weapon. Charlotte was right about that. But then, I was also hopin' the sight of it might keep Nan's man from double-crossin' me.

At the very least, it would make sure he died if he did.

The door to the saloon had been propped open on account of it bein' mid-afternoon, and I stepped through it like I owned the place. My gaze swept the floor in search of the man with the droopin' handlebar mustache. The place was fairly full, and the general buzz of banter and conversation dimmed as eyes fell on that giant gun.

The hush rippled outward, startin' with those closest to me and the door, and travelin' all the way to the back of the joint.

The barkeep stopped polishin' his glass.

Several hands dropped toward their weapons. Ready, just in case I was gonna start trouble.

But there was only one man in the vicinity I wanted to start trouble with.

I noticed the place seemed all put back together from our gunfight here a week ago. All you could see of it now were some fresh bullet holes in the walls. "I'm lookin' fer the man who answers to Nine-Fingered Nan," I said.

The bartender gave an amused snort. "Ain't that everyone in the Territories?"

I glared at him from under my hat brim. "No. It ain't."

"He's lookin' fer me," came a voice from the back.

Everyone sober enough to grasp what was happenin' turned to look at him.

And it was him, all right.

Sittin' at a poker table with his legs stretched out in front, ankles crossed, slouched in the chair like he had not a care in the world. He studied me fer a minute, then studied his cards. Then he heaved a sigh and threw his cards to the table.

"You save my seat, hear?" he told the man to his right.

The man gave a grave nod, and Nan's man took his time in standin' up, pushin' his chair back so that the legs screeched on the wooden planks of the floor. He stretched. Then waved me over. "Come on, boy. Come to my office and let's talk business."

My fingers tightened around the rifle. If I didn't need him to set up my meetin' with Nan … if I thought I could find her without him … I'da shot him down right then.

But instead I walked across the saloon, slow and deliberate so my limp weren't as bad, never takin' my eyes off him, though I surely felt all the other sober eyes in the saloon followin' me.

His eyes watched me, too. And then, as I got closer, they slipped down to the rifle briefly before comin' back up to my face. His expression didn't change, but I saw his hand go to casually rest on his own gun grip. "This way," he said. He turned and led me through a door at the back of the saloon, then up a creakin' staircase to another door, which he opened and gestured me through.

I did as he beckoned, but went sideways, so as to still keep an eye on him.

That made him smile.

I did not return the sentiment.

He came in after me and shut the door behind him, then strolled over to a table set toward the far wall. A single window let in the light of the afternoon, throwin' bars of white gold on the floor. He went around the table and then turned to face me, crossin' his arms. "Well?" he prompted. "Ya got my money?"

"You got my sister?"

He lifted a black eyebrow. "Not till I see that money."

I walked closer to the table, then set the rifle down, proppin' it up against the table's edge. I pulled the saddlebags from my shoulder and opened 'em, grabbin' up the stacks of cash. I made a pile toward the left side of the table. "That's the ten thousand fer you." Then I made another stack, a much bigger stack, on the right side of the table. "And there's the twenty-five thousand fer Nan. Fer my sister."

Both his eyebrows lifted now. He stared down at the money, one hand strokin' his mustache. Then looked up at me. "What happened to yer face?"

My left eye was still bruised and swollen, that gash still fresh and the other one in my head still fulla stitches. But none of that were his business. "Doesn't matter," I snapped. "I got the money. Now go tell Nan I want my sister back."

He pursed his lips and looked back down to the money. "You got all thirty-five thousand dollars in a week?"

I hooked my thumbs into my gun belts. "What can I say? I'm resourceful."

He grunted. "Well, a course I'm gonna have to count it before I take it to Nan. You just make yerself comfortable. That's a lotta cash. Might take me awhile."

The grin he flashed me then made me wanna put a bullet right in his teeth. I resisted the urge … barely. I still needed him to set up the meetin' with Nan.

There was only one chair in the room, which he pulled up to the table and settled down into. Then he pulled one stack of bills toward him and began to count.

Very slowly.

There was nothin' else in the room. No other decoration, no other furniture, and I realized with a flash of irritation and dismay that his invitation to 'make myself comfortable' was just him fuckin' with me. Again.

I ground my teeth, my fingers twitchin', itchin' to draw my pistol.

But instead I drew in a slow, calmin' breath and exhaled evenly. If he wanted to play that game, then fine. I'd waited nine years fer this. This was the closest I'd ever been to gettin' Ethelyn, and I wasn't gonna quit now on account of him wantin' to jerk me around.

I could wait a little longer. I picked up the giant rifle, makin' a show of it fer his benefit, and settled myself against the opposite wall. I stared him down, unwaverin', unrelentin', holdin' that rifle at the ready.

Two could play at this game.

I didn't know how long he counted that money. Didn't know how much time had passed. I watched that patch of white-gold sun move across the floor, and said nothin'. He took as long as he could possibly take, I was sure, hopin' to test my patience. Maybe hopin' to break me. Maybe hopin' I'd swing that rifle around in his direction so he'd have a chance to gun me down. Have a chance to keep all that money fer himself.

I wasn't generally a patient man, true enough.

But he'd underestimated my resolve. Holt coulda told him I was more stubborn than impatient any day. I wasn't gonna let this bastard win this one.

So eventually he gave up, with a great, theatrical, disappointed sigh, and finished countin' that money. "Looks like it's all here," he said. "All right. She said if you actually brought the money to tell ya to meet her up in the Bone Spur Mountains, near the holdin' tank pool. Ya know the spot?"

I straightened from the wall, shiftin' the rifle in my arms. The muscles were startin' to tire after so long, the burns still afire beneath their bandages. "Not particularly."

"Guess you'd better figure it out, then. That's where she'll meet ya fer the trade. Tomorrow, high noon."

"I'll be there."

"I'll tell her to expect you." He reached a hand out toward the money again, and that's when I swung the rifle in his direction. He paused, his other hand droppin' to his own gun. "Don't do anythin' stupid now, boy."

"Put the twenty-five thousand back in the bags," I ordered. "I'll take it to Nan myself." Holt thought me a fool fer makin' this deal in the first place, and maybe I was, but I weren't *that* big of a fool to trust this cur with that kinda money. It'd never get to Nan. And I'd never get Ethelyn. I knew that much.

He hesitated, eyein' my rifle again.

"This thing'll chew up this whole room and you with it," I warned. "You can't spend that ten thousand if yer dead."

He smiled. "And ya can't get yer sister back if *yer* dead." His finger tapped against his gun.

"How good's yer aim when you got a chest fulla lead?" I pulled back on the trigger, just a bit. Just enough to start that signature heavy whine, that unholy sound that heralded an incomin' storm of bullets.

His smile widened into a yellow-toothed grin,

and he lifted his hand from his pistol, holdin' it up in surrender. "Ya know, I'm kinda startin' ta like you, boy."

"Can't say I feel the same about you."

"All right. All right. Take it easy. You can take the twenty-five thousand yerself. Nan'll still kill ya if she feels like it."

I had no doubts about that, so I only shrugged.

He chuckled and swept Nan's large pile of cash back into the saddlebags. He buckled 'em up, then tossed 'em over to me.

I bent to pick 'em up and settled 'em on my shoulder again, never lettin' the rifle barrel lower from aimin' square at his chest. Then I backed toward the door. "See ya around," I said, though I had no intention of ever seein' the likes of him again. Not if I could help it.

He gave me a salute, still with that sly smile plastered beneath his mustache. "Maybe," was all he said.

I opened the door and backed through it, too, then turned and headed quick as my metal leg would allow down the stairs and back into the saloon proper.

The conversations hushed again as I went through, and all the eyes followin' me bored into my back. But I paid them no mind. All that mattered was gettin' outta there before the mustached man—or anyone else—decided to stop me.

But they didn't. Yet.

I mounted up in a hurry and turned the horses down the street toward the post office.

I didn't intend on stayin' around Bravebank fer long. There were too many people here I didn't want to run into again. I planned to head out toward the meetin' place just as soon as I could.

There was just one more thing I had to take care of first.

I handed the post master a small package I'd wrapped in brown paper and tied tight with twine. Didn't want anyone gettin' greedy. "For Doctor Balogh," I instructed him. "Will you see that he gets it?"

The man shrugged as he took the parcel from me. "Sure. The doc comes here to collect his mail regular enough. He'll get it."

"Thanks. And tell him … tell him that's fer what I owe him."

"All right. Sure." He tucked the brown-wrapped rectangle in one of the mail cubbies behind him and pulled a piece of paper and pencil toward him, preparin' to write. "And who should I say the package is from?"

That gave me pause. My name weren't on no posters here, but that didn't mean there wouldn't be other people lookin' fer me. There was always someone out there somewhere lookin' fer me, it seemed. "No name," I said. "He'll know who it's from."

The man rolled his eyes and pushed the paper and pencil away. "Suit yourself. I'll tell him."

I tipped my hat to him. "Thanks, Mister."

"Don't mention it."

"Oh, uh … you happen to have a map of the state on you?"

He lifted an eyebrow. "Sure. I got a map." He reached down under the counter and produced a large, folded paper map. He spread it out in front of us and turned it around to face me. "Wanna take a look?"

"Yes. Thank you." I perused it fer a minute, findin' Bravebank easy enough. Then my eyes went outward, searchin' in ever-widenin' circles fer one of the many nearby mountain ranges to be labeled **Bone Spur**.

To my relief, it weren't too far. Westward again.

I tapped my finger on the Bone Spur Mountains. "You know where there's a place here they call the holdin' tank?"

The post master leaned his elbows on the counter and cocked his head to look at the upside-down map. "Up in the Bone Spurs? Sure. The stage-coaches sometimes stop there for water. It's off the main road that goes up through there. Should be easy enough to find. It's the only standin' pool of water in the area. Can't miss it."

I nodded. "Good. Great. Thanks again, Mister."

"Sure." He pulled the map toward him and started to fold it up again. "But listen, if you're fixin' to head up that way, be careful. Lots of bandits and thieves in the area, waitin' for the coaches to stop at the pool. Lots of good nooks and crannies they can shoot at you from 'fore you even know they're there."

I sighed. Of course. "Thanks. I'll keep that in mind. You have yerself a pleasant evenin'."

"And same to you, sir."

I turned from the post master and caught a

glimpse of the evenin' sun out the window. I'd been too long here already. But at least now the guilt over that damned mule and saddle were eased. Holt had a little less money fer it, since I'd taken the cost of the animal and saddle outta his share … but still, makin' out with almost fifteen thousand dollars weren't no small thing, neither.

Dr. Balogh and his family could get another mule to pull their wagon and replace the saddle I'd taken, Holt would still get most all his share of the money, and I could stop feelin' like I'd betrayed that poor kid Radley.

Though I had a feelin' that money wouldn't make that kid feel any better. At the least I hoped his parents hadn't figured out he'd been the one to bring me back my guns. And if they had, I hoped he hadn't gotten whooped fer it. I hoped in that case they'd put the blame all on me … the no-good drifter who'd sweet-talked their innocent child into becomin' an accomplice to mule rustlin'.

I sighed again as I stepped out from the post office into the evenin', then turned toward the horses —and ran straight into a fist.

IN THIS TOGETHER

The blow hit me in the jaw and knocked me back against the wall of the post office. I staggered, caught completely off guard, and then hands grabbed the front of my shirt and hauled me around the corner into the alleyway, tossin' me to the ground.

I rolled and came up again almost immediately, but my metal leg was still sluggish and I tripped on it, nearly goin' right back down to the dirt. I stumbled, reachin' fer my gun. Another fist landed in my jaw, then one to my right wrist knocked the pistol outta my hand, my fingers numb. I got shoved back into another wall, and my curse was cut short by the forearm that landed across my throat.

I groped fer my left pistol, only to remember I'd given it to Charlotte. So instead I sent a fist of my own hard into my attacker's gut.

He grunted and doubled over a bit, and as he did my left hand went to his right hip, aimin' to relieve him of his gun.

That was when I felt the barrel of another gun shove hard into my ribs, and the forearm pressed harder against my throat. "Hands off the pistol," he growled. The one shoved into my ribs twitched in warnin'.

I choked and gagged, abandonin' my attempt at freein' his second gun to use both hands on his arm, tryin' to pull it away so I could breathe.

"Insolent, ungrateful bastard," he whispered harshly, "I oughta kill you where you stand."

That voice. I knew that voice. I blinked, focusin' on the face of my attacker fer the first time since runnin' into his fist. His clear blue eyes were narrowed beneath the bushy gray brows. Glarin' like I'd never seen.

I tugged at his arm, suckin' in a thin gasp of air. For an old, angry bastard who was thickenin' around his middle, he was stronger than he looked. "Holt," I choked out. "Let … let me explain…"

"*Explain*?" The gun in my ribs pressed in harder and I grimaced. "You already done explained things, boy. You *explained* you was gonna take the money I got … the money I'm *owed* … and give it to that shriveled up cunt Nine-Fingered Nan on some fool's quest to get yer sister back!"

"I left … yer share…" He wasn't makin' it easy on me to talk. Every word, every breath was a struggle, raspin' through the little space I could make with my efforts to lighten the weight he leaned on my throat. "Didn't … didn't you get … the note?"

He leaned on me harder, his face inches from mine, his glare fierce. "I ain't no child to be placated with riddles, Van. What'd you think, I was gonna go off on some half-assed treasure hunt? No … I *earned* that money, and I ain't gonna go wanderin' around lookin' fer it, yer gonna take me straight to it."

Black spots danced in my vision. I could have gotten to his gun still, maybe we woulda traded shots into each other and both died there in that alley.

But I didn't want to have to kill him. I wondered if he really wanted to kill me.

"Holt." I couldn't rightly tell if I were speakin' aloud or not; all I could hear in my ears now was a rushin' sound and the frantic, panicked beatin' of my heart as it starved fer air. "I … I didn't … let her … shoot you."

He just stood there fer a second stranglin' me, and the blackness slowly closed in on the alley until I could hardly even see his face.

Then, suddenly, his arm let up and I could breathe again.

I fell to my hands and knees, gaspin' and gaggin', suckin' in air so greedily I choked and fell into a coughin' fit.

Holt picked up my dropped pistol and stuck it into his waistband. "Take me to my money, Van. All of it."

I was still breathin' hard, my heart still racin', my head throbbin', but I sat back on my heels and looked up at him. I swiped at the blood runnin' down my chin now from the split in my lip and shook my head. "You know I can't do that."

He shifted on his feet, his lips formin' a hard line. "Why?" he demanded. "Why do you insist on doin' this? We could take that money … live out the rest of our lives on that cash!"

I looked straight at him, knowin' full well that weren't true, not with the way he spent money when he had it. But that weren't the point of this argument, either.

"Look at you!" he went on, not givin' me a chance to reply. He paced back and forth in front of where I knelt in the dirt. "Look at you! You've nearly killed yerself already in pursuit of this idiotic venture … several times over now. How much longer you think yer luck'll hold? Huh? You said yerself … yer pa weren't so lucky there in the end, was he? Why you so eager to fall into the grave after him?"

I shook my head. "I don't care what happens to me. Long as I get Ethelyn free first."

Holt threw up his hands in exasperation. "Always about yer sister, and you don't even know if she's—"

"I promised her!" The words belted out loud and desperate in the narrow confines of the alley. I shoved myself to my feet and faced Holt square, hands balled into fists. "I promised her, Holt. I promised I would come back fer her, and I don't care how long it's been, I ain't gonna abandon her now."

"But you don't even know if she's—"

"I have to try." I cut him off. I couldn't bear to hear him insist she was only a ghost any more. Not when I was so close. Not after I'd already sacrificed so much to get this far. "If there's even the smallest chance, Holt, I have to go. I have to try."

"And what if Nan takes all the money and still don't give you yer sister, or don't even have yer sister?"

"Then at least I'll have the satisfaction of killin' Nan."

Holt gave an amused and skeptical snort. "I don't think even yer pa could beat Nan's draw these days."

I remembered how she'd downed my horse, shot the gun clean outta my hand, put a bullet in my thigh. All before I'd registered what was happenin'. I swallowed. "Well. Then at least I'll die knowin' I tried. I can't go off and try and live a life knowin' my sister might be out there somewhere, made a slave—

or worse. I can't. And you should know that, Holt. You should know that."

He sighed heavily and shoved his drawn pistol back into its holster. "Yeah. Guess I do. Guess I just hoped maybe after all these years you'd wise up."

"I ... I can't give you the whole fifty thousand we—*you*—got from Blessing. If you need to shoot me fer that ... you'll just have to shoot me." I hoped I'd read his bluff right. If not, well, I wouldn't get the chance to try and free Ethelyn or kill Nine-Fingered Nan at all.

He looked at me fer a minute, contemplatin'.

And fer a heartbeat I thought I'd guessed wrong.

But then he sighed. Rubbed a hand over the short gray beard on his chin and shook his head. "God damn it all, kid. I don't wanna shoot you. Never did."

I exhaled quietly.

"But my money ... I *am* real pissed about my money..."

"We can rob another bank," I offered. "After I have Ethelyn. Do it together from the beginnin' this time. Get yer money."

He rolled his eyes and started pacin' again. "Naw. Soon as you get yer sister back, you'll go straight. I can see it in ya. You've never been a natural killer. That's why I was able to get the jump on you so good just then." He gestured lazily back toward the post office porch.

I clenched my jaw against the retort and felt the ache of the bruise that would be darkenin' there 'fore mornin'. "Lloyd Renneker might not agree with you on that point," I muttered.

Holt grunted and shook his head. "I didn't say

you were against killin', Van. I know you can do it … I seen you do it plenty of times. What I'm sayin' is that yer choosy about yer killin'. And once ya get yer sister back, you won't have much reason to go about it no more."

Well, maybe that was true. But what did it matter, anyway? I didn't need to be no natural killer. I'd done just fine like I was. So instead I said, "One last job. I'll stay fer one last job, fer you. To get you the money yer owed."

He stopped pacin' and faced me. "What if Nan kills ya?"

I shrugged. "Well, then … I guess you've proven you can pull off a bank job yerself, in that case."

A smile pulled at one corner of his mouth. "Well … maybe I woulda had a harder time of it if I hadn't of had a partner to distract the law fer me."

Some of the tension in my coiled muscles relaxed at that admission. If he was willin' to admit that now, maybe it was true he didn't really want to shoot me. Maybe he'd finally realized him gettin' that money wasn't truly a one-man job, and I was entitled to it as much as he. Maybe he'd finally get it through his head that I was gonna meet with Nine-Fingered Nan to trade twenty-five thousand dollars fer my sister, no matter how it all worked out in the end.

"So," I said, "we'll do one more job then? After I get my sister. Together."

He pursed his lips and exhaled a long, slow breath through his nose. His hands were on his hips again, the fingers tappin' on the sides of his double holsters. "That means you gotta stay alive through another meetin' with Nan, kid. I told you the first time you went off to see her … I didn't spend all that time lookin' fer ya and raisin' ya just to watch you charge off to die."

"So maybe meetin' Nan ain't a one-man job, either," I said.

He tilted his head fractionally to the side. "Meanin'?"

"Come with me. Give me another gun in the fight." I'd asked him to come with me the first time, too. He'd refused, sayin' he weren't gonna watch me throw my life away on somethin' so foolhardy. Nor was he gonna risk his own neck fer a ghost. I wasn't sure this time would be any different, but I had to try.

Maybe if he'd been backin' me up that first time I'd confronted Nan, things would have ended up different.

Or maybe they'd have ended up the same, except with him dead.

It was hard to know. All I knew is that I'd feel a lot better going into those mountains tomorrow with another gun on my side.

"The meetin' place is up in some mountains not too far from here," I said when he stayed silent. A kind of plan was formin' in my mind now … a plan I thought he might approve of. "The post master said there's a lot of hidin' places up in there. So we get you a rifle. A sharpshootin' rifle. And we put you up high somewhere where you can see the meetin' spot. You can cover me. And give 'em hell from on high if things go south."

He scratched at his bearded chin and grunted. "You got any idea how expensive those rifles are?"

"You can take Baron Whittaker's rifle, too."

He looked surprised at that. "You still got that monstrosity?"

"Yeah."

He glanced around the darkenin' alley, as if lookin' fer someone. The sky over the tops of the surroundin' buildin's had turned a navy blue, night comin' on quick now. "Speakin' of, where's the girl? She didn't come to save you this time."

I straightened, choosin' to ignore the jab. Choosin' to ignore the anger that stirred in my gut. "She's on her way home. Sent her off last night."

"Ah, well, good riddance." He spit into the dirt.

"She helped us," I said stiffly, not likin' his disregard fer Charlotte. *And if not fer her, I woulda suffered a helluva lot more hurt at the hands of Baron Whittaker. And probably be dead.* I wondered how painful that death woulda been, too. From the way it'd been goin', I imagined it woulda possibly been one of the worst ways to go in this world.

"She also tried to kill me," Holt said flatly.

"She thought you were gonna shoot me."

"I was thinkin' about it."

"Then it seems her actions were justified."

He looked steadily at me. "Yeah. Maybe so."

"Yer welcome, by the way."

He frowned then. "Fer what?"

"Fer savin' yer life. When she tried to kill you."

He barked a short laugh and shook his head. "Kid, if you think that makes us even, you've got a long way to go yet. Fer all the times I've pulled you outta scrapes ... fer gettin' you off the streets and gettin' food in yer belly—"

"And that's why I didn't let her kill you," I cut him off before he could continue his list. I didn't need to hear it again. I'd heard it all before. Many times. "I'm grateful fer everythin' you've done fer me, Holt, I am. Yer an insufferable, self-centered bastard—"

"And yer a reckless, hard-headed fool."

"—but I am grateful. So. We in this together, or not? What do you say?"

He grumbled somethin' and spit again, hookin' his thumbs in his belt. Then he heaved a sigh and pulled my pistol from his waistband, holdin' it out to me butt-first. "Guess we'd better make a proper plan."

Course, I wasn't sure how proper of a plan it was, really, considerin' there was only the two of us, and who knew how many Nan would bring with her. I remembered clear enough those lieutenants of hers she had hidden in the rocks durin' my first encounter with her.

I suspected somethin' of the same this time, too.

But at least this time I'd have Holt.

We sold the baron's fancy horse and got a fair amount fer her, to my surprise. The hostler didn't ask no questions; he barely even glanced at her brand. I was beginnin' to understand a lot more about Bravebank now.

I was beginnin' to understand it was a town loyal to Nine-Fingered Nan.

The realization made me uneasy, no matter that it had worked in our favor this time, and we left the livery in a hurry. Then we got Holt a sharpshootin' rifle just before the gunsmith closed. It weren't the best on offer, but it was the best we could afford. It would do just fine. Holt took his geldin' back, givin' me another glare fit to flay a man—he'd been real sore about havin' to ride that mule into town—and we made what time we could that night, ridin' even after dark.

I kinda would rather have kept the baron's horse, truth be told, but it was still a risk, even with the modified brand. And she seemed to run kinda hot, which weren't necessarily a good thing when you were out and about in the wilds where there was always the chance somethin' bad could jump out at you.

And anyway, the mule was mine now, bought and paid for.

He plodded along slow and steady under me, and we rode on till the moon was high, cold camped, and went on again at dawn.

We saw 'em long before we reached 'em, the rocky hills those around here called mountains. They rose up outta the surroundin' flat scrubland and climbed up toward the bright blue, cloudless sky.

The Bone Spur Mountains.

We angled to approach them from the south and enter along the road there, like I'd seen on the map. The coolness of the mornin' was burnin' off by the time we reached the foot of 'em, and then we reined up our mounts.

Holt took off his hat and swiped at the sweat startin' to glisten on his brow. "Well," he said. "Guess this is it."

I peered up at the side of the nearest one. They looked like most other mountains in the area I'd seen, only in these, some of the big rocks up toward the top were a lighter color. Not red or black, but a grayish white.

Like bones.

"Guess so," I said. I took a moment to breathe, settle my nerves. This was it. This was what I'd been waitin' fer for nine long years. I closed my eyes and opened them again. Readjusted my hat. Cleared my throat. "Well, let's go." I kicked the mule, and he moved forward obediently.

Holt trailed after me, the sharpshooter rifle in its scabbard glintin' in the late mornin' sun.

BODIES AND BONES

The road gradually sloped upward as we went, deeper and deeper into the mountains. The rock walls on either side of us grew higher and higher, until we rode mostly in shadow. Shadow that slowly shortened as high noon approached.

We picked up our pace as much as we could manage.

The pale rocks surrounded us now, tumbled and jagged, makin' plenty of good hidin' spots, just like the post master had said. Some of those rocks had drawin's on 'em. Ghostly images of animals and shapes, near lost to time, but still visible if you looked close enough.

And I couldn't help but look close enough. It was eerie, to see those pictures suddenly appear amidst so much wilderness, no other trace of civilization around for miles and miles.

I heard Holt mutter a curse behind me. "What is this place?"

I could only shake my head. I didn't know no better than he.

We pressed onward, and came upon the pool close to noon. The post master had been right about that, too. You couldn't miss it.

Though it weren't much of a pool. There hadn't been a rain for some time, and as such there weren't much water left for the pool to hold. But it was there, all right. Greenish and tepid in the growin' light of day.

Holt grunted. "Good spot fer an ambush."

I raised my eyes from the pool to look at him. He, in turn, was studyin' the cliffs around us. I followed his gaze. The area here by the pool was relatively large and open, flat. A good spot fer stoppin' coaches to get water, sure. But the road in and outta here was narrow, and the walls on all sides sheer and tall.

It'd have been easy enough to block the ways in and out, and anyway, there surely wasn't enough room even here by the pool to turn a coach. Lucky fer us, we weren't in a coach.

It still woulda been a good spot fer an ambush, though. Even just on horseback. Unease prickled at my skin. "You'd better go," I said, lookin' up at the sun. "Plant yerself atop one of these walls. Should give you enough height."

Holt craned his neck back to look up at 'em. "I'd say."

"There was a side trail a little ways back that looked like it'd take you up there."

"I saw it." He blew out a breath through his teeth and looked at me. "All right, kid. This is it. Don't fuck it up. And ... be careful, damnit. You hear?"

I nodded. "I'll do my best."

"Mm-hrm." He looked at me a second longer, as if thinkin' of sayin' somethin' else. But then he only reined his geldin' around and headed back the way we'd come.

When he'd disappeared around the bend, I walked

my mule around the clearin' a few times and back down the trail a ways before comin' back to the pool to confuse the tracks a bit. The floor of the area was mostly bare rock, but there were a spot or two of dirt and gravel that would show a horse print, and I preferred Nan and her company to think I'd come alone … or with a little hidden army of my own, maybe.

Then I waited beside the pool. Alone.

I stayed atop the mule, nerves hummin' with restless energy. I kept one hand on the reins, one hand on my gun, watchin' the road ahead and the rocks around me, listenin' fer any sound.

These mountains were quiet. Far too quiet.

Beside me, the surface of the small pool was still as glass.

Above me, the sun moved higher into the sky, until it beat down upon me full force, shinin' squat in the middle of that great ring of bone-colored rock.

That's when my mule perked his ears and lifted his head, and I tensed.

Far away, faint, I heard the approachin' clip-cloppin' of hooves. Lots of hooves.

My heart quickened, throbbin' in my throat. My fingers tightened around the grip of my gun, already slick with sweat. I fought to control my nerves, my anticipation, my relief, my rage … too much feelin' threw off yer aim. Made you sloppy. That's what Holt always said, and experience had proved him right more often than not.

The cleanest kills, the easiest kills, always came when the killin' was instinctive, a reaction, a muscle-memory response to a threat.

That, or when the rage went on long enough it settled into somethin' hard and flat and numb.

So I waited and breathed through all the things jumpin' around in my gut … waited fer one of those two things to happen. Either I'd have to react, or the rage would settle. I wondered which might happen first.

Horses appeared on the path ahead.

My mule gave his signature bastardized whinny in greetin'. Sounded like somethin' was killin' him. Here in this quiet place, among the bones of the earth and so many ghostly drawin's, the unnatural sound seemed to strangely belong.

But the horses didn't deign to answer him. They entered the clearin' two by two, which was all that could fit abreast on the road at a time.

Two women riders came first, and my heart jumped fer a second, then fell again as I quickly realized neither of 'em were Ethelyn. They split as the road opened up into the pool's clearin' and went alongside the rocky walls, past the pool, to take up positions behind me.

Blockin' the way out.

I swallowed and took another breath. It didn't matter. In truth, I'd never expected anythin' less.

And I still had Holt, hidin' up there somewhere, watchin' all this through his scope.

I hoped.

Four more riders came then, all men. They took up positions on either side of me, reinin' up their horses near the sheer walls. The two on my right had their horses' hooves nearly in the water. They turned their mounts to face me, hands restin' casually atop the pistols at their hips.

My attention was pulled away from glarin' at 'em by the single rider who came next.

It was the bastard from the Stag Saloon with his handlebar mustache. He eyed me as he rode in and smiled, touchin' the brim of his hat.

I glared him down.

But it was the shaggy chestnut pony he led after him and the figure sittin' atop it that made my breath catch. It was a woman, her wrists tied in front of her, one of the hands that gripped the saddle horn missin' three fingers. She had a burlap sack over her head, but long black hair spilled out the bottom of it.

Long black hair like Ethelyn's.

Fire leapt up in me then, nearly blindin'. I laid the fist grippin' my reins on the saddle horn to hide the tremblin' in my body and fixed my eyes on the mustached man.

It was all I could do not to shoot him down right then.

But there were an awful lot of hostile eyes on me right now, and an awful lot of fingers ready to pull triggers. If I drew now, we'd all die. Me and the man with the mustache would die first, but the rest Holt would get with his rifle, or they'd get hit in the crossfire of ricochetin' bullets, I had no doubt.

This mighta been a good spot fer an ambush, but it weren't such a good spot fer a gunfight.

So I waited. I waited and watched fer my chance.

Behind him came two more riders, one man and one woman this time, and they halted in the mouth of the road there, rifles already drawn and laid across the fronts of their saddles. Blockin' the way ahead.

And that was it.

No one else was comin'.

There was no Nine-Fingered Nan.

But as long as I got my sister, I could settle with just killin' the mustached bastard in front of me.

"Howdy," he said cheerfully, grinnin' from ear to ear. "Guess I'm seein' ya around again sooner than we thought, eh?"

I kept my hand on my gun and my eyes on him, no matter how desperately I wanted to look at my sister, who I hadn't seen since she was a scrawny girl of ten. And I spoke only to him, too, though everythin' in me wanted to call out to Ethelyn and tell her everythin' was gonna be all right, that I was here now, that I was sorry—*so sorry*—fer leavin' her alone all those years ago, even if it was only supposed to be fer one night.

"Where's Nan?" I asked flatly, swallowin' back all those feelin's.

Now wasn't the time.

Too much feelin' threw off yer aim. And I was gonna need all my wits about me fer this one.

He shifted in his saddle. "Ah, you know. Somewhere else. Doin' more important things."

I swallowed again. ***More important things.*** Well, it didn't matter. I'd find her someday. I'd find her someday and make her pay, too.

"So?" he prompted. "Ya wanna make this trade or what? Ya got that money with ya?"

"Of course I do," I snapped.

He pushed up the brim of his hat with a thumb. "Well, let's see it, then."

"Hand over my sister first."

He chuckled and looked over his shoulder toward Ethelyn. Then turned back to me and shook his head. "Boy, you ain't in no position to be makin' demands. Yer lucky I brought yer sister at all. What's to stop me from just tellin' my crew here to shoot ya down? Then I could take the money *and* yer sister. Come to think of it, that's probably the better deal. Fer me."

His lewd grin turned my stomach, but I held his gaze. Resisted the urge to look up at the rocky walls. Resisted the urge to try and pick out any sign of where Holt mighta perched himself. "Yeah, but yer forgettin' somethin'," I said hoarsely.

"Am I?" His right hand slid over toward his gun.

"Sure."

"And what's that?"

I let go my reins and lifted my left hand slowly. And prayed Holt was settled up there, watchin'. I was countin' on him to be my angel, here. "Yer forgettin' … I got friends, too."

The mustached man laughed. Or started to.

Until I gave Holt the signal.

The sharpshootin' rifle cracked like lightnin' hittin' an old tree, and the bastard sittin' in front of me went clean off his saddle, his left shoulder explodin', nearly severin' his arm. He hit the ground screamin'. His horse reared.

My mule threw up his head, eyes rollin'.

Fer a second, none of those ready trigger fingers surroundin' me moved, frozen in startled confusion.

I jumped off the mule in that split second and swung to my right, workin' my own trigger, fannin' the hammer.

Two bodies fell from their horses and hit the water with a splash.

Holt's rifle cracked again, near ear-splittin' in the bowl of those rocks.

Another body hit the ground.

And that was all the time we had before the rest of 'em woke up from their surprise.

I ducked behind my mule as the first one of 'em fired. Least they weren't shootin' wild—they knew the danger of a ricochet same as me. And thankfully fer my mule, it seemed they didn't want to waste their bullets on an animal, neither. They were makin' their shots count.

Holt fired again, and the head of one of the women ridin' toward me just plain disappeared in a spray of red mist.

I turned away as the headless body slid from her horse, wincin'. And glad Ethelyn couldn't see none of this. Least, I hoped she couldn't see anythin' through that burlap sack.

My mule took off, the traitor, barrelin' through the chaos to disappear down the road, and I threw myself to the ground just in time to avoid the fire of three of the five left. Their bullets missed, some of 'em pingin' back again against the rocks before finally stickin' in somethin' or breakin' apart.

Riderless horses shrieked and galloped wildly around the pool's clearin', stirrin' up the ones that still had riders, and one of 'em headed right for me. I curled myself into a tight ball as the hooves thundered at me and they only barely missed, ringin' against the rock only inches from my head and then runnin' off down the road after my mule.

Holt shot again, and then there was only three left ridin'.

I uncurled myself with a curse and looked fer

that shaggy chestnut pony carryin' my sister. It was still in the clearin', prancin' wild-eyed and draggin' its lead, half-buckin' now and then as my sister clung to the saddle horn with white-knuckled hands.

One of the riders still livin' was tryin' to catch it. Another of 'em was aimin' his pistol at Ethelyn.

I pushed to my knees and fired, hittin' the one aimin' at Ethelyn in the side. He yelled and reined his horse around to face me instead, his pistol quickly followin'.

I fired again and got him in the throat.

He went off his horse backward.

"Tell your man to stop shootin'!" barked the only man still left standin'. "Stop shootin' or I'll kill her!"

I swung around to face him, still on my knees, pistol outstretched. But my finger stilled on the trigger.

He'd dismounted his horse and pulled Ethelyn off the pony, and now held her with an arm hooked around her neck, his gun pressed against her temple. She whimpered, but the sound was muffled. Sounded like she might be gagged.

That's when all the rage inside me settled. It went all flat and numb. My harsh breathin' slowed. My nerves stilled, a strange, detached calmness comin' over me.

The other rider still livin', a woman, fought to control her frantic horse, but she kept her seat well enough and kept her gun trained even, too. On me.

"Put your gun down," the man ordered. "And tell your man up top to stop shootin'. Or I swear I'll—"

The crack of Holt's rifle ate the rest of his words, and half his head, too.

I didn't wait fer his body to drop. I fired two quick shots at the woman remainin' even as I dove fer the ground again. Her bullet grazed my right shoulder as I ducked, but both of my bullets hit home.

She jerked in the saddle as blood painted the front of her vest, then wheeled her horse around to flee. Guess she'd decided—too late—she'd had enough of this mess. The horse tore off northward with her leanin' sideways in the saddle, barely stayin' on.

I let her go, pretty sure I'd got her through the heart. She wouldn't live fer long.

And anyway, I had Ethelyn. That was all that mattered.

A gunshot echoed from behind me.

Fer a minute I didn't understand. It didn't make sense. There weren't no one left standin' to shoot. And anyway, at this range, I surely woulda felt the bullet.

My fingers tightened around my own grip, but I'd emptied the chamber. Frownin', I turned.

The mustached man still lay where he'd fallen, his mangled shoulder leakin' bright blood to stain the bone-colored rocks, his face ashen gray. He writhed there, moanin' and groanin', but laughin', too. Cacklin'. Manic. He held his pistol in his right hand. And he laughed. And laughed and laughed.

From the corner of my eye, I saw Ethelyn fall.

LAND OF THE LIVING, LAND OF THE DEAD

Everythin' in me shattered.

I ran to her, horror in my throat, my empty pistol clatterin' to the rock as I dropped it, forgotten.

I hit my knees at her side, gatherin' her up into my lap.

Holt's rifle fired one last time, silencin' the mustached man's cacklin' laugh.

But all I saw was the bloom of crimson spreadin' across the breast of Ethelyn's dress; all I heard were the short, choked gasps comin' from under that sack. "No," I whispered. "No no no."

Tears blurred my vision, streaked down my face. I yanked the blood-splattered burlap off her head and threw it away. Pulled the tied cloth outta her mouth. Cradled her face.

Blood trickled from between her lips. She looked up at me with wide, terrified eyes.

Eyes that were the wrong color.

Ethelyn had always had our mama's eyes. A sea-green shade. The color of jade, our pa used to always say.

This woman had dark eyes. A warm, soft brown. Kinda like my own.

But my sister and I had never looked very much alike.

I stared down at her. Stared down at this girl I held in my lap. This dyin' girl. This girl who weren't my sister.

This girl who weren't Ethelyn.

I couldn't comprehend. Couldn't understand. My body felt numb again. My head too light.

She tried to speak. Coughed and choked. Blood bubbled up in her mouth.

I shook my head, tried and failed to speak myself. Tried to swallow down the sickness risin' in my insides. *I'm sorry*, I wanted to say. *I'm so sorry*. I wanted to comfort her somehow, this poor girl who'd suffered and was gonna die fer nothin', but the words were stuck. I was findin' it hard to breathe … much less talk.

If this weren't Ethelyn … then where the hell was my sister?

Was all this a trick? A double-cross?

Or was this the girl Nine-Fingered Nan had had the whole time, and all this just a terrible case of mistaken identity?

It all made me sick. All of it. My heart beat too hard, too fast, pulsin' out in my ears a frantic, desperate rhythm.

There was nothin' else I could do 'cept hold her as she exhaled a long, rattlin' breath and then went still, her warm brown eyes goin' cool as they stared past me to the sky.

Fresh tears ran trails down my face as I eased her off my lap and laid her down against the warm rock. Tears fer her, whoever she was, and a life wasted fer no reason, and tears fer my sister, who was still out there somewhere.

Maybe still with Nine-Fingered Nan.

Maybe not.

The idea of startin' my search for her over fresh was almost too much to bear.

I closed my eyes against the surge of panic and forced myself to breathe. *Focus. Focus, Van.* First, I needed to figure out what had happened here. First, I needed to figure out who else was gonna die fer this.

Anger sparked again in my chest, slowly buildin' back up into that familiar rage, burnin' away all the numbness of the shock at not seein' my sister under that burlap sack. I stood and backed away from the girl who weren't Ethelyn, lettin' that rage warm my limbs.

I turned to face the flat space of the holdin' tank pool, suddenly hopin' someone had lived. Bodies lay everywhere. A few of the horses had stayed and were mostly settled now, snortin' at the ground and lookin' to me curiously.

I stalked forward, hardly limpin' now, and scooped up my pistol. I reloaded quickly, studyin' each body in turn, lookin' fer breathin'.

There were two.

"Holt!" I barked. My voice echoed up against the cliffs. "Holt, get down here!"

Maybe he was already on his way. But if not, now he would be.

We had some business to take care of.

I went to the nearest body still breathin', a man, lyin' face down and bleedin' somethin' terrible from a big hole in his gut curtesy of Holt's sharp-shootin' rifle. I dug one toe under his shoulder and kicked him over onto his back. He was un-conscious.

Well, if he thought he was gonna get to go so peacefully, he was sorely mistaken.

I caught a fistful of the back of his shirt, drug him over to one of the cliff walls, and propped him up sittin' against it. I freed him from all his weapons, tossin' 'em into the pool, then slapped him. Hard.

He stirred, but didn't wake.

I slapped him again.

His eyes fluttered open. Then he choked and cried out in pain. His hands went to the ragged hole in his belly, his face deathly pale. His gray eyes found my face eventually, glassy and unfocused.

I gave him a smile. "Howdy, mister. Welcome back to the land of the livin'. Fer a little while, anyway. We need to have a talk."

His eyes left my face and wandered around the scene of death spread out behind me. They paused fer a bit on the body of the girl, then stopped altogether on the body of the mustached man.

"Yeah," I said. "He's dead. But that ain't my problem. My problem…" I pointed to the body of the girl, "my problem is that she ain't my sister."

His eyes followed my finger, then came back to my face, a little more focused now. A grin split his lips, showin' off bloodied teeth. "I know," he gurgled. Then he chuckled. And choked, coughed, and winced.

I straightened, glarin' down at him. The pistol was heavy in my hand, warm against my palm. "That amuses you, does it?"

"Yeah." He choked out a few more chuckles. "You thought it was her, though, didn't ya? Thought it was yer sister?" He coughed and cried out, then spit a wad of blood in my direction. "Wish I coulda seen yer face when she went down. Or did ya already know it weren't yer sister by then?" He could hardly keep his eyes open, his breath wet and labored, but that didn't stop him from grinnin' up at me.

I put a bullet through his right knee.

His scream got amplified by our rocky surroundin's, ringin' up into the sky, bouncin' back over itself. He sagged against the wall, and fer a minute I thought he might pass out on me again.

I stepped forward and leaned down to slap him again to keep him awake, then took a fistful of his shirt to hold him upright against the rock. "Where's my sister?" I growled through my teeth. "My *real* sister? Does Nan have her?" I shook him. "Does Nan have her or was this a ruse from the beginnin'?"

He rolled his head up to look at me. His eyes wouldn't focus, and he blinked slowly. But he was still smilin', damn him. "Nan ain't gonna ... give up ... yer sister," he said weakly. "Deal's ... deal's too good. And ... and anyway ... Nan thinks yer dead." He tried to laugh again, but it came out a wheeze.

I let go of his shirt. I remembered what the mustached bastard had told me durin' our first meetin' in the Stag Saloon ... that he'd told Nan I was dead. But I wasn't dead. And I'd paid him ten thousand dollars extra to go back to Nine-Fingered Nan and tell her he'd been wrong about that. I swallowed hard, all the pieces startin' to fall into place.

Humiliation crawled up under my shirt collar and burned worse than the noonday sun beatin' down upon us. "He never told her I showed up in Bravebank."

The man bleedin' out in front of me grinned all the wider. "Desperation ... makes a man ... a fool,

Taggert said. Guess he was right." He choked out another chuckle.

My mind was racin', goin' back through everythin' I had done to get to Bravebank, and to get that thirty-five thousand dollars. All of that and thirty-five thousand dollars I thought would get my sister back. Instead, it had all been fer nothin'.

A fool's errand set upon me by one of Nan's crew who'd decided to use me to make himself and his closest allies rich.

I'd been played all right, jerked around like a puppet on strings, just like Holt had said.

Only it hadn't been Nine-Fingered Nan doin' the pullin'.

Unless … unless the man bleedin' out in front of me now was the one lyin'. Unless *he* was the one fuckin' with me now, tryin' to get in one last stab before headin' off to Hell. I squinted down at him. "The fingers," I said. "They had a note from Nan."

He shook his head and tried to spit more blood at me, but it missed. By a lot. "Did it? Funny. Don't remember … there bein' a signature."

He was right. There hadn't been a signature. In truth, anyone coulda written that note. Hell, anyone coulda written that note even if there *had* been a signature. I'd never seen Nine-Fingered Nan's writin' before. I had no way to know. I'd just assumed it had come from her, given the circumstances.

I spun away from him and paced a few steps, runnin' a hand over my face, careful fer the swollen lip Holt had given me the night before. *You fool. You goddamned fool!*

"Taggert … just wanted to … to dissuade you … from killin' any more … of his guys. And said …

said it would … motivate you. Guess he was … right about that, too."

The wheezin' laugh came again, but this time in short, hard gasps. He weren't gonna last much longer.

"Sure, Nan woulda … woulda done the same … if she'd known about it."

He thought it all real funny, laughin' even though it musta hurt somethin' awful. Takin' great pleasure in these last few moments of his life lettin' me know just how big of a fool I'd been.

Well, I figured I should make his last few moments more comfortable fer him in return. I turned and put a bullet in his other knee.

This time he didn't have enough air to scream. He only grunted, his face goin' even more pale, chokin' and gaggin' as his eyes rolled back in his head. I holstered my pistol and went to him, slappin' him around to consciousness one last time. "Wake up, you no good sonuvabitch."

He did, but there weren't much of him left by now.

"Yer gonna meet the Devil with yer eyes open, mister."

His glassy gray gaze found my hard glare. His lips tried to smile one last time, but in the end he couldn't do it. Between the hole in his gut and his ruined knees, he was down too deep in a world of hurt.

And he was still there when the life went outta him, the expression frozen on his face in death not smilin' at all, but instead a grimace of pain. Pain, and some fear, too. That fear men feel when they die slow and have the chance to count their sins before takin' their last breath.

I had a feelin' this man had a mighty long list of sins.

Maybe I shoulda given him a little more time to count them.

Maybe then he woulda been a lot more scared to leave this land of the livin'.

I wouldn'ta minded seein' him realize what he'd have suffer there in the depths of Hell. Wouldn'ta minded seein' him realize that poor girl they'd kidnapped and tortured and brought here to die would get her justice … whether in this life or the next.

But fer now I supposed I'd have to be satisfied by what justice I'd given her in this life.

I left him there and made my way toward the second one still breathin', grabbin' the reins of one of the horses on the way and leadin' it after me.

Hoofbeats gallopin' up the south road behind me rose into the silence and I turned to train my pistol on the narrow opening between the cliffs, ready fer whoever might be comin'.

Holt exploded into the clearin' on his black geldin' and reined it up into a hard stop, his pistol pointed at me in turn before we both took fingers off triggers and lowered our weapons. "Van! You all right? I heard shots…" He circled his horse, lookin' fer anyone else with a pistol in their hand, but found none. He stopped cold at the sight of the girl's body and then turned to me with a look of distraught alarm on his face.

Ah, so he did care. All that talk about not wantin' to go after a ghost, but it turned out he didn't much like the thought of bein' right about that.

"Yer ... yer sister," his words came out a stran-gled whisper. "Is she ... is she...?"

"That ain't her." I resumed my walk to the single remainin' survivor of our shootout, this one a woman lyin' face up, sprawled out near the pool. She had a nice big hole in the right side of her chest. She was unconscious, too, her shallow breaths already quick and raspy.

"Wha?" Holt asked from behind me.

"That ain't her," I repeated, louder. "I was had by that mustached bastard from the Stag Saloon. Nan don't even know about this deal. She still thinks I'm dead. She..." I shook my head, waited till I could bite back the bitter surge of feelin's. "She still has Ethelyn."

Unless it was too late now.

Unless that deal had already been done.

All this time I'd wasted...

I sucked in a shudderin' breath and pulled the lasso off the saddle of the horse I led. I couldn't think about any of that now.

All that mattered was that I didn't waste any more time.

I left the raspin' woman where she lay. She wouldn't last more than three or four hours with a hole like that in her chest, not long enough to be any use to me. I coulda put her outta her misery, I suppose, but then, she had sins to pay for, too.

And who was I to interfere with the work of the Devil?

Instead I went over to the dead man with the mustache. Taggert, I guess his name was.

Holt was just starin' at me. "That ... that ain't yer sister?" He looked back to the girl's body.

"No."

"Who is it, then?"

"I don't know." I blinked hard, shovin' down those goddamned feelin's again. "She died before she could say anythin'."

"Maybe ... maybe they got the wrong girl by mistake?" Holt ventured.

"No they didn't." My voice was hoarse, rough. "They knew exactly what they were doin'. They used her to use me to get their money. They were never gonna trade. This was a trap. Fer all of us." I pulled my knife and went to work on the the dead Taggert, dressin' him out like he were the carcass of an animal I'd just killed in a hunt.

"What the hell are you doin'?" Holt asked.

"We got a ways to travel," I said. "And this desert sun is hot. Don't want him gettin' too ripe 'fore we get there." I finished my grisly work, wiped my knife and my hands on Taggert's shirt tail, sheathed the knife, and leveraged the body up onto my shoulder, ignorin' the way it made all my burns flare up into sharp agony and the nice red stain it left on my own shirt. Then I threw him over the saddle of the horse I'd caught, a dapple gray, and tied him there.

By the time I was done, sweat was drippin' off my nose.

Holt was still starin' at me. "Before you get where?"

I walked over to grab the reins of another abandoned horse, a chestnut with tall white socks, trailin' the one holdin' Taggert's body after me. I swung aboard the chestnut and pulled it around to face Holt. "I'm goin' to pay Nan a visit," I said. "And get my sister back."

Holt looked at me as if I'd gone ravin' mad.

And maybe I had.

"And just how do you plan to do that?" he demanded.

"I'm gonna make her a new deal."

He tilted his chin downward, sendin' me a warnin' glare from under the brim of his hat. "Van, damnit, last time you said somethin' like that and rode off to find Nine-Fingered Nan she all but outright killed ya!"

"But this time I'll be bringin' her a gift." I swept out my hand toward the dead Taggert.

Holt's eyes went wide.

I swung the chestnut mare around and kicked her into a trot, headin' northward in hopes of findin' my mule and all that cash he carried.

"Van!" Holt yelled out in my wake. "Goddamnit! All this and you ain't learned nothin'! You ride in there with the corpse of her man on yer heels and—"

"Be sure you bury the girl," I called back over my shoulder. "Leave the rest of 'em to rot."

"Van! Van, goddamnit, *get back here*!"

I ignored him, lettin' the sound of my horses' hooves drown out his shoutin' and cursin' as I went on down the road, weavin' through the towerin' rocks with my grisly caravan. I needed to find that mule and that cash and head fer Nan's rocky oasis of a hideout, and fast.

I wondered if Holt would follow and try to stop me.

Let him, if he wanted.

I weren't gonna stop. Not this time. Not any time. Not till I got back to Nine-Fingered Nan.

Not till I got Ethelyn back.

ALL THE CARDS ON THE TABLE

My mule hadn't gone too far, turned out.

His social nature wouldn't let him stray too far from his fellows. And they were all there, all the horses who had bolted in terror once the shootout started and their riders fell, all clustered in a group where the road curved around to the northeast and opened back out into the gentle, slopin' hills that were the feet of the Bone Spur Mountains.

I dismounted the chestnut mare and retrieved my mule, walkin' him back to my borrowed mounts. The saddlebags on him were still intact, the cash still buckled up safe inside.

I let the other horses be, leavin' the mare to join 'em, knowin' they'd eventually find their way back to wherever they called home … or at least back to whoever tended to feed 'em most. Then I climbed back aboard my mule, leadin' the gray behind us. I pointed him east and kicked him into motion, pickin' up into a canter.

I had a long way to go, and I didn't want Taggert's body gettin' too ripe before we got there.

Three days ridin' under the sun was makin' me feel pretty ripe by the end of it, and I weren't even dead.

On the outside, at least.

I'd stopped along the way in Bravebank to get a few supplies fer the journey, but then I'd headed off again. I pushed the mule and the gray as hard as I dared, workin' 'em up into a lather before slowin' down to let 'em cool off.

The ride coulda gone faster if not fer all the damned mountains that littered this part of the Territories. There weren't no straight road to be found fer more than a few miles at a time. I went east sure enough, but then had to pick my way north and then south again to get around the biggest peaks in this particular cluster, which the locals had dubbed the Superstition Mountains.

Superstition. Maybe those worshippers of the dead in Grave Gulch shoulda settled in these mountains, instead. Woulda suited them just fine.

As it were, maybe it was just fittin' enough that Nine-Fingered Nan had chosen this place to be her home. There were some mighty interestin' stories circulatin' about her, too.

If this really was her home, anyway.

Truth be told, I didn't know if she'd still be at this particular hideout of hers or not. But I had a feelin' someone would be, and that someone could take me to Nan, wherever she might be. Surely. And if they were reluctant to do so, I was fully prepared to persuade them, one way or another. Whatever it took.

On the evenin' of the third day, I topped a ridge and saw the river snakin' out below me, nestled down along the craggy feet of the Superstitions. The sun was already droppin' in the west, makin' the water shine like liquid gold.

My mule was blowin' hard, the gray the same. I patted his sweaty neck. "Easy there, boy. You done good. We'll go down in the mornin'."

I mighta been ravin' mad, but I weren't stupid enough to walk into Nan's lair in the dark.

I made camp there on the ridge, but had no fire. Nan's people mighta spotted me already. But if they hadn't, I didn't wanna make it any easier on 'em.

I didn't sleep much that night, on account of several factors:

Part of me still expected Holt to show up blusterin' mad in efforts to stop this latest affront to his cautious self-preservation sensibilities.

Part of me expected some of Nan's crew to manifest outta the darkness and either try and kill me, or truss me up to drop me like some neatly delivered parcel at Nine-Fingered Nan's feet.

And part of me expected some kind of vulture of the animal variety might take a sudden interest in the pounds of slightly aged meat I carried with me. The buzzards had followed me most the way here, hopin' fer an easy meal. I wondered how much longer their patience would last.

Though, the birds were a manageable annoyance.

Considerably less manageable would be the big mountain cats that prowled this area. If one of those were to take an interest in Taggert's overripe remains … well, that fight would be quite a bit more hazardous to my health than a disagreement with the buzzards.

So I settled back against my saddle to wait through the long night and pulled my hat low over my face, though I kept my eyes uncovered. And half-open.

And I kept my hand on my gun.

At last, mornin' came.

Holt, Nan's crew, and the lions did not.

Some mighta called that luck. But I didn't believe in luck. So I packed everythin' back up, saddled up, hauled Taggert's carcass back onto the dappled gray, and then took a minute to catch my breath and let the agony in my angry burns fade again.

Least my metal leg was farin' better now. And the nick across my right shoulder I'd gotten in the shoot-out at the pool wasn't hurtin' so much anymore. But Charlotte had said those burns would take a few more weeks to heal up. Guess I couldn't ask fer too much.

I climbed aboard the mule, and we went slow and careful down the side of the mountain toward the river.

Last time I'd met Nan here, it'd been right outside an impression in the cliff face that resembled a cave, only it weren't a cave at all. There'd been buildin's carved outta that rock. Nan hadn't done that herself, of course. No, those rock dwellin's had been there a long, long time, long before us. Maybe done by the same people as had done those drawin's out in the Bone Spurs.

Or maybe it had been someone else.

Either way, the makers of those cliff-carved buildin's had long since gone. Some of the walls were crumblin' now, some of the stairs worn away to nothin'. But that didn't stop murderers and thieves like Nine-Fingered Nan from usin' what was left of 'em fer shelter.

I picked my way down the same path as before, until about halfway between the ridge I'd camped on and the river, I saw ahead the big hole carved outta the cliff and the pale face of those crumbled walls.

I drew the mule up short. Studied the brush and cacti and boulders that littered the land around me. But nothin' moved. The mornin' was still and quiet.

The mule blew a snort and shook his head, jinglin' his bit.

There were hoofprints in the soft red dirt of the path. Fresh ones. Someone was here, all right. They just weren't wantin' to show themselves. Yet.

I loosened my pistol in the holster, kept my fingers wrapped around its grip. I settled my seat in the saddle and drew in a slow, calmin' breath.

This was either gonna be the day I got my sister back ... or the day I died.

As soon as I opened my mouth now, there'd be no goin' back. I'd be puttin' all my cards on the table.

Well ... I'd always been shit at poker.

"Nan!" I bellowed out. "Nine-Fingered Nan! I got somethin' fer ya!"

My words carried up loud and clear to those crumbled buildin's and echoed away out over the river. Both the mule and the gray perked up their ears and lifted their heads at the sudden noise in the quiet.

The only thing that answered me was the heavy drone of flies buzzin' around Taggert's body.

Swearin', I nudged the mule into a canter, makin' my way up the narrow path as it switched back and forth toward the carved-out dwellin's. "Nan!" I yelled again. "Get out here! I got business to talk with you!"

And then she appeared at the top of the hill, Nine-Fingered Nan, her horse standin' across the path. He was a tall, lean bay with a white star in the middle of his forehead, watchin' us approach with bright eyes.

Nan watched us approach, too, her double pearl grips glintin' in the sun.

I pulled the mule to an abrupt stop, the gray slidin' up behind me. But I didn't draw. Didn't even try. Not this time. I was here to make a deal, not to die.

Her eyebrows lifted in the shadow of her wide-brimmed hat. "Well, well, well," she drawled. "Look who's still breathin'. Taggert told me you were dead."

I yanked my knife from my belt and leaned over to cut the body free of the gray's saddle, then gave it a push. The lifeless corpse thumped to the ground in a cloud of dust and the dappled horse side-stepped away from it, bumpin' into me and the mule. "That Taggert?" I jerked my head in the direction of his body.

Nan's eyes narrowed as they went to him, then came back to me. "Yes. That Taggert."

"He lied," I said harshly.

"I can see that."

"He double-crossed you. Lied to you and made a deal with me himself fer the return of my sister. Had a couple of yer other guys and gals with him, too. Wanted me to get him a lot of money. I don't suppose he meant to share it with you."

Two of her lieutenants rode up behind her then,

two men armed with rifles. They took up positions to either side of her, squintin' glares at me.

Nine-Fingered Nan eyed me coolly with that pale gaze of hers. Her weathered face was shadowed by her hat, her hands restin' light on her reins. She weren't concerned at all. "How much money?" Her voice, as clear and hard as the first time I'd heard it, rang against the cliff face.

How much money. There was that thing she loved most again. Cold, hard cash. A flicker of hope rekindled in my chest. Maybe this was gonna work. "Thirty-five thousand," I said.

A grin split her wrinkled lips. She chuckled. Looked back over each shoulder to her two lieutenants in turn. Then she faced me again and shook her head. "I always knew Taggert was an underachiever. So? What of it? Did ya get the money?"

"Yeah. I got it."

"Let's see it, then."

I swallowed. Forced myself to ask the question. "You got my sister?"

"What, you mean Taggert didn't have her?"

"No." I couldn't tell if she was bein' serious or just fuckin' with me. "He didn't."

"Imagine that."

She was fuckin' with me. I ground my teeth. I looked to each of her lieutenants, countin' my odds. I wanted desperately to draw and put a bullet right into that calm, smug face of hers, but I surely wouldn't be gettin' out of that alive.

Of course, stayin' alive only mattered if I had Ethelyn. "Where," I repeated, slow and gruff, "is my sister?"

Nan spit off the side of her horse. "I told you

before and I'll tell you again. She's safe enough fer now. Long as you do as I say. Long as you show me that money."

I stared at her and she stared at me, and my breath came too fast and my heart beat too hard. But I couldn't just take her word fer it. Not after what'd happened with Taggert and that poor girl he'd killed. "So I give you the money and you give me my sister, then?"

"Sure."

I want to see her," I blurted. "Show me Ethelyn and I'll show you the money."

Nan smiled. "No."

A sick feelin' crawled into my gut. I shifted in the saddle, and the mule shifted, too, chewin' at his bit. All I could hear in my head then was Holt, screamin' at me fer the fool I'd been twice over now, ridin' straight into this trap. "How do I know you have her, then?" I managed to choke out. "How do I know she's still alive?"

Nan shrugged. "You've seen the proof. If that ain't enough fer you … well, then … I guess you got to make a choice. But, I gotta tell ya," her right hand, the one with the missin' index finger, slid smoothly to her right pearl grip, "I ain't the most patient of women. So make yer choice quick, boy."

I *had* seen the proof. What little there was of it. And half of it had already proven to be false, just like Holt had warned. But what was the greater gamble, here? Believe it to be true, believe Nan did have Ethelyn, and bargain fer her freedom? What could I lose by believin' such a thing, aside from twenty-five thousand dollars? Or I could believe it to be false, decide Nan didn't have Ethelyn, and leave here empty-handed or stay here and die bleedin' out into the dirt, and risk bein' wrong and doomin' Ethelyn to a life of slavery overseas in a foreign land.

There really was no choice at all.

I growled a foul curse and dropped my reins, then picked up the saddle bags holdin' the cash and tossed 'em at her. They hit the path about mid-way between us, stirrin' up their own cloud of dust.

Nan looked at 'em, then arched an eyebrow. She clucked her tongue in admonishment. "Well now. You won't get too far with those kinda manners. Pick 'em up and bring 'em to me, boy. On yer feet."

I glared at her, but her even stare didn't blink.

A pair of clicks echoed out into the mornin' as Nan's lieutenants thumbed back their hammers and aimed at me, just in case.

Scowlin', I dismounted carefully, though that was mostly 'cause of my burns and metal leg more than from a fear of gettin' shot. I limped up to where the bags had landed and pulled 'em outta the dirt, then went to the side of Nan's tall horse and held 'em up toward her. "Here," I spat. "Here's your damn money."

She smiled down at me. A horrible, triumphant smile. And took the saddle bags. "Thank you." She laid them over the front of her own saddle and proceeded to open 'em, riflin' through the contents. "There's only twenty-five thousand here," she said after a while. She counted a lot faster than her man from the saloon. "I thought you said you got thirty-five thousand?"

"I did. Taggert took ten of it earlier. Don't know what he did with it."

She grunted and closed up the saddle bags.

"Well. Twenty-five thousand ain't near enough to get back yer sister."

"Then how much?" I demanded. "Name yer price."

She looked down at me again, sizin' me up.

I pushed on. "You told me if I made it to Bravebank alive and with my wits intact you'd discuss terms. Well, I did. I got to Bravebank. I made a deal with Taggert and delivered what I promised. He didn't follow through on his end of the deal, and now he's dead. He was double-crossin' you. I did you a favor cuttin' out that rot from yer gang … now I'm here to make a new deal. A legit deal. With you. Directly. When I came here before, you said I hadn't proved myself yet. Well, I have now. So we gonna bargain, or what?"

Nan was quiet fer a long minute. The only sound in the silence was the drone of the flies around Taggert's body. Her gaze dropped down to my left leg. The leg she'd put a bullet in. "Looks like that leg healed up all right."

I shifted on the metal foot, glad she couldn't see what most my left leg was made of now. "Well enough," was all I said.

"Musta found yerself a real good doctor."

Somethin' in her tone I didn't like. My mind went to thoughts of Dr. Balogh and his family, a spike of worry lancin' into my heart. But she couldn't know. She couldn't have known he'd been the one to find me in the desert. The one to fix me up. She'd thought I was dead. Taggert had said so. She'd said so. And anyway, what interest could she have had in a doctor?

Old World tech.

That damned doctor was gonna get himself killed flauntin' that stuff around. "Good enough." I made it sound casual, dismissive. Didn't let my eyes slide back in the direction of Bravebank. Kept 'em on her. "My sister," I said again. "You want that other ten thousand? I can have it to you in three days."

"Yer face, though," she said, squintin' down at me. "That doesn't look so good. Run into some trouble gettin' this money, did ya?"

I ran my hand over my chin, feelin' the start of somethin' near a proper beard now under my palm. Sweat prickled under my hat brim and between my shoulders. "Somethin' like that," I said. "But I got it."

"So you did," Nan mused. "Thirty-five thousand dollars in the space of … how long it'd take you to get Taggert's money?"

"From the time we made the deal to the time I delivered it? A week."

"And you say you can get me ten thousand more in three days?"

"That's right." Might mean Holt wouldn't hold back in shootin' me, after all, but she didn't need to know we already had extra cash stashed away fer ourselves.

She gave a low whistle. "Well, Mr. Delano … it seems I may have underestimated you. When I shot you last time … well, I never expected to see you again. Least, not alive. Thought maybe bein' raised in a nice, warm, lovin' home woulda made you soft. Thought maybe up to this point in yer life, you'd just been lucky. Like yer pa. And yet … now here you are. Not dead. And with twenty-five thousand dollars."

"I just want my sister back. Like I told you before."

She nodded. "Sure, sure. Seems you wantin' yer sister back is a mighty powerful motivator."

I had nothin' to say to that, so I only stood there glarin' up at her, fists balled at my sides.

She looked away from me to gaze down along the path I'd come in on as if ponderin' somethin'. "Ya see, I'm just sittin' here thinkin' to myself ... well, hell, if Lucky Logan's boy is gonna be so eager to please ... so resourceful and efficient ... why waste such potential?" Her eyes came back to me then, hard and glitterin'. "You still willin' to owe me, Mr. Delano?"

I didn't like the look on her face. Not at all.

But I'd already given her the twenty-five thousand dollars. Already told her I was here to make a new deal. Already put all my cards on the table. So I forced myself to hold her greedy stare and gave a nod. "You set my sister free and I'll owe you whatever you want."

A slow smile spread across her face. "Very noble of you, Mr. Delano. But I think I'll hold on to yer sister fer now ... fer safe-keepin'. And to be certain you stay *properly motivated*, ya understand."

An image of those severed fingers flashed into my mind. Those hadn't been Ethelyn's fingers, no, but I also remembered what Taggert's man had said about 'em. *Nan woulda done the same thing.*

I swallowed back the bile that rose in my throat, tried to breathe through the fire burnin' in my chest.

"I want to see her," I said again. "I want proof you got her."

"And I told ya no. Look, you've lasted this long, boy. Don't push yer luck. This money," she patted at my saddle bags, "and the body of that traitor over there," she nodded toward Taggert, "bought you another chance. Bought yer sister more time stayin' off the boat. But you want to see her? Yer gonna have to make it worth my trouble to get her here, understand? You do a few things fer me and manage to live through 'em, I'll consider it. Till then, don't ask again. Them's my terms. That's the deal I'm willin' to make. You can take it or leave it."

There was rushin' in my ears again, my chest too tight and my head too light. I held her stare fer as long as I could while I considered my greatly limited options. Then I tore my eyes away from her and glanced at her two lieutenants. They were both still sightin' down their rifles at me.

But no one had shot me yet.

Not even Nan.

And I'd already been willin' to make this deal before, a horse and a leg and a month ago.

Why not now?

"Daylight's wastin', Mr. Delano," Nan prompted. "What'll it be?"

I stepped back from her horse and gave a nod. "Fine. I'm in."

"Very good." Her maimed gun-hand slid off her pearl grip and went back to her reins. "Good to see yer finally usin' those smarts of yers. Musta got those from yer mama, yeah? She were a smart woman, weren't she? 'Cept fer the fact she married yer pa, of course. That didn't get her very far, did it?"

I took a few more steps back from her horse, heart poundin' and fingers itchin' at her goadin'. *Don't do it. You just made a deal. This is your best chance yet ... don't ruin it.*

How many times had I said that, now?

Maybe this one would finally come through fer me.

Or maybe it was all another lie. Another trap. I had no real way to know. But I was still almost certain Nine-Fingered Nan had Ethelyn. Somewhere. If she was gonna let me do some business fer her, maybe I could do some pokin' around of my own and see where she might be holdin' my sister.

And if I could find that out, I could take things into my own hands.

No more payin' debts. No more playin' games.

"Just tell me what I owe you," I growled.

"Oh, I'll think about it. In the meantime, why don't you make yerself comfortable in Bravebank. I'll put in a word with the sheriff that yer to be granted ... *permissions* ... to conduct my business. Now, a'course I can't promise the same kind of leniency in all other towns in the Territories—yet—but that'll be somethin' we'll work on. So see that you don't get yerself arrested durin' the conductin' of my business. You do, and ain't no one will come to save you from the noose." She nudged her horse forward till she was beside me once again, loomin' over me. "Unless you go sayin' things to the law you shouldn't, of course. Then we most certainly will come to save you from the noose. And deliver you into somethin' a great deal more unpleasant. Understand?"

I remembered well what I'd suffered at the hands of Baron Whittaker, and wondered if there could be much else worse than that. I didn't think so. But then, I surely didn't feel like findin' out, neither. I lifted my hands, slow and careful so as to not prompt her lieutenants' trigger fingers into firin'. "Sure."

"Good. Then I look forward to seein' what else you can do fer me. I'll have someone fetch you when I decide what that's gonna be. Till then..." she tipped her wide-brimmed hat to me, a corner of her mouth quirkin' in a smirk, "pleasant day to you, Mr. Delano."

She kicked her heels into her horse's side and he leapt forward into a canter, headin' down the path toward the river. Her two men holstered their rifles and followed after her, thunderin' by me on either side and startlin' my mule and the gray, makin' 'em trot off a ways.

I was left alone, coughin' in the swirl of red dust they left behind.

Alone, with no money and no sister and only a dead body and its flies fer company.

All I had left now was hope.

Hope that Nine-Fingered Nan was actually the one holdin' my sister in the first place. Hope that she weren't lyin' to me about that. Hope that if all that were true, she'd keep her end of the bargain better than Taggert had and set my sister free.

Hope that Ethelyn was truly safe enough fer the time bein', fer however long it took Nan to feel we were even.

Hope that I'd survive any of this.

I hung my head, blinkin' away the grit in my eyes, then turned my face toward the sun, still risin' in the east. I trudged toward the mule and took his reins, then gathered up the dappled gray, too. If they were gonna leave me the horse, I could at least get a little somethin' out of all my troubles here.

I mounted the mule and led the gray behind, and pointed us back west.

Toward Bravebank.

I didn't want to wait in Bravebank as a lackey fer Nine-Fingered Nan, millin' about aimlessly till she came to fetch me. But I supposed I didn't have much other choice. At least, not fer now.

The mule ambled back down the switch-back path, and I thought I'd have felt a lot happier about makin' a solid deal fer my sister. After all, if everythin' worked out, I'd be gettin' exactly what I wanted.

If everythin' worked out.

I sighed heavily, suddenly feelin' every place on my body that hurt. And there were a lot of places that hurt. I glanced over my shoulder to the sun as it warmed my back, then closed my eyes against its light.

Hope.

That soul killer.

EPILOGUE

A BARON'S BASTARD

Charles Miller paced a slow circle around the man hanging from the ceiling.

He'd been hanging down here for three days now. Alone, in the dark. No food, no water. He squinted now in the dim light created by the lantern Charles had set on the small wooden table to his right. The air reeked of excrement, still and damp, moisture seeping through the cracks in the stone-brick walls.

The man looked terrified. He was so pale. His breathing fast and haggard.

Charles shook his head. Clucked his tongue in admonishment. He had hoped this man would be harder to break. He'd seen his father do this kind of thing plenty of times ... he'd been looking forward to trying some of the same strategies. He was sure he could have equally as satisfactory results.

Except ... he wasn't sure now he'd get the chance to hurt this man.

He looked ready to talk again. Unprompted.

Charles stopped in front of him and sighed heavily. He clasped his hands behind his back.

"I ... I told you," the man gasped. "I already told you everything I know, I swear!"

Charles frowned, sucking on his top teeth. "Mmm."

The man's dangling feet hung only inches above the floor's damp cobblestones. The skin of his wrists showed raw and bloody in the lamplight. He'd been struggling to get free these last three days, it seemed.

Alas, no one had ever escaped from this cellar. Not in Charles' lifetime, at least.

"I see," Charles said quietly. Patiently. "So you're telling me it was just one man who did all of that?" He pointed upward, up through the yards of earth that blanketed them, toward the surface. Toward the three burned-out husks of barns, and the once-splendid manor with its now-charred beams and ruined furniture, and the horse barn that was still half empty, the rest of the highly bred and very expensive animals still missing.

Stolen, most likely. Or kept by whoever had chanced to find them, more likely.

Anger kindled deep within, and Charles drew in a slow breath.

"Yes!" the man blurted. His voice cracked. He must have been so thirsty. He struggled in the chains, and his body swung gently back and forth. "And a woman, like I said. I swear, I'm telling you the truth!"

Charles nodded. He knew about the woman. She had been identified easily enough by some of the household staff, as well. A known trouble-maker. A rebellious soul.

If it had been up to him, she would have hanged months ago.

But his father had always had difficulty letting go of his prettiest possessions.

Charles would not make his father's mistakes. "I know the woman," he said curtly. "I'm not concerned with her. If I know her, I can find her. And trust me, I will find her." He began his slow circling again, hands still clasped behind his back. "No, what concerns me is this man you speak of. No one seems to have gotten a very good look at him. No one who is still alive, anyway. No one seems to know who he was."

The man now hanging from the ceiling shook his head vigorously. Long, lank strands of dark hair fell across his face. "No, I didn't know him, neither. Never seen him before."

"And you're *sure* it wasn't another of my father's slaves?"

"Yes. Yes, sir. He surely wasn't!"

Charles stopped in front of him again and shook his head. He went to the table where the lantern sat, and studied the tools lined up neatly atop it. He picked up the crowbar. One of his father's personal favorites. "It's just ... I find it terribly disappointing that so many of my father's slaves were so eager to abandon him ... to betray him ... after he did so very much for them. The Territories are such a dangerous place." He tested the crowbar's weight and balance in his hand. Gave it a few half-hearted, experimental swings. "Do you think any of you would have survived for long out here without his protections? Without all the things he provided you?"

The man shook his head again, his eyes growing wide. "No, of course not, sir. That's why I came to you first! I didn't abandon the baron! I didn't betray him! Please, you must believe me!"

"Yes," Charles said. "Yes, you did the right thing,

coming to me and telling me about these people … these *murderers*. I will see justice done for my father's death." He set the crowbar down gently, and lifted a knife. He studied the fine edge of its blade in the lantern's light. "It's just, well, I *really* need to know more about this mystery man."

"I'll tell you," the man hanging from the ceiling blurted as Charles stepped close. "I've already told you! I swear, I told you everything! You don't need the knife. Don't need anything. Just ask! I'll tell you again! Ask whatever you want to know and I'll tell you!"

"Mmhmm." Charles leaned down to slice away one of the man's tattered trouser legs. He always liked to start with the tendons in the legs and work his way up from there.

"He—he was not from any of the other families," the slave babbled on. "I think he was one of those freedom fighters. He wanted to free the baron's slaves, certainly. He was working with the woman!"

"Mmmhmmm." Charles had already heard all of this.

The man tried to jerk his leg away from Charles' grip, but three days of no food and water had weakened him considerably. Not that he'd been in spectacular condition to begin with, anyway. Charles tightened his hold on the grimy ankle. "Now, now. Hold still, would you? Don't want this blade to slip…"

"Please," the man gasped, "please, you don't have to do that. I'll tell you anything you want to know!"

Charles rolled his eyes. Just as he'd suspected. This one had no spine. And would therefore be no fun at all. Oh well. He'd do what he could, anyway.

The slave had come to him voluntarily, yes, and supposedly told him all there was to know about that horrible night, and yet Charles still felt there was something missing from the man's story.

People didn't just show up out of the dark of night to set a baron's house on fire and free his slaves … not even those blasted, bleeding-heart freedom fighters would have had the stones to make such a direct attack against his father.

There had to be some other motive at play here. Either this man who had helped that troublesome woman slave was a brilliant mastermind playing at some game Charles didn't yet understand, or he was just colossally stupid, led by a pretty face into something that would guarantee his death.

Charles snorted in amusement at the thought as he set the knife's sharp edge against pale skin, made all the more pale by so much time spent underground in those Old World ruins. *Certainly wouldn't be the first time a young man followed the pull of his loins into death.*

"He—he musta been demon-touched!" the slave shrieked.

Charles paused. The skin beneath his knife blade remained unbroken. He straightened and stepped backward. That part was new. "*What* did you say?"

The man trembled in terror. His wide eyes gleamed in the lamplight behind strands of greasy hair. He tried to wet his cracked lips, but had no spit for it. "He musta been demon-touched, sir."

Charles cocked his head to one side, intrigued. "And why is that?"

"B—because, sir … on account of his … on account of his m—metal leg, sir. His metal leg."

Charles bit back an impatient sigh. *Oh, of course.* The metal leg. The thing he personally found most interesting about this whole affair. After all, it wasn't every day you saw a man walking around with a metal leg.

It wasn't something you saw in general. Ever.

No one had ever used Old World tech in such a way before. No one had even *considered* using it in such a way before. But if this was really true … if there was someone out there who had succeeded in fusing that kind of tech to their own body…

The thrill of the potential, the possibilities, took his breath away. Which was exactly why he needed to find this mystery man who had murdered his father.

To exact justice … and to claim such a thing for himself.

"It…" The man hanging from the ceiling swallowed visibly. Or tried to swallow. His throat nearly spasmed. Poor man desperately needed a drink. Too bad he wouldn't be getting one. "It … it ain't natural," he husked at last.

Charles resisted the urge to roll his eyes this time. If he had a nickel for every time he'd heard someone in these parts mutter those words, he wouldn't have needed the rights to his father's fortune to live a comfortable life. "Now, now, Mister…?"

"George," the man answered breathlessly. "George Gillham."

"Mr. Gillham. Of *course* it ain't natural. It's *metal.*"

"Sir … but … please … that tech … it's the Devil's work. We shouldn't be messin' with it. And he … he had it … *attached* to himself. Sir…" The man's eyes were wild, his already extremist beliefs fueled by delirium, most likely. "What if he comes for me, next? Or—or *you*, sir?"

Charles gave a short huff of impatience. "George, you said my father captured this man for a time."

He nodded.

"And did he bleed?"

George blinked. "Well … y—yes. Yes he did."

Charles stepped closer. "And my father had him branded?"

"Y—yes, sir. Several times."

"And did his flesh burn same as everyone else's?"

Again the rapid blinking. "It … it seemed so."

Charles took another step closer. "Exactly. He is not a demon. He is not demon-touched. He is a *man*, George. A mortal man who dared to attack my family, who helped to murder my father. And I will see to it that he is properly repaid for the atrocities he committed here that night. And you are going to help me, George, aren't you?" He hooked his hand around the back of the man's neck, holding him steady as he brought the knife's edge to rest against the gaunt cheek. "You want to tell me every single little thing you can remember about this man so I can hunt him down and send him straight to Hell, don't you?"

George Gillham trembled in Charles' hold, taking short, shallow breaths. He dared not nod again, not with the knife pressed so firmly against his skin. His dark eyes didn't blink now. They were wide, wide open, begging Charles silently for mercy. "Yes," he breathed, in a voice hardly louder than the guttering of the oil lamp in the darkness. "Yes, I'll help you. I told you, sir. I told you everything I know!"

Charles granted the man a friendly smile. "Well. Let's just be sure about that, shall we?"

George's face went so pale as to look positively sickly in the dim lantern's light.

Charles released him and stepped back again, but allowed the blade to pull across the man's cheek as he did so, leaving behind a bright line of blood.

George gasped.

Charles ignored him and resumed his circling. "So. This metal leg. Which leg was it, again?" He remembered which leg it was. He remembered every detail this slave had recounted to him about that night, in fact. But he still wasn't entirely convinced the man was telling him the truth. That he hadn't been making up stories in attempts to gain himself a better position within the estate. Or, if all of this *was* true, that the slave wasn't holding back some vital piece of information out of fear … or spite.

"The left one!"

Well, that was what he'd said the first time, too. But no harm in being absolutely certain. "I see. His left leg was made out of metal? The whole leg?"

"No, j—just from the knee down. Like I told you before."

"And you believe it was Old World tech?"

"L—looked like it, sir. Your father thought so."

Charles considered this, as he'd been considering it since the moment this man had first come to him. With something so rare as a metal leg, and *working* Old World tech, surely someone, somewhere, had to know something about it … had to have seen this man around... "You're absolutely *sure* this man didn't say where he'd gotten that metal leg?" he asked. "My father never got it out of him?" That seemed hard to believe. For as long as Charles had known his father, there had never been a man—or woman—he couldn't break.

Eventually.

But George shook his head vigorously again. "No, sir," he rasped. The blood from the cut on his cheek made red lines down his face and dripped off his chin to splatter the stones beneath his feet. "Your father ... he tried. But the man ... wouldn't say. Then—the woman—she came. She came and killed them all."

Charles stopped pacing at that, fury flaring in his chest and burning up his throat. Yes. The woman. Charlotte Harrison.

But she would pay. He'd see to that. He already had some of his most loyal people tracking her down. And she shouldn't be that hard to find. He knew her name and her face. He knew she'd come from the east. And he knew she'd had proper breeding. That had been quite clear as soon as she'd arrived.

That's what had endeared his father to her so completely.

But it would also be her undoing. Charles was sure of it. There were only so many proper ladies from the east named Charlotte Harrison. He would find her, all right. It was only a matter of time.

As for this man, however ... the mystery man with the metal leg ... the man who had resisted his father's interrogations for just long enough ... well.

Charles would be damn sure he was found, too. Whatever it took.

He turned toward George Gillham and lifted the knife once more. "Isn't that a shame? You see, Mr. Gillham, I really must find out where this man is now, and where he got that leg." The man's eyes got real wide again as Charles stepped close once more. "Let me just see if I can't help you recall any details you might have forgot..." He grabbed George's ankle again.

"No," the man whispered, kicking and struggling. "No, please, I swear! I swear, I t—told you all I know! P—please, sir!"

Charles ignored George's pleas and went to work, calm and sure, just as he'd seen his father do so many times before.

George's begging turned to shrieks and screaming.

More blood ran down to paint the cobblestones.

And still, relentless, Charles carved on.

It went on for hours, long into the night.

George Gillham desperately babbled his whole story again and again, and sometimes, Charles would ask more questions. To which he would receive the same answers as before, only less and less coherent, of course.

Eventually, George wasn't making any sense at all, lost in a haze of pain and blood loss.

Charles stopped his work then, and set the knife back on the table. He picked up the white linen towel and wiped the blood from his hands, even more disappointed now than he had been when he'd started this process.

Mr. Gillham had been telling the whole truth about the night of Baron Whittaker's murder from the start.

There'd been no lies, no omissions, after all.

Charles grunted and tossed the soiled towel to the table.

How very rare.

How very … *disappointing*.

"Fire…" the slave muttered. He hung limp from the chains now, too weak to struggle, too weak to even lift his head. "Fire and thunder…" His greasy hair hung in a curtain around his bloodied face.

Fire and thunder, yes. The weapon that red-haired bitch had stolen from his father had often been described as thus by the household staff, on the rare occasion the baron would deign to fire it. The staff was terrified of it. The slaves were even more terrified of it.

And Charlotte Harrison had taken that from his family, too.

Charles ground his teeth and picked up the lantern. Just another thing to recover and reclaim for his family—for himself—once he found Ms. Harrison and ended her.

"Demons!" George gasped suddenly. "Demons … comin'. They're … d—demons! Comin' fer us … comin'…"

Charles lifted the lantern to take one last look at the pathetic mess of a man who hung before him. "Yes, Mr. Gillham," he said softly. "Demons, indeed."

Then he turned and made his way out of the cellar, leaving the dying man in darkness. Not that he'd notice, most like. He'd finish bleeding out soon enough.

Charles would have to send someone down to clean up the mess later. But for now, he had some organizing to do. He climbed the stairs up toward the surface quickly, already forming a plan.

If the folk around here wanted to think a man with a metal leg was a demon, why, Charles Miller would let them. The masses were quick to turn on a person perceived as evil, after all, and their hatred and suspicion got ugly in a hurry if that person could be said to be doing the Devil's work.

Superstition could be a very useful tool, indeed. It was a tool his father had often used to keep his staff and slaves in line. It had proven quite efficient.

Charles might not have gotten as much information as he would have liked out of George, but he'd gotten enough. Enough to have some wanted posters drawn up. Enough to start spreading whispers about a demon-touched man with a limp and a metal leg, set loose upon the Earth to slake his bloodlust on the innocent. That should stir up the locals, all right.

And he'd make the reward for the capture of this demon high enough everyone in the Territories would be looking for him.

Didn't matter that Charles didn't have access to the family's fortune ... yet. Once he got his hands on that metal leg, and recovered his father's Old World rifle, he'd have enough. He'd exact his revenge on his father's murderers. And then he'd take care of his meddling half-brother, and finally take his rightful place as head of the Whittaker family.

It was all just a matter of time.

He came to the cellar's door and threw his shoulder up against it, swinging it open, then stepped out into the night. He turned to push the heavy slab of wood shut again, then set off across the yard, past the ruins of Whittaker manor toward his own, much more humble abode.

Even still, there was a spring in his step as he marched across the grass, and he inhaled the night's fresh air deeply. Anticipation swelled in his chest.

It's time to do some demon hunting…

THE END

READ ON

FOR A SNEAK PEEK AT
BASTARD OF BLESSING! ...

Don't forget, if you'd be so kind, to leave a review for this book on your favorite platform! The number of a book's reviews directly influences how visible the retail platform makes it to other readers! And leaving a few sentences about what you loved most about the book will help others decide whether or not this book might be for them, too! Also, you'll have my eternal gratitude!

You can also find *Bargain at Braveback* on audiobook – narrated by none other than the amazingly talented Roger Clark (of Red Dead Redemption II fame)! Visit https://jrfrontera.com/ allaudiobooks/ to learn more!

ACKNOWLEDGEMENTS

This book could not be what it is today without two specific people, for certain.

The first is Jamie Davis, a former paramedic and nurse, who was of infinite help when it came to severely injuring my characters. ...Which apparently I do quite a lot. I can't thank Jamie enough for saving me from the hours and hours I was spending on the internet researching skeletal traction and intramedullary nailing, etc. (If you want to give yourself a headache, just Google that one!) So thank you, Jamie, thank you *thank you* so much for all of your medical wisdom, which I certainly (I hope) put to good use in this book!

The second is Matt Carlson, a firearms expert, who was kind enough to give me a crash course in 1800s era guns via email... which I imagine was no small feat. Matt also saved me probably years of my life lost on the internet in feeble research attempts, and it is thanks to him that this book has any sort of accuracy when it comes to firearms. But, a disclaimer! I have, in certain instances, taken a wee bit of artistic license with the weapons and their actions in this book... so if you are the sort who might spot those instances of slight deviation from reality... know those were done *on purpose, with reason, after careful consideration*, and in no way do those brief instances reflect Matt's completely accurate advice! Even still, Matt *did* save me from making some rather embarrassing gun-related mistakes in this book... so thank you, Matt!

And a special shout-out to my patrons from Patreon, especially Pat Stevens and Vicky Meyer, whose contributions directly affected this book's production, and made it so much more awesome! Thank you!

THE LEGACY OF LUCKY LOGAN
BOOK 2

ACES HIGH

The sonuvabitch was cheatin'.

I may have been shit at poker, but I'd learned enough about it in the last few weeks to know when a man was cheatin'. And the sonuvabitch sittin' across from me at the table right now was cheatin', sure enough.

So when he laid down his winnin' hand with a cocky grin and made to grab for the stash of money in the middle of us, I put my hand over the top of it first. His grin slid fast into a murderous scowl, and the other four men sittin' with us pushed their chairs back a mite, not wantin' to get caught in the middle of this. They glanced to each other, then toward the barkeep, but I paid 'em no mind.

This here was the Stag Saloon, under the ownership of none other than Nine-Fingered Nan, the oldest and most feared outlaw in the Territories, and around here, I was Nan's man.

No one had much wanted to pick a fight with me before, and they certainly didn't want to do so now. So I kept my glare on the man across from me, my hand atop his money, and he glared right back. His left hand was below the table, but I happened to know he only wore one gun, and it was perched on his opposite hip. If he tried to draw, I'd beat him easy.

"I don't much like cheaters," I said.

His face reddened.

The other four sittin' with us pretended to look surprised, but I had a hard time believin' they hadn't suspected somethin'. I was shit at poker, and the room was on the verge of spinnin' on account of all the whiskey I'd downed since sun-up, but even I had seen it.

Maybe I was shit at poker, but this fella was even more shit at cheatin'.

"Yer drunk, Delano," he said. "You should mind the words comin' outta yer mouth. Might getcha into trouble."

"Might," I agreed. "But I still don't much like cheaters. And yer a cheater. And a bad one, at that. If yer gonna do it, you should at least get good at it before you come in here tryin' to rob me and the rest." I tilted my head toward the others at our table. "So why don't you go ahead and get outta here. Before yer cheatin' gets *you* into trouble, yeah?"

His face got even redder, and his eyes darted from me to the other fellas sittin' round. They were watchin' him, tense on their chairs, ready fer him to try somethin'. Or fer me to try somethin'.

His eyes finally came back to me, glarin' somethin' fierce. "I ain't no cheat," he hissed. "You shut yer lyin' mouth 'fore I gotta teach you some manners!"

The conversations nearest to us faltered at his shoutin', people turnin' to see what the commotion was about.

I smiled at him. Truth be told, I was itchin' fer a fight. But then, it seemed I was always itchin' fer a fight these days. Three weeks I'd been holed up in Bravebank now, waitin' on word from Nan over what she wanted from me in exchange fer my sister —beyond that twenty-five thousand dollars I'd already given her.

Three weeks of waitin' with nothin' to do but drink, sleep, and gamble. And avoid goin' near Dr. Balogh's shop, which I'd discovered was set up over on the east edge of town.

All that time, and not a word yet from Nan.

Holt were convinced no word would come. He figured she'd said such things just to get me outta the way. Just to fuck with my head while she sold Ethelyn off, anyway.

That coulda been true. But if that's what she'd wanted, it woulda been easier for her to just gun me down three weeks ago when I'd showed up at her cliff-side hideout with the gutted body of one of her men in tow.

She coulda just ended it all then.

But she hadn't.

I had to believe she wanted more from me. I was bankin' on her greed. Bankin' on the fact that would be enough for her to keep her word, enough to save my sister.

But there was always that doubt in the back of my mind, made manifest in Holt's conviction of Nine-Fingered Nan's dishonesty, and his certainty she was only manipulatin' me.

That, and the fact no one in this damned town seemed keen to talk when I inquired as to the details of Nan's operations, was enough to drive a man to madness. So I only smiled at that cheatin' sonuvabitch across the table, and stood slowly from my chair. I rocked a bit as the room tilted, but reached out to steady myself on the table. Well, maybe I'd had more whiskey than I remembered.

"I'm gonna give you one more opportunity, Mister," I said slowly. "You can leave now on your own two feet, quiet-like, or we can make a nice scene and I'll throw you out."

He stood then, too, but fast, knockin' his chair over.

More people turned to look now, and I saw his right hand dip toward his sixgun.

I coulda drawn then and put him down, even drunk, but there was too much fierce anger roilin' around inside me, and it wanted out. So instead I grabbed the edge of the poker table and flipped it over toward him just as his gun was clearin' leather.

He had to jump back to keep from bein' hit by it, throwin' off his aim. Cards and money went everywhere.

The other four men sittin' there yelled and dove fer the money, likely tryin' to recover their share of it before anyone else could claim it.

Someone somewhere shouted out in alarm.

And then the cheatin' bastard recovered his balance and took aim again. I launched myself at him, tacklin' him just as his gun went off.

It was loud, right in my damn ear, but I still heard the barkeep swear and yell for us to take it outside.

Too late.

We crashed to the floor, and a commotion erupted all around us. Seemed the other patrons were quick to pick sides in this fight ... or quick to get the hell outta there.

The cheater's pistol jarred out of his hand as he

hit the ground and went spinnin' off across the floor. And all his aces fell outta his sleeve. But I ignored all that, rollin' over the top of him to land a few good fists into his face before he could bring up his forearms to block my pummelin'.

He struck out with a fist of his own and caught me on the chin, ringin' my bell pretty good. I fell sideways and caught another fist to the jaw, then I was the one on the floor. He made a grab for my left gun but I twisted away outta his reach, and then the other four fellas we'd been playin' cards with found him and hauled him up to his feet.

From the beatin' they proceeded to lay on him, seemed like they'd sided with me.

Hands found me then, too, grabbin' my upper arms and draggin' me upright. I winced as their fingers dug into the mostly healed burns on my right bicep. The burns were mostly healed, sure, but the skin there was still kinda sore, and I didn't much like people diggin' into it.

Too bad fer me, they weren't friendly hands. Seemed the cheatin' bastard had some people on his side, too.

A fist landed in my gut and I doubled over, the breath goin' out of me. Then another cracked into my face and I staggered sideways before bein' caught again by more hands.

I ducked the next blow and sent my own fist into someone's middle, then reached out fer a half-empty bottle on the closest table and came up swingin' it, catchin' the nearest man on the side of the face.

The bottle shattered. The man howled and spun away as blood painted his cheek.

His friend stepped up to take his place, and another fist sailed at my face.

I dodged that one, too, but stumbled. Damn the whiskey. I'd drunk more than I thought. The room was spinnin' now, and I caught the back of a chair to keep from pitchin' over onto the floor again.

Someone was yellin' fer the sheriff, and the barkeep was cursin' all of us.

A blow landed in my right kidney and sent me down to my knees, but I let myself roll with the momentum even as I gasped in pain, and took the chair with me to use as cover.

The next fist punched the solid wood of the chair back instead of me, and then that man was the one cryin' out in pain as he shook out his hand. I kicked at him with my left boot, the one that had a metal foot in it, and made solid contact with his right shin.

It knocked his leg out from under him and he fell forward. His face smashed into the chair on the way down and I grimaced. *Ouch. That had to hurt.*

Sure enough, he wailed and rolled away with his hands over his nose.

It was probably broke.

Well, at least my metal leg was cooperatin' better these days. It almost even acted like a real leg now.

Three men loomed over me then, one of 'em a big, burly fella with a bushy beard. He didn't look friendly, neither.

I threw the chair at 'em, but the big guy knocked it away easy and it bounced off his meaty forearm to crash into another fella and knock him sprawlin'. Then the big guy reached down and grabbed the front of my shirt.

Well shit.

He pulled me up as easy as he'd knocked away the chair and grinned into my face. "Hey there, Delano," he drawled. "Remember me?"

I frowned at him as the fightin' went on all around us, the sounds of yellin' and shoutin' and shatterin' glass makin' a real ruckus. I had a feelin' I shoulda remembered him, and he had the kinda build that was hard to forget, but I couldn't recall crossin' paths with him before. "No," I admitted.

But then, I *had* been awful drunk lately…

Maybe the swill was startin' to affect my mind.

Maybe I needed to lay off a bit.

"Well then, let's see if we can't refresh your memory," he said.

He drove one of his big, meaty paws into my middle hard enough to send black spots burstin' across my vision, and then I was on the floor on hands and knees, retchin' and gaggin' fer air.

He didn't give me time to catch my breath.

He caught the back of my shirt and lifted me again, then threw me at the nearest table.

I crashed into it and knocked it over, and what food and drink had been left atop it clattered to the floor, addin' to the mess. I landed myself in a tangle of chairs, but I still couldn't breathe. I rolled onto my side, gaspin', tryin' to blink the black from my eyes.

A pair of boots stomped up next to me, but they didn't look like the big fella's boots.

Then a shotgun roared out over the noise of the fight, and I flinched at the closeness of it. I fumbled fer one of my own guns, but all the damn chair legs was in the way.

"All right, that's enough!" a familiar voice boomed into the little hole of quiet the shotgun blast had bought him. "All of you, that's enough! Party's over!"

I shoved some chairs outta my way and rolled over onto my back, a hand over my achin' stomach and feelin' like I might vomit. I looked up into the angry face of Sheriff Earl Jennings, the man who passed fer the law around these parts. So those boots had belonged to him.

He stood over me with his shotgun ready, three of his deputies fanned out behind him.

The sound of people runnin' quick out of the saloon marked the hasty retreat of several of the fight's worst offenders, and the sheriff motioned fer his deputies to go after some of 'em. I hoped that blasted cheater wouldn't get away.

I wasn't quite sure what to hope for that big, burly fella. On the one hand, I wouldn't mind him spendin' a few days in a cell while I recovered my wits. On the other hand, if the sheriff had scared him off now, maybe he wouldn't chance comin' around again if he managed to escape this time.

Least, I was pretty sure Sheriff Jennings had scared him off. He weren't comin' fer me anymore, anyway. And fer that, I was grateful. I smiled up at the lawman standin' over me and ignored his scowl. "Howdy, Sheriff. Mighty nice timin' you got."

His frown deepened beneath his gray mustache, and his dark eyes glittered. He looked awful angry this time. "Delano," he growled. "You start this again?"

"No, sir." I touched gingerly at my jaw, already

feelin' a spot swellin' up. "I didn't start nothin'. Only called out a man fer cheatin' at cards, is all."

"He started it, all right," the barkeep called from across the room, and I pushed myself up sittin' to glare at him.

He was glarin' back at me, and his slicked-back hair and hooked, narrow nose sure made him look somethin' like a vulture, waitin' to pounce on a meal.

"He was *cheatin'*," I said again. "You wanna harbor cheats at your establishment? I thought you wanted to be a respectable place of business?"

He scoffed, throwin' up his hands as he looked around the saloon. "Respectable place of business? Delano, look at this place! You've trashed it!"

I gave the room a glance-over. Everyone else able-bodied had cleared out now, leavin' only me, the barkeep, and the sheriff. It *was* quite the mess. Tables overturned, chairs broken, glass and shattered bottles all over the floor, and some bodies, too. Looked like they was all breathin', at least, though they'd likely have some awful bad headaches in the morning.

It seemed things had escalated, sure enough. But I hadn't been the one to cause such a mess. I'd only called out one man fer cheatin'. "What was I supposed to do?" I asked. "Let him rob me and the others? That don't seem smart. All I did was call him out, give him a chance to leave quietly." I prodded at a new split in my lower lip. "He refused my offer. But ya can't say I didn't give him a chance."

"This is the third time I've had to come in here 'cause of brawlin' in just as many weeks," the sheriff said. "And every time it seems I find *you* in the center of it."

He was lookin' at me.

I lifted my hands and shook my head, then winced as that made the room start spinnin' again. "No, sir. I ain't at the center of nothin'. Seems there's just an excess of cheats and swindlers in this town. Maybe you should work a little harder on cleanin' them up, yeah? Then we wouldn't have so much of a problem."

One of his thick gray eyebrows lifted up into his hat brim. "All right," he said. "We're gonna go have a little talk."

He grabbed the collar of my shirt before I could protest the notion, and I found myself once again hauled to my feet. Sheriff Jennings was an older man, but he'd lived in the Territories all his life, and the sun and the heat and the outlaws he'd been chasin' most that time had whittled him down into a hard, unyieldin' man.

It made me wonder what Nine-Fingered Nan had on him, to bend such a man to her whim.

I had no such leverage, least not yet, and so he was none-too-gentle as he dragged me across the mess of the saloon floor to the back door and shoved me through it.

I tripped across the threshold, partially 'cause of too much whiskey, and partially 'cause of that damnable metal leg, and landed hard in the dirt on the other side. All the places I'd been pummeled in this most recent tussle started to make themselves known, and I groaned as I picked myself up onto hands and knees.

I was gonna be one sore mess soon enough.

But for now … for now I had to decide what to do about Sheriff Jennings.

He rounded on me in the back alleyway behind the Stag, and I noticed he kept his shotgun in-hand, as if unsure whether or not he might need to use it.

Smart of him, 'cause I wore both my own six-guns, and I weren't sure whether or not I might need to use those, neither. I sat back on my heels and regarded him through a haze of alcohol and a deep, throbbin' pain that was startin' up in my temples.

"Listen here, you cocky little shit," he snarled. "You might be in Nan's fold now, but that don't mean you have free rein to go around causin' trouble whenever you damn well please!"

I scoffed. "Don't it? Thought you and her had an *understandin'*." I remembered clearly the sneering face of Taggert, the handlebar-mustached bastard who'd double-crossed Nan and me both the first time I'd tried to make a bargain in this town. He'd also been the first to clue me in to the fact Brave-bank was ruled by Nine-Fingered Nan.

And now, he was dead.

"Yeah, we got an understandin', all right." Sheriff Jennings stepped up closer to me. "We got an *under-standin'* that this town is gonna run business as usual. None of her crew goes around shootin' up folk or causin' trouble, and we let some of her questionable business practices go unnoticed, let her use the place as a base of operations for her industry expansion out further west."

"Industry expansion?" What the hell was he on about? The only industry Nine-Fingered Nan seemed interested in was robbin' and murderin' and the sellin' of innocents as slave labor, and that was an industry I was keen on bringin' to an end.

"Yeah," the sheriff said. "And you're givin' the Stag a bad reputation, Delano. Word's startin' to spread that it's a good place for bad men, and that's just what we *don't* want. Word like that scares away the honest folk and brings in people who might be lookin' to move in on Nan's territory. You startin' all these fights and wreckin' the saloon every week is *bad for business*, got it?"

I only scowled at him. Frankly, I didn't give a damn about the success of his business, or the Stag's business, or Nan's business. Far as I were concerned, they could all go to Hell. But I was stuck here, bidin' my time, until Nan sent word on what she wanted next from me.

And if most of the town was loyal to Nan, it wouldn't do much good to make enemies out of 'em all. Not yet.

Maybe this Sheriff Jennings was the one I shoulda been tryin' to talk to about Nan's operations these last few weeks. Seemed he knew an awful lot about 'em. I wondered how loyal he really was to their *understandin'*, given he was a lawman and all.

He was at least loyal enough to be upset over my recent public disturbances, I supposed. I wondered if he'd tell me anythin', either, in that case.

"If there's one thing Nan hates most," he said now, "it's people gettin' in the way of her business. You best watch yourself, Delano. She ain't got no qualms about cuttin' loose dead weight. You best make yourself of more use and less trouble, else…" He broke open his shotgun and made a show of pullin' out the spent cartridge, puttin' in a new one, and snappin' it closed again. "Else she's gonna cut you loose, and then there won't be nothin' between you and the law. Nothin' between you and me. Understand?"

I grumbled and scrubbed at my eyes. It all made sense, sure. Made sense I'd backed myself into a nice, tight corner, and I didn't much like that feelin'. "Yeah," I growled. "Sure."

"Glad we have an understandin' now too, then," Sheriff Jennings said. "Cause I'm gonna need you to come back to the jailhouse with me. Take a little time to cool off and sober up."

I stared up at him, pretty sure I'd heard him wrong. "You wanna lock me up?"

"That's right."

He was starin' down at me steadily, shotgun in hand. Close-range. Real close. If he wanted to take me in, there weren't much I could do about it. But even still, that restless anger flared again inside, heatin' up my blood. Why should he go after *me*? I weren't the one cheatin', or tryin' to kill a man over cards. And I'd had nothin' to do with what anyone else did in that saloon. "Like hell—"

He didn't give me time to finish.

He whipped that shotgun around and cracked its butt into my skull, and I went out cold.

AVAILABLE NOW!

https://jrfrontera.com/bastard-of-blessing

ABOUT THE AUTHOR

J. R. Frontera is an Outlaw Storyteller who dares to write the stories she personally loves most for the readers out there who are looking for something different, and not for the algorithms, sales numbers, or the most recent popular trend. She has been telling stories in some form or another since she could hold a crayon and draw, and her love of science fiction and fantasy originated with her early exposure to the worlds of Star Wars, Star Trek, Lord of the Rings, and Dune. Exploring the potential and pitfalls of humanity in future or fantastical worlds is a temptation she's just never been able to resist. She co-founded a local writing group known as The Wordwraiths in 2013 and is co-owner of their publishing imprint Wordwraith Books and their newly minted entertainment branch Wordwraith Studios, under which she'll be producing her first film in 2025. When she's not writing, filming, momming, or working at her full-time job, she's often horseback riding, playing videogames, or cosplaying. She lives in rural Missouri with her husband, son, and more animals than she'd prefer to disclose. You can find out more about J. R. Frontera, her books, and her films by visiting her website at https://www.jrfrontera.com.